The Rottweiler Howls at Midnight

A Cascade Canine Club Mystery: Book 1

By: Rachelle Orcelletto

D1738328

Acknowledgments

A heartfelt thank you to my first readers: Nicole, Dottie, Melissa, Marnie, Morgan, Beth, Lori, Sam, Nikki, Emily H., Evita, and Lissa. Your feedback and encouragement were invaluable.

Cover Design by: Birdie Book Covers

Edited by: Linda Orcelletto - Orcelletto Communications

Dedicated to the memory of my mother, Becky Hein, who instilled in me a lifelong love of books and storytelling. I miss you every day.

Chapter 1

I opened my eyes. That was my first mistake. Rule number one for waking up in the middle of the night in an unfamiliar place. Don't open your eyes. Nothing good ever comes of it.

Case in point. I opened my eyes, just for a second, just to get my bearings in this too big, too dark room. And spotted a shadowy figure at the foot of the bed.

I tensed. The soft, memory foam topper I'd been grateful for just a few hours earlier now seemed akin to quicksand, weighing me down and impeding my movement. Not like in the Green Machine, where I could slip out of my sleeping bag and be out the door in a step. Where even was the door in this place? I felt so disoriented.

A slither of movement sounded from near the window, and the figure advanced. I squeezed my eyes shut. Was this how it was going to end? Here in my sister's guest cottage, unable to defend myself because my bed was holding me prisoner?

The attack came sooner than I'd anticipated, in the form of a forty-four-pound deadweight dropped directly onto my abdomen. I gasped for air, my eyes flying open to find a mouthful of sharp, pointy white teeth just inches from my nose. And just as suddenly as I'd panicked, I relaxed.

"Rush!" I groaned, fumbling for my phone on the nightstand. "What are you doing?"

My Australian shepherd, delighted at finally having woken me, leapt off the bed, spun in a quick circle, and then jumped back up, his lips once again peeled back from his teeth in an ingratiating grin as he crawled toward me on the bed. Simon, my border collie/whippet cross, sat up on my other side, throwing disdainful looks in Rush's direction.

I finally located my phone, swiping my thumb across the screen to bypass the true crime podcast I'd been listening to earlier, and checked the time. Six a.m. Okay, so maybe not quite the middle of the night. But it was still only a little more than three hours since I unloaded everything from the Green Machine and collapsed into bed. This was supposed to be my day to sleep in and enjoy the luxury of a bed in an actual house. Or, cottage, at least. Though, by my standards, Maeve's cottage might as well be the Taj Mahal.

And hey, no shade on the Green Machine. The campervan, as far as I was concerned, was part of the little family that I put together over a decade spent journeying from state to state, learning everything about dog training and behavior that I possibly could, and, of course, picking up two canine misfits along the way. The Green Machine had gotten the dogs and me out of countless scrapes and sticky situations. Still, though, he was no match for the comfort of an actual bed.

That's what I kept trying to tell myself, anyway, as I lay cocooned in a nest of blankets and a comforter, the faint smell of woodsmoke in the air, courtesy of the black, round-bellied stove in the corner. This was supposed to be comfortable. Luxurious, even, if only by comparison. The Green Machine wasn't like those tricked out vans you see on Instagram. My version of #vanlife was definitely no frills.

So, I shouldn't have been feeling trapped inside these sturdy oak walls or smothered by the thick rug on the floor. This was the first day of the rest of my life. Eleven years after I graduated high school, I was finally becoming an adult.

Or so my mother liked to say.

Rush nudged my hand with his liver-colored nose, leaving a wet swipe across my palm. He was usually more polite about mornings, which could only mean that his need to go outside was becoming urgent.

"Fine, fine," I muttered, finally managing to free myself from the bed. I padded along behind Rush and Simon as they raced to the back door, toenails clacking on the gray-toned laminate floor.

"Holy shih tzus!" I exclaimed, looking out over the white blanket of snow that covered Maeve's backyard. Three hours earlier it'd just been dry desert.

Rush and Simon went nuts when I opened the door, rocketing around the cottage's small, fenced enclosure like two furry comets. The space was hardly adequate for proper snow zoomies. After a few seconds of watching through the window, I shed my pajamas and threw on a pair of jeans and a couple light layers, topping everything off with my favorite *Connection, Not Correction* hoodie. I tried to ignore the way the jeans were a little more difficult to button than they were the last time I'd worn them, telling myself I'd start my diet tomorrow, for sure.

I only had to dig through two boxes before finding my snow boots. One advantage to a decade spent living in the Green Machine is that I certainly hadn't accumulated much in the way of excess junk. It had taken just a half an hour to move all of my stuff into the cottage.

I tugged the boots on over my odd socks; the right decorated with pink and purple elephants, and the left sporting a handful of cavorting whippets. My socks have only ever matched by accident. It used to drive my mother crazy when I was a kid, but in the years since I left home, my socks had been pushed way down on the list of reasons of why I was a disappointment.

Stepping out into the small, fence portion of the yard, I forced the image of my mother's displeased expression from my mind and made a mental note to ask Maeve if I could expand the space a little. After all, the arrangement was supposed to be long term. Semi-permanent. It wasn't so long ago that those phrases would have been enough to send me into an anxiety attack.

This morning, though, I merely swallowed hard as my heart gave a panicked thump in my chest. Just one. This was a good thing. Settling down was good. Putting down roots was good. This was nothing like the childhood I'd been running from all these years. Maeve and the kids needed me. After everything she'd done for me, I owed her at least this much.

The dogs provided a welcome distraction, with Rush uttering an unearthly wail of excitement, and Simon bringing the two of us to eye level with one bounce. I looked around as I buried my hands in Rush's thick red coat. We stood in the middle of a mass of churned together earth and snow. I really needed to expand the space before the dogs completely destroyed it.

"Ready for a walk?" I asked, placing one hand on the makeshift gate. Rush screeched again, and I shushed him this time, not sure how far the sound would carry. There didn't seem to be any neighbors in close proximity, but I didn't want to take chances.

The gate swung open, and both dogs' eyes locked on me in anticipation, the border collie half of Simon's DNA in full display as he sunk into a half crouch. I waited a beat, then released the dogs with a quiet, "Okay."

They sprinted out of the enclosure, sending a spray of snow against my shins. The sun was still working at making itself visible over the horizon, but what little light there was reflected off the snow, and visibility wasn't too terrible. I headed away from the house and cottage in the direction of the woods, if you could call it that. The forests I was used to were lush and green, dense with vegetation and moss-covered trees. Here, gnarled and twisted juniper trees, looking more dead than alive, dominated the landscape. The sandy soil was dotted with fat, round sagebrush. That morning, all of it was coated in a layer of fluffy white powder.

Rush and Simon sped past me, chasing each other in ever-widening circles. Simon, channeling his sighthound half, now, stretched out low, his long, effortless strides eating up the ground; his eyes focused on his prey, Rush. Simon's lean physique may have given him a slight physical advantage over Rush, but Rush had drive enough to make up for it. He was little more than a red and white blur as he flew past me, keeping Simon on his toes with tight turns and sudden feints and starts, following a complex route that he'd no doubt mapped out in his brain the instant his feet had hit the snow.

We walked for about a half hour, pausing for a few minutes to watch the sun rise over the white-topped Cascade Mountains in the distance. I wasn't entirely sure of the exact boundaries of Maeve's large property, so I proceeded with caution, turning back when I saw the slightest hint of a *No Trespassing* sign in the distance.

Upon emerging from the woods, I saw that a light was on at Maeve's. I hadn't seen Maeve and the kids in what seemed like forever, and last night I arrived too late to even say hi. I knocked lightly on the back door and stepped back as a series of thumps, shouts, and barks sounded from within the house.

Someone flung the door open, and my niece and nephew, along with Gentle Ben, Maeve's service dog, spilled out into the yard. Ben made a low roo-ing sound from deep in this throat, his entire rear end wiggling along with his stub tail. He lived with me for nearly a year and a half during his training, and he always recognized and seemed excited to see me.

"Aunt Nell!" nine-year old Liam shouted, launching himself into my arms. I gave him a bear hug, lifting him up off the ground and swinging him back and forth as he shrieked with laughter.

"Wow, I love your hair!" twelve-year old Julianne exclaimed from just behind him. My hair hung past my shoulders, with a little bit of natural wave if I let it air dry. I was pretty sure that Julianne was reacting more to the color than the style, though. I changed colors regularly, and I was currently sporting a deep, dark purple that ended at my cheekbones, followed by a vivid bright pink, which transitioned to a fiery reddish/orange, and ended with a buttery, sunshiny yellow. Eye-catching to say the least.

"Can you do mine sometime?" she asked, craning her neck to see the effect of the color combination from every angle.

"Me too!" chimed Liam.

"Ah," I said, looking past them, to where Maeve was slowly making her way down the hall with her cane. She shrugged.

"Sure!" I said. "We'll see what we can come up with this weekend, maybe."

Cheers erupted, and I got to feel like a rock star for a little while longer before Maeve interjected, "Come on, guys, let's let her inside, it's freezing out there."

We lingered a little longer, though, watching the dogs as they got reacquainted. Australian shepherds, both, Gentle Ben and Rush were half-brothers, though you'd never know it to look at them. Rush was moderately sized and compact, built for speed and agility. Gentle Ben was several inches taller than Rush, pushing the limit of what's typical for size in the breed. His thick coat was a marbled pattern of varying shades of red, broken up with large swaths of white, including most of his left ear. Rush's coat was mostly solid red, with copper points on his face and rear legs. His white markings were confined to all four feet, a blaze down his muzzle, and a full white collar over his neck and chest.

I watched carefully as the dogs circled and sniffed. Simon could be a little tetchy with unfamiliar dogs, and it had been nearly a year since they'd all seen each other. Gentle Ben's name was more than apt, however, and he ignored Simon for the most part, giving him space. Satisfied that everyone was heading in the right direction as far as interdog dynamics went, I herded them inside, closing the door firmly behind me.

"Glad you made it," Maeve said.

"Me too," I replied, folding Maeve into a light hug, careful not to throw her off balance or squeeze anything too hard. Just like Gentle Ben and Rush, you wouldn't have known that we were related at first glance. Maeve was shorter than I, and slender, with hazel eyes and fine, light blond hair. It'd been a while since I'd seen my natural hair color, but last time I checked, it was a shade or two darker than Maeve's; more of a dirty blonde. Really, the bright rainbow topcoat was probably the most interesting thing about it.

Maeve returned the embrace, and I frowned slightly as I felt sharp angles beneath her bulky sweater.

"You know, the last thing I want is to sound like Mom, but you need to eat more," I said.

Maeve pulled away, steadying herself with her cane on one side and Gentle Ben on the other.

"It's just stress, that's all," she said, with a meaningful look in the direction of the kids. She'd warned me ahead of time not to say anything derogatory about Frank in front of them. I wasn't sure exactly when the divorce would be final, but in my opinion, whenever it was wouldn't be soon enough.

We reached the kitchen, and Maeve settled into a seat at the round oak table. The coffee maker burbled on the counter, filling the kitchen with the homey aroma of fresh brew. I grabbed Maeve's empty coffee mug and found a clean one from the cupboard over the sink. Maeve was a creature of habit, and everything seemed to be in the same place it was the last time I visited. I set Maeve's steaming mug of coffee in front of her and took the seat next to her, with Liam and Julianne sliding into the two remaining chairs and the dogs arranging themselves around us on the floor.

"There's creamer in the fridge," Maeve said.

"I'll get it!" Liam jumped up and retrieved the carton from the refrigerator.

"So," I said, changing the subject in deference to Maeve's wishes, "I got here last night and not a hint of snow in sight. This morning, it's a winter wonderland. What gives?"

"Welcome to Central Oregon," Maeve said, watching as I added a dollop of creamer to my cup. It was hazelnut, my favorite. "If you don't like the weather, just wait a few minutes."

Liam slumped in his chair.

"I'm sick of snow," he moaned. "Winter is supposed to be over!"

"It's only March, stupid," Julianne said. "There's still plenty of time for snow."

"Okay, you two," Maeve said. "You're both kind of right. Everyone's ready for spring this time of year, but this is also when Old Man Winter likes to get in his last licks."

"Old Man Winter is a jerk sometimes," Liam muttered.

"Well, I'll probably agree with you next year," I said, trying to ignore the way my stomach flipped at the idea of being in the same place an entire year from now, "But I was traveling all over the south this winter. Georgia, Florida, Louisiana, and Texas. So I'm kind of glad to see some snow. It's pretty."

"Yeah, you say that now," Maeve said, taking a sip of her coffee. "Just wait until you have to drive. They don't maintain the roads at all around here."

"Sometimes they lay down cinder," Julianne piped up.

"So, I need to leave a little early for the job interview today," I said, sampling my coffee. It was good. "Noted."

"At least it's toward the end of the season, and people have mostly figured out how to drive in the stuff," Maeve said. "If it were October, I'd really be worried."

She glanced at the clock above the stove. It was new since the last time I'd been here and that, more than anything else, really did seem to signify Maeve's marriage was well and truly over. Frank would never have allowed the *Stargate* themed clock, with its glowing blue center and hieroglyphs instead of numbers, to be displayed. Maeve was such a nerd.

"Kids, you better finish getting ready for school," she said, noticing me gazing at the clock and flashing a smile. "I'll have breakfast ready for you when you're done."

Julianne and Liam left the table, disappearing down the hall. I got to my feet as well, motioning for Maeve to stay put as she started shifting in her chair.

"I'll get breakfast," I said. "That's what I'm here for, remember?"

"I don't need a maid," Maeve snapped, the sudden change of mood and the uncharacteristically hard edge to her voice giving me pause. "You're just here so that Frank can't claim there isn't an able-bodied adult in the house and use that against me in court."

I turned away from the fridge, where I'd been searching out breakfast options, and returned to the table. I could count on one hand, including my years as an obnoxious teenager, that Maeve had ever spoken to me in that tone of voice.

"I'm sorry," Maeve said immediately after I reclaimed my place at the table.

"Don't be," I said, and meant it. Maeve had always been fiercely independent, pushing the limits of what she was capable of physically rather than ask for help. I wouldn't even have known about Frank's unscrupulous bid for custody if it wasn't for our mother's penchant for gossip. And for taking Frank's side.

"It's just so humiliating," Maeve dropped her gaze to her lap. "I'm perfectly capable of caring for my children."

"Obviously," I said. "You're pretty much solely responsible for me surviving until adulthood. And look well I turned out." I flashed her my most winning smile, glad Mom wasn't here to put her two cents in. "You are a million times more capable than Frank could ever be. And he knows it. He just wants to make things difficult for you. He's a —"

"Don't." Maeve lay a hand on my arm. "Please don't, Nell."

I bit back the insult with difficulty. Maeve was, quite possibly, the kindest, most caring person on earth. That Frank was stooping so low, going to such lengths to gain custody of kids he'd never shown any interest in before just to hurt her, enraged me. I slid my chair back, walked over to the refrigerator, and pulled out a carton of eggs.

"It'll work out," I said. "You'll see. Julianne and Liam aren't going anywhere. But for now, let's start slow, and get some protein into you."

Chapter 2

"Hello!" a voice sounded.

I half-turned away from the Green Machine, where was making sure Rush and Simon had everything they needed while they waited during my interview. I'd seen photos of the Cascade Canine Club online, of course, during the research I conducted before responding to the job posting. But even that didn't prepare me for the sheer vastness of the property; the sprawling paddocks, well-tended buildings, and lava rock-lined trails leading enticingly off into the trees. For a moment I was lost, distracted by all the beauty around me, and couldn't pinpoint where the voice was coming from.

"Over here," the voice called again, and I turned in the opposite direction. A woman with dark brown skin and a head full of grey, almost-white curls strode energetically in my direction, a long-haired German shepherd pacing at her side in a perfect heel.

Rush whined in excitement, shifting his weight forward slightly, eager to greet both the woman and her dog.

"Not now," I said to him quietly, and he sank back onto his haunches.

"Are you Nell McLinton?" the woman asked, stopping a polite distance from the van. Her dog halted when she did, gazing up at her in adoration. Gotta love a German shepherd. They'll make you feel like a celebrity every moment of every day. I motioned for Rush and Simon to stay and stepped away from the Green Machine, closing the distance between us.

"I'm Deanna Welton," she said, offering her hand. "And I'm the director of obedience training here at the Club."

"Hi, yes, I'm Nell," I said. The shepherd watched attentively as the two of us shook hands but didn't move from her position at Deanna's side. "Your dog is beautiful."

Deanna smiled down at the shepherd. The dog's tail swished once as they made eye contact.

"She is, isn't she? Her name is Kasha."

Deanna's gaze shifted to a spot over my shoulder. "Are those your dogs? They're adorable. Or, the smiler is, anyway. I can't really see the other one."

I glanced back. Simon appeared to have flattened himself against inside of the Green Machine's door, with just the tip of his little needle nose poking out. Rush, on the other hand, was in full display, trembling with the effort of holding his sit, his lips peeled back in a toothy grin that was visible even from our vantage point, a dozen odd feet away. Goofballs, the both of them. I refrained from rolling my eyes with difficulty.

"He's a little over-eager," I said.

"He's an aussie, right?"

"That's right. He didn't get the memo that Australian shepherds are supposed to be aloof toward strangers."

Deanna laughed.

"That's not the worst thing," she said. "Anyway, it looks like his friend over there is aloof enough for both of them. Or is he worried?" Her brow wrinkled in concern.

"He's the snooty one of the pair," I nodded in agreement with her first statement, though it was her second that delighted me. I loved working with trainers who didn't hesitate to question a dog's mental state if there was the possibility of an issue. "And I don't think he's too worried about anything right now. He just doesn't approve of Rush's excitement. He's a border/whippet," I added, by way of explanation.

"Ah," Deanna said. "Say no more. Felicia, our agility director, has two. I think they're her favorite sport mix."

"It's a cool cross," I agreed. "Though I'm not sure if Simon was an intentional mix. He turned up injured at a humane society I was working with a few years ago. He had a history of escaping and was unlucky enough to get hit by a car. That was the last straw for his owners. They were in way over their heads."

"Sounds like Kasha's story," Deanna said. "Minus the hit by a car part." She motioned toward one of the buildings. "We should get going before they all think we've decided to just do the interview out here. Do you need to bring your dogs inside?"

"No, they're fine," I said. In truth, I would have loved to bring the boys inside to meet everyone, but I was already nervous enough about this whole ordeal. I didn't want the dogs picking up on that and thinking this was a scary place. "The van is the only home with me they've ever known. Just give me a sec to make sure they're settled."

I jogged over to the Green Machine. Rush leapt to his feet.

"Sorry, buddy," I said, dropping a kiss onto his freckled muzzle. Simon slipped under my arm and gave my ear a slurp. I tickled him under his chin. "You two are going to hang out here for now."

I re-checked their water pail, straightened their blankets, and ensured that their favorite chew toys were in easy reach. The windows had already been rolled down two inches, enough to provide some fresh air without compromising security. Even though there was snow on the ground, I still made sure to park beneath a large tree. By the position of the sun, I estimated the Green Machine would be fully shaded for the next few hours.

I hoped the job interview wouldn't last that long. I didn't think my nerves could take it. After double-checking that the doors were securely shut and locked, I trailed behind Deanna and Kasha as they entered the largest building.

"This is our main training arena," she said, flicking a light switch just inside the door.

The room was huge, easily the largest space I'd ever seen devoted to training classes. The entire floor was covered in black rubber mats to ensure proper footing. Large windows set near the ceiling let in natural light, but were too far from the ground to provide a distraction to the dogs while they worked. Between windows, framed photos of various dog and handler teams filled the remaining wall space. Some equipment had been pushed off to the side of the room, out of the way. There were several tunnels, some jumps, a few flyball boxes, and some other miscellaneous obstacles used for confidence building and conditioning.

"Wow," The word slipped out before I could come up with something more eloquent. But the place was fantastic.

"We use this building for our pet training classes, conformation, obedience, rally, flyball, and nosework. We also do special events and seminars in here," Deanna continued. "There's another indoor arena for agility training. We just put in new turf flooring, and it's amazing. There's also an outdoor area for agility, but we don't use it much over the winter. We'll probably start getting out there again later this month, though."

All I could do was stare around the room in awe. If I'd been asked to design my ideal training facility, this would be it, right down to the photos on the walls. Deanna and Kasha continued across the room, so perfectly in sync that they almost appeared to be moving as one. It was mesmerizing to watch.

"Do you do freestyle?" I asked before I could think better of it. The way they moved together reminded me of a dance, and canine freestyle was the closest sport there was to an official dog and human dance.

"Not yet," Deanna said, sounding amused. "But I think it would be something fun to try after we get our OTCH."

OTCH, or Obedience Trial Champion, was the highest obedience title that was offered. It was an incredible achievement. And obviously a more likely pursuit of the director of obedience training. A part of me wished that silly comment would be enough for me not to win the job. Anything for an excuse not to continue down the path of permanency.

"We'd better head up," Deanna said, nodding to a staircase at the far end of the room. "Everyone's dying to meet you. And I promised I wouldn't be late. I'm what they call punctually challenged."

I chuckled and followed Deanna and Kasha up the stairs.

"Upstairs is mostly office space and some more storage," she said, pausing at the top and motioning for Kasha to move to her other side, right next to a long table full of miscellaneous training equipment and bags of treats.

"There they are!" A tall, athletic looking woman with bright red hair and a smattering of freckles dotting her pale skin poked her head out of a doorway near the end of the hall.

"Only ten minutes late," Deanna said. "That's practically on time!"

The redhead grinned at what seemed to be a familiar exchange between the two of them.

"Come on in," she said, sweeping an arm dramatically through the doorway.

Deanna and Kasha entered first.

"Hi, I'm Nell," I said, offering my hand as I approached the door.

"I'm Adrienne Santi," she responded, and returned my handshake firmly. "I'm the vice-president of the Club. I love your hair, by the way."

I'd plaited my hair in a neat French braid, and the resulting swirl of color contrasted dramatically with the grey dress shirt I wore.

"I want to see!" called a voice from inside.

"Yes, please let the girl through, Adrienne," another voice, calmly authoritative, sounded.

Adrienne immediately stepped aside. Deanna and two other women were gathered around a long table in the center of the room. One of them, a slender woman with soft white hair that fell to her shoulders, stepped forward.

"Hello, Nell," she said, pleasantly causal, though it was clear from the way she held herself that she was used to being in charge. "I'm Clarice Abernathy, and I'm the Club president and owner. It's so nice to finally meet you!"

We shook hands. Her grip wasn't as firm as Adrienne's. Up close I was surprised to see she was older than I'd initially thought, possibly in her late sixties or early seventies.

"Have a seat," she offered, indicating the chairs grouped around the table.

I grabbed the nearest one. Deanna pulled out the chair across from me, and Kasha settled at her side. The woman next to Deanna motioned for me to turn so she could see my hair.

"Love those colors," she said. "It's like a sunset."

"Exactly what I was going for, thanks."

"Bet the maintenance is a pain."

"It is. But it's worth it to see my true self in the mirror when I look, you know?"

It wasn't my typical response to the question, but I had a

feeling that she would understand what I meant. Her black hair was cropped pixie-short on the back and sides, but the top was longer, swept off to the left in a faux hawk. Her mascara was heavily and elaborately applied, and two silver studs, one in her right eyebrow and the other in her left nostril stood out starkly against her bronze skin. She'd been eyeing me warily, but her expression relaxed a little after my last comment.

"Absolutely, I get it," she said. "I'm Felicia Yin, by the way. Director of agility training."

She reached across the table to shake my hand. What I'd initially taken for an abstractly designed top was actually a sleeve tattoo, all in black, of twisting tree limbs that looked like something out of a Tim Burton movie intertwined with paw prints and various names written in swirling script.

"Beautiful artwork," I said. "Is it local?"

She nodded.

"I can get you the name of my guy, if you want."

"Sure! I don't have plans for any others right now, though. I just have the one."

I rotated my arm, showing her the underside of my wrist where the pawprint of my first dog, Sebastian, had been inked in shades of blue, purple, and turquoise. I'd adopted him from the local humane society just before graduating high school. A month later we hit the road together. Working through his issues had awakened my interest in all things behavior.

"All right, now," Clarice said, from where she stood at the head of the table. "Everyone can compare tattoos later. We've all seen Nell's resume and credentials, but she hasn't had the opportunity to familiarize herself with us. Let's rectify that, shall we? How about we all introduce ourselves. I'll start. I've had salukis for over forty years, and my interests are in breeding, exhibiting, and lure coursing."

"Such elegant dogs," I said. "I'll confess, though, I haven't encountered many professionally."

"Clarice will tell you it's because the saluki is too aristocratic and refined to need any training," Adrienne said with a grin, sending a sideways glance in Clarice's direction. Clarice shrugged.

"Sighthounds tend to be naturally quiet and well-behaved. I always say they're the best kept secret of the dog world."

Yeah. Tell that to Simon. Though, to be fair, one could make the argument that it was his border collie half that was responsible for his quirks.

"I still don't believe it," Adrienne shook her head. "Naturally well-behaved doesn't exist."

"Says the lady with the huskies," Clarice said with a chuckle. There were grins and smirks around the rest of the table as well. I could tell this was a well-worn joke amongst them all. "At one point I had seven dogs living in my house. My closest neighbors at the time refused to believe it. We've gotten off track, though."

The women around the table settled, and Clarice cleared her throat and continued, "I founded this club a little over twenty years ago. I was interested in something more inclusive than the local kennel club, something less focused on breeding and exhibiting, and more open to a wider variety of dog owners. Apparently, I wasn't the only one who felt that way. We've become more successful than I could have imagined, with the revenue from our membership dues, pet training and performance classes, shows, and trials supporting our annual expenses, something I didn't think would ever happen in the beginning. People really like that we don't discriminate. Everyone is welcome, whether they rescue or breed, compete in sports, or just want to enjoy their pets."

"Well, we do have one rule," Adrienne broke in, "And that is: No matter how you're involved with dogs, you maintain ethical and responsible practices. That goes for trainers, breeders, rescuers, and everyone in between."

It sounded almost too good to be true. No sooner had the thought entered my mind than Felicia muttered, "With one glaring exception." Her eyes shifted toward Clarice.

Clarice met her gaze coolly.

"Let's just keep things on topic," she said smoothly. "Adrienne? Would you like to go next?"

Adrienne started to answer, but Felicia cut her off.

"Actually, I would really like to hear from Nell before we go too much farther. I know we've all seen her resume, but I'd like to hear, in her own words, what her training philosophy is."

Clarice's tone turned positively icy.

"My thought was that we could all get to know each other a little before launching the Spanish Inquisition," she said.

Deanna cleared her throat.

"Clarice, I'm curious as well," she said. "I'm sure Nell appreciates your efforts, but really, for Felicia and myself, it's going to come down to the training."

"And you know why," Felicia added darkly.

Chapter 3

My eyes ping ponged between the three of them as they spoke. Everyone looked tense, even Kasha. What in the world was going on? I'd never encountered anything remotely like this in a job interview. Adrienne gave me a sympathetic smile but remained silent.

Clarice took her seat.

"Okay, then," she said. "Nell?"

Four pairs of eyes focused intently on my face. Well, five if you counted Kasha. But I was used to it from dogs. It was a little unnerving from a handful of people in such close quarters. I took a deep breath.

"I am a ..." I mentally ran through the list of adjectives trainers commonly used to describe their methods. Purely Positive? Balanced? Force Free? All were so politically charged, so divisive in how they categorized the various professionals in the field. To be honest, I didn't really care for any of those terms; didn't feel any were truly accurate.

"I'm a ..." I said again, stalling, still frantically considering and rejecting various descriptors. By their own admission they'd all seen my resume. They should have an idea of my philosophy just based on my credentials and education. But it seemed that wasn't enough. One of my first mentors had cautioned me that the only thing two trainers can agree on is that the third is wrong. It had quickly become apparent how frighteningly accurate the joke really was as I gained experience. So, what was I supposed to say? And then it came to me.

"I am a LIMA Being," I said at last.

Deanna and Felicia visibly relaxed, leaning back in their chairs. Adrienne's smile broadened. Only Clarice seemed confused.

"Leema?" she asked.

"LIMA stands for Least Intrusive, Minimally Aversive," I explained, as Adrienne nodded in agreement at my side. "When working with all species. Even people. Dogs are easier by far, though. Takes a little more effort with the humans," I added, remembering the conversation about Frank earlier. I definitely hadn't been in a LIMA mindset then.

Felicia's expression progressed from guarded to elated in the span of seconds.

"For sure," she said. "It's much harder with people."

"You don't say," Clarice said drily.

Felicia gave an apologetic shrug. Adrienne clapped her hands.

"Well," she said. "Now that's out of the way, we can continue with the intros. Like Clarice said, I have huskies and they aren't well-behaved. Naturally or otherwise. Luckily, I'm far out enough that I don't have any close neighbors, but if I did, I'm pretty sure they'd think I had dozens of dogs instead of just eight."

The remaining tension around the table broke, and Deanna, Clarice, and Adrienne herself chuckled at the joke.

"I love mushing and skijoring," she continued. "Basically anything that gets me and the dogs out and running in the snow. I do some workshops at the club from time to time about winter activities for dogs, but I don't teach any classes. My dogs keep me too busy for that."

"Adrienne is an unofficial one-woman husky rescue," Deanna said.

"You're brave," I said in admiration.

"It's on a very small scale," Adrienne said. "I usually just work with one dog at a time. All the humane societies in the area know me, and they'll give me a call if a particularly challenging husky or mix comes along. I'll foster for a few months and make an assessment about what type of environment would be best suited for the dog before seeking out adopters. People get sucked in by how beautiful the dogs are, you know. But not a lot of people are really equipped to give them what they need in terms of exercise and enrichment."

True enough. I'd seen that firsthand during my time spent at various humane societies and animal shelters.

"I'll go next," Felicia said. "Obviously, I love agility. Which is great, because it seems that all of Central Oregon does as well. Every time I add a new class, it fills immediately. I also work part-time at Leaps and Bounds, the local dog rehabilitation and fitness center. I'm pretty much all over anything to do with canine fitness and injury prevention."

"It's a fascinating specialty," I said. "I'm glad there's a local place offering that kind of care."

"We're filling a need, for sure," Felicia said.

"What kind of dogs do you have?" I asked. "Deanna mentioned border/whippets? I have one named Simon. I kind of stumbled onto that mix, but he's such a cool dog. I'd love to meet some others."

"Yes, I have two border/whippets," Felicia said. "I also have a border collie/papillon mix, and a real mixy mix of border collie, border/whippet, Staffordshire bull terrier, and rat terrier. He's wild. I do pretty much everything with him. And I also have a plain old border collie. I'm really captivated by the sport mixes, though. It's this whole subset of dogs bred purely for health and function, with almost no consideration for looks at all."

"Yes, the movement is gaining more traction," I said. "It'll be interesting to see where things are at in a few years."

Clarice checked her watch.

"While I appreciate everyone's enthusiasm for the sport mix discussion, we will absolutely be here all day if it continues. Deanna, would you like to talk a little about your interests?"

"Sure," Deanna said. "You've already met Kasha, of course. I found her when she was about six months old, while volunteering at the local shelter. She was more than her owners had bargained for when they brought the cute, fluffy puppy home. They did the best they could, though, and I'm glad they had the foresight to seek out a more appropriate home for her when they realized they couldn't provide her with what she needed. I still keep in touch with them, and they love to hear about all of her adventures."

"Aw, that's so nice of you," I said. "I wish there wasn't such a stigma about rehoming. In so many cases it's the best thing for both the dogs and the people."

Deanna nodded emphatically.

"It certainly was in this case. And Kasha has been the best obedience partner I could have ever hoped for. We got our Utility Dog Excellent title last month, and like I said earlier, we're going for our OTCH. Hopefully we can get that in the next year or two."

"And then freestyle?" I asked.

She grinned at the joke.

"Possibly. My wife and I also have a little chihuahua mix called Delany that we're doing some scent training with. And, of course, there are my classes here. I handle the competitive obedience and rally classes. Lately, I've been taking on some reactive dog classes and some puppy training as well." Deanna wrinkled her nose at the last sentence.

"Not a puppy fan?" I asked.

"Not a fan of other people's puppies," she clarified. "I don't have the patience for pet training. I'm more than ready to pass those classes off to you."

"Well, no one asked you to steal the classes from me in the first place," a deep, indignant voice rumbled from the doorway.

Chapter 4

Judging from the reactions from around the table, you would have thought Voldemort had materialized in all his red-eyed reptilian glory. I saw clenched hands and set jaws. Deanna subtly shifted her chair so she was firmly planted in front of Kasha.

I turned to look for myself and was surprised to see that the man standing just beyond the doorframe looked perfectly ordinary. He was tanned and healthy looking, probably around the same age as Clarice, with a salt and pepper goatee and close-cropped gray hair. Muscular and fit, he held himself with the air of someone who had served in the military as he stood, arms crossed over his chest, glaring into the room. An unleashed Rottweiler stood at his side, unnaturally still, it seemed to me.

"Bryan," Clarice said, a hard edge to her voice that wasn't there a few minutes earlier, even when she'd been reprimanding Felicia, "I don't recall that you were invited to this meeting."

"Well, I should have been, considering you're hiring my position right out from under me, don't you think?"

"Nonsense," Clarice said, rising from her seat with queenly grace. "You were given every opportunity to educate yourself and adapt your methods to fit with how the other trainers work and with the expectations of our clientele. You've repeatedly refused, even after being informed that the consequence would be your removal from this position."

"Client expectations?" Bryan's voice grew louder with every word. "Do you need me to read the positive reviews from online? How people were hopeless -- on the verge of giving up on their dogs -- before coming to see me?"

The Rottweiler beside him grew agitated as Bryan's tone betrayed more of his anger. The dog stiffened. He flicked his tongue, and his eyes widened enough that I could see the white's flash as he scanned the room for the source of his owner's distress.

Adrienne leapt to her feet, her chair screeching against the floor as it slid back. The Rottweiler uttered a low growl. Bryan's arms shifted slightly, and a barely perceptible tremor ran through the dog's body. The growl abruptly ceased. I narrowed my eyes, taking a closer look at the pair. And sure enough, there, just visible beneath the folds of skin under the dog's chin was a black plastic box. Shock collar. My eyes flicked back to Bryan and found the remote concealed in his right hand.

"You want to talk reviews?" Adrienne said, her green eyes flashing. "How about those who go beyond your pet training classes to some sort of sport, and are completely confused when the instructors request that they remove their choke chains and shock collars? What about those dogs that you claimed were *one hundred percent reliable* that lost their minds once they realized the electric collar was off?"

Bryan waved a hand as if swatting a fly, dismissing Adrienne entirely. The Rottweiler flinched.

I frowned. Though electronic collars weren't a tool I

personally utilized, they were able to be used effectively. Or misused. It wasn't hard to see which category Bryan fell into. Clarice spoke up.

"It's all about consistency, Bryan. The lack of it is hurting our bottom line.

Pet class enrollment is down. Our competition instructors are being put in an awkward position when clients ask why they're being told the opposite of what was learned from you."

"And you think this girl with the crazy hair is going to help your image?" Bryan pointed a finger first and me and then at Felicia. "Trust me, people aren't going to take you seriously if they find a clown instructor in one class and then a punk rocker instructor in the next."

Felicia rolled her eyes.

"Tell me you're a Boomer without telling me you're a Boomer," she muttered.

Adrienne snickered.

"Is there an issue with Baby Boomers you'd like to bring to the table, Felica?" Clarice asked. "Condemning an entire generation over one person's comment doesn't seem very LIMA of you." Without waiting for a response, she returned her attention to Bryan, leaning forward and placing her hands on the table.

"Bryan, we've had this conversation before. This is not the time or the place to have it again. If you'd like to continue discussing the matter, then please wait for me in my office. But I can assure you, nothing is going to change at this point. If you are so unwilling to explore other training methods, why not open your own business? No one here is going to stop you. You have my blessing."

Clearly done with Bryan, Clarice returned to her seat, shuffling the stack of papers in front of her and placing my resume on top.

"Tell us about your time at the Karen Pryor National Training Center," she said.

Adrienne retrieved her chair and sat back down. Everyone else turned away from Bryan and fixed their attention on me. I rotated my chair so that I faced the rest of the table.

"It was amazing," I said, deliberating keeping my back to Bryan. "Working with animals other than dogs and cats really helps you to improve timing and develop the ability to break specific behaviors down into small pieces. It's always so tempting with dogs to lure or to physically place into position, but you don't have those options as much with goats, llamas, donkeys, or chickens."

I allowed myself a glance at the doorway. Bryan and his dog had gone.

Chapter 5

The interview didn't last much longer after that. We'd gone over the rest of the work experience I'd listed on my resume. We then discussed our individual training ideas and discovered that we all pretty much ascribed to the LIMA philosophy. We didn't all train in exactly the same way, of course. But the differences we all had were inconsequential, and likely wouldn't confuse clients who wished to train in a variety of disciplines.

Adrienne fell into step beside me as the group dispersed.

"Sorry about all that with Bryan," she said. "He's always been arrogant, but ever since we started phasing him out of training he's become downright impossible. Clarice is considering having him banned from the premises, but she doesn't want to take such a drastic step just yet."

"Why not?" I asked. "He seemed pretty over the top. And if the way he treats his own dog is any indication, I wouldn't want to see how he works with clients' dogs."

"You saw that with the shock collar, huh?"

I nodded, squinting a little as we transitioned from the building to the bright sunlight. Adrienne sighed, making sure the door had closed firmly behind her.

"It would be one thing if he used it properly, but he doesn't. The way he uses it is quick and easy for him and seems to get results. That's all Bryan cares about."

We moved away from the building, dodging the occasional clump of snow that hadn't yet melted away from the blacktop.

"Bryan and Clarice go way back," Adrienne continued. "He was one of the first people she took on, back in the day. In fact, I don't even think she paid him those first few years. And at the time, he was on the top of his game. The way he trained was actually considered more humane than most of what was happening out there, you know?"

I did. Behavior nerd to the core, I'd soaked up pretty much every book, article, or seminar on training I could find. That included the ancient history of Koehler and Wood-house to current generation of Clothier, Fenzi, and Stremming. Though much of the evolution of our understanding of dog behavior, and the resulting development of different training methodologies and techniques had taken place before my time, I'd wanted to understand every facet of that journey.

"It's gotta be hard, hearing that the way you've done something your entire life is no longer acceptable," I said, trying hard to see it from Bryan's perspective.

I headed in the direction of the parking lot, but Adrienne waved me toward a curving, blacktopped path.

"I'll give you the rest of the tour," she said. "Did Deanna tell you about the new turf in the agility building?"

"Ooh, yeah, let's go look."

Adrienne led the way toward the next closest building, nearly as large as the one we were just in. She walked with the smooth, long strides of an athlete, and I nearly had to jog to keep up.

"See, on one hand, I do kinda feel sorry for the guy," she said. "But on the other hand, isn't it your responsibility to keep up with everything current in your profession? I'm a personal trainer, for exmple."

No surprise there.

"I read all of the latest studies and publications. I go to seminars. I keep myself as up to date as possible; not just for my own knowledge, but for the sake of my clients. Clearly, you do the same."

Adrienne stopped at the doorway to the second building and fished a ring of keys out of her pocket, making a frustrated noise as her large keychain caught on her beltloop.

"Well, sure," I said, as she finally freed her keyring and began flipping through the keys. "But I can understand that not everyone can drop everything and travel across the country to take advantages of workshops and internships as they come along."

"Oh, of course," Adrienne found the key she was looking for and unlocked the door. "And I know dog training is almost completely unregulated. There's really only one organization that you can get certified through, right?"

"Yeah, it's the Certification Council for Professional Dog Trainers. Holy shih tzus!" I exclaimed, as we stepped inside.

The turf surface looked as green and lush as grass, and beautifully set off the blue and yellow painted contact obstacles: dog walk, A-frame, and teeter totter. White plastic jumps accented with different colored stripes painted on the frames and bars were positioned around the arena in what looked like a challenging course. A set of twelve weave poles had been incorporated into the course, along with several tunnels, a tire jump, a pause table, and a broad jump. Two by two disconnected sections of weave poles, spare jumps and tunnels, and various wood-carved structures designed for contact work had been moved out of the way alongside the walls.

"I don't think I've ever seen such an absolutely perfect agility facility," I said, looking around the large space in awe.

"The space is actually large enough for a full course, and there's plenty of extra room for teaching and for the other teams not running. I almost never see that in an indoor arena. And your course is so well-maintained."

Adrienne laughed.

"Yeah, Felicia is a stickler for proper equipment care."

"No kidding," a voice sounded from the vicinity of the A-Frame. A gangly, sandy haired boy slid out from beneath the triangle shaped obstacle, a can of WD-40 in one hand.

"Kyle!" Adrienne exclaimed, placing a hand over her heart theatrically. "You scared me! I didn't know anyone was in here."

"Sorry," Kyle straightened and shifted the can from one hand to the other. "Felicia asked me to take care of a couple things before the next class."

"Don't apologize," Adrienne said. "I don't know what we'd do without you here." She turned to me. "Nell, this is Kyle Gilmore. Handyman extraordinaire and, apparently, secret ninja. Kyle, this is Nell McLinton, our new trainer."

That was news to me. Clarice offered me the job, true, but I hadn't yet accepted.

"Hi," Kyle said. He offered his hand before seeming to realize it was greasy and hastily dropping it to his side.

"Nice to meet you, Kyle," I said. "What's your breed?"

"Um …" Kyle's gaze suddenly dropped to his shoes.

"He's got a little labby girl who's a fantastic gundog," Adrienne offered, smiling.

"She's just a mix from the shelter." Kyle mumbled.

"Hey, now," Adrienne wagged a finger. "Shelter mixes are plenty awesome. I found my best mushing dog at the humane society up in Madras."

"The dog I use most often for demonstrations is a shelter mix," I added. "Great dogs can come from anywhere."

"Not to mention, I seem to recall reading in the last club

newsletter that your little Remi kicked all the purebreds' butts at the last field trial," Adrienne said.

"Not all," Kyle corrected, but the faint blush creeping up his neck seemed to indicate he was pleased with the compliment. "We got third place."

"Well done," I said, impressed.

"What classes are you going to be teaching?" he asked, clearly eager for a change of subject.

"Nell is going to take on the pet manners classes, puppy classes and reactive dog classes," Adrienne jumped in.

"Doesn't Bryan teach those classes?"

"Bryan is going to be stepping back from classes for a bit."

"Oh." Kyle finally looked up from his shoes. "Well, I've got a few other things to get to before work, so I'll get out of your hair. Nice to meet you, Ms. McLinton."

"Oh, it's Nell, please," I said. "And nice to meet you, too, Kyle."

Kyle waved his can of WD-40 as he left.

"He seems like a nice kid," I said to Adrienne once the door closed behind him.

"He is," Adrienne said. "Just turned eighteen, what, six months ago? He volunteers his services here whenever he has a moment between his two paying jobs in exchange for instruction from our hunt and field instructor, Jerry. That little dog of his is a dynamo. She's mostly lab, I think, but with a little something extra in the mix. I swear there's some husky in there. Something about the eyes. She's cute as heck."

"He didn't seem too happy about me taking over Bryan's classes."

Adrienne shrugged and bent over to pluck a speck of lint from the otherwise pristine turf.

"I'd imagine he's not super thrilled about it. Bryan was the first contact he made at this club, back when he adopted Remi from the shelter. He's the one who convinced Clarice to let Kyle work in exchange for classes."

I nodded, checking out the photos on the walls which, like the other building, featured teams of dogs and handlers, though in this building the focus seemed to be solely on agility. I saw Felicia with an ever-changing roster of sport mixes and border collies, Deanna and a little black chihuahua, and even one of Adrienne with a red and white husky captured flying through a tunnel.

"Nice," I said, pointing to the photo.

"That's Denali, my problem child. That was when Felicia first started here. Until then, I hadn't been having much luck with training. Huskies just aren't fans of the whole, *do it because I said so*, philosophy."

"Nope," I agreed, having worked with my fair share of huskies and other northern breeds at various animal shelters and humane societies. Super smart dogs, but independent and resilient. Definitely not easily intimidated.

"I started Denali in agility because he was driving me nuts," Adrienne went on. "We were mushing upwards of ten miles a day, sometimes more, but he was still just wild. I enrolled in Felicia's class out of desperation, trying to find something that would hold his attention. Well, I nearly died when Felicia took this dog who only wanted to run, who never paid any attention to me, even when I popped him with a prong collar, and had him running complex courses off leash. Once I stopped worrying about how to punish Denali when he misbehaved, and figured out to motivate him to work with me, it was amazing how quickly we progressed to competing in agility and obedience trials. And winning, no less!"

"That's so cool," I said. "Denali sounds hilarious. I need to meet this dog."

"Yes! Though he's nearly thirteen, now, so a little slower, but still up for ALL of the mischief."

Adrienne ushered me back outside and locked the building behind her. We continued down the path, past a giant fenced paddock off the agility building.

"Outdoor agility arena," Adrienne said. "It's half an acre."

"Wow." I was just so in awe of the size of the facility, of all the space afforded to each building and outdoor enclosure. The cost of running the place must have been astronomical. And yet, Clarice claimed the club more than paid for itself. Fascinating.

"Anyway," Adrienne said as we continued on our way. "Certification. Felicia is certified with the CCPDT. And so are you."

I nodded.

"Yes, I have both the trainer and behavior consultant certifications."

"Don't you think there should be some sort of requirement, then, for trainers to be certified? To maybe weed out the Bryans of the world?"

I hesitated, gazing over the snow-blanketed buildings and paddocks, the mountains just visible against the horizon.

"I don't know," I said. "I mean, I was so lucky to be able to do what I did, living out of my van and traveling and gaining all of that experience. Certifying with CCPDT isn't quick, easy, or cheap. I know plenty of amazing trainers, some I would consider mentors, who aren't certified. I'd hate to think of the dog world being deprived of those people just because they don't have a bunch of letters after their name. If training were more lucrative, maybe, but most trainers train on the side. It's a small percentage of us who are able to make a living at it."

"That makes sense," Adrienne said, nodding. "Deanna and the other people involved in training are all so talented and knowledgeable. They all deserve their positions. Bryan just made me so mad, and then that was all I could think about."

We walked in silence for a bit, until we arrived at another building, much smaller than the first two.

"What's this?" I asked.

"It used to be the grooming shop."

"Used to be?"

Adrienne shrugged.

"We're between groomers right now. The last one decided to pack up and move back to California. We'll get someone else in there soon, but for now it's vacant. We're allowed to use any equipment we want, though, so long as we clean everything up. Which is nice. Blowing out husky coats at home is not my idea of fun."

We passed another large building that turned out to be kennels, though the club didn't yet offer boarding. There were several more fenced paddocks, and trails leading off to the trees. Clarice's house, though not quite a mansion, but large and beautifully designed, sat up on a hill overlooking the entire facility.

It all seemed too good to be true, I reflected as I steered the Green Machine back down the crooked drive to the road, an episode of my favorite true crime podcast, RedHanded, playing in the background. As soon as the thought entered my head, I admonished myself. Any trainer would kill to work here. Thinking that this was anything other than the opportunity of a lifetime was just plain silly. Wasn't it?

Chapter 6

Once safely back on the road, I checked the clock on the Green Machine's dashboard. It was nearly lunchtime. I should have headed back to Maeve's, but I felt so unsettled from the interview and the scene with Bryan that I wasn't quite ready. And so, instead of heading back to Tumalo, the little hamlet just outside of Bend that Maeve called home, I made my way further into town and pulled into the parking lot at the Pilot Butte trailhead.

The butte was the cinder cone remnant of an extinct volcano, smack in the middle of the city. It was kind of a tradition for me to take a hike up to the summit whenever I was visiting. I used the hike to gauge my fitness level (or lack thereof) from year to year, as the trek to the top of the butte was steep.

The trail was popular, and even with the recent snowfall, was fairly crowded at that time of day. I put Rush and Simon on leash, and they pranced in place beside me as I made sure everything in the van was in place before locking it. Well, Rush pranced. Simon executed a series of gravity defying leaps at my side, never once coming into contact with either me or the van, but literally jumping for joy.

We set off at a brisk walk up the lava lined path that circled the butte. As the snow from the night before melted, the sandy earth became hard-packed and slightly slippery in places. On the side of the butte that got the least amount of sun, sheets of ice added an element of danger to the hike.

I tried to clear my head as we climbed; to not think of the space Maeve had freed up for the Green Machine in her garage, or the job I'd been offered but hadn't formally accepted, or the years, _years_ ahead of me -- all spent right here in this touristy mountain town. The image of my mother sitting placidly as my father delivered yet another lecture of how a woman's place was in the home, of how my path to fulfillment was to be in the service of some man popped into my head. I couldn't force it out.

I pushed faster, starting to pant, and then gasp as the angle of the trail steepened. My heart pounded, and I started to feel tightness in my quads and hamstrings. Somehow, over the years, I'd equated any kind of permanency or stability with my father's beliefs. Logically, the I knew the two were not the same. I _knew_ that. But the urge to run, to keep pushing forward and never look back, was always there.

About three quarters of the way up, we came upon a pull out with a wooden bench overlooking the city. I collapsed onto it, struggling to catch my breath. Rush and Simon danced around me, not even the slightest bit winded.

"Sure, rub it in," I wheezed. "You guys are a lot younger than I am, you know."

I leaned back against the bench tipping my head back to gaze at the clear, blue sky. Rush leapt lightly onto the bench beside me, settling himself so that his front half was draped over my knees and his head rested on my right wrist. I buried my left hand in the shining white fur on the back of his neck.

Simon sprang up onto the bench next to Rush, and the three of us watched a hawk glide lazily over the treetops. It switched course, heading west, growing smaller and smaller as it drew away to places unknown and unexplored; until it was little more than a dark speck against the lone wispy cloud that dared spoil that endless blue. I sighed, wanting nothing more than to keep heading west, just like the hawk.

Instead, knowing that Maeve was waiting, I heaved myself to my feet, standing just off the trail, adjusting the leashes in my hand. A large group meandered past us.

"Oh, what a beautiful aussie! What's his name?" exclaimed one of the women.

I smiled at her. People were familiar with aussies around here, I'd noticed. In other places I'd traveled, no one seemed to recognize the breed at all.

"His name's Rush. You can go ahead and pet him, he's friendly."

The entire group paused to fawn over Rush, and he went from person to person, accepting the attention as his due. Simon fidgeted beside me, bored. If he were human he'd have been checking his watch.

One of the guys looked past Rush, to where Simon stood watching the display haughtily.

"Whoa," he said. "What's that?"

I smothered a laugh. I was used to the difference in people's reaction to the two dogs. Simon's narrow head, large brown eyes, and long, skinny legs made for an interesting combination of features. I'd heard him described as a stick insect more than once. His demeanor didn't help, either. While Rush plastered himself against the shins of his admirers, smiling up into their faces, Simon remained aloof. He wasn't nervous or scared, just disinterested.

The viewing area at the summit was filled with hikers. The dogs and I circled around the low stone wall a few times, glancing at the informational plaques and taking in the view of the city and the mountains beyond from several different angles. I spotted the house that Maeve and Frank had lived in when they'd first moved here. It was several blocks away, just beyond a cemetery. I recognized the dark green roof.

"That's Mount Bachelor, I think," the woman next to me said, pointing. "That's where we were skiing this morning."

"No," her companion said. "I'm pretty sure that's Mount Hood."

I trained my eyes in the direction they were pointing, at a white-capped crest in the quintessential shape of a mountain; the type of rugged triangle you'd see in a Bob Ross painting.

"That's actually Mount Jefferson," I said. "It's my favorite. Love that dramatic peak."

"Oh, of course!" said the first woman. "So, where's Mount Bachelor?"

I gestured over her shoulder.

"It's Bachelor, and then the Three Sisters, Faith, Hope, and Charity." The name of each mountain rolled off my tongue as though they were old friends, familiarity born of the many years spent visiting Maeve.

"There's Broken Top, that shorter, uneven one, and Mount Washington with the smaller peak. Black Butte has hardly any snow, and then Jefferson, and there, way, way out in the distance, that one you can barely see, that's Mount Hood."

The second woman actually clapped her hands with glee.

"Oh, how perfect!" she cried. "How do you manage to keep them straight? Do you live here?"

"No," I said automatically, and my hand clenched around the dogs' leashes. I took a deep breath. "I mean, yes. Kind of. Maybe."

Smooth, Nell. Real smooth.

Chapter 7

On my way back to Maeve's, I swung by Parilla and picked up lunch for the both of us. Locals seemed to be divided about the place, with some touting it as *the* best after skiing snack spot, and others decrying it as an insult to food. I was a fan. Let the local food snobs fight me; they'd never change my mind on that.

The snow had mostly melted by the time I got back to Maeve's place. I left the Green Machine parked in the driveway and sent Maeve a text letting her know I returned. Rush and Simon raced ahead of me, doubling back when they saw I stopped at Maeve's door. I knocked twice to announce my presence, then let myself in.

Gentle Ben greeted us in the hall. Bobtail wagging madly, he lifted his muzzle and let out a low, rumbling *roo*. Rush and Simon gamboled around him, but Ben made a beeline for me, leaning against my legs and raising his head, presenting me with his snowy-white ruff, his favorite place to be petted. He *roo*-ed again as my fingers found the perfect spot, and I could feel the vibrations under my hands.

"Who's the sweetest boy?" I cooed, while both Rush and

Simon stared at me, affronted. I shrugged at them. Rush and Simon were plenty sweet, of course, but there was just something special about Ben. Initially, I was skeptical when his breeder, Deb, recommended him for Maeve. Herding dogs don't typically make the best service dogs. Their tendency to feed off their owners' emotions could interfere with tasks. In addition, mobility assistance dogs tended to be much larger than the average aussie.

I had to hand it to Deb, though. She knew her dogs. Everything from Ben's size to his temperament had turned out to be the perfect match for Maeve's needs.

"Where's Maeve?" I asked him, after a few moments passed and she hadn't made an appearance.

Ben took off down the hallway, Rush and Simon in pursuit. I brought up the rear. He led us through the kitchen, dining room, and family room to Maeve's office, a small, cozy room that overlooked the backyard. Maeve's desk faced the window, and that's where she sat in her custom designed office chair, hunched over her computer.

"Hey, Shakespeare!" I called, and she jumped a little before swiveling the chair around to face me.

"Since when are you so stealthy?" she asked.

I snorted.

"Stealthy? The dogs made a huge racket in the hallway just now. Didn't you hear Ben talking?"

Maeve shook her head.

"I guess I was really focused on the book."

I peered over her shoulder.

"What are you working on?"

"Final edits," she said. "Book's supposed to be released next month, but it's fighting me every step of the way."

"Which one is it again?" I asked. Maeve typically had three or four books in progress at once, and I read the first drafts of them all before she sent them to her editor.

"The one with the alien/human hybrids fighting against the evil slave traders."

"Oh, right. I really liked that one! What's the trouble?"

"Nothing really," she said. "Just tightening some things up. Normally I'm pretty ruthless about trimming the fat, but it just so happens that I really, really enjoy a lot of the fatty parts of this book. So, it's hard."

"So, leave it," I said. "If I remember correctly, the so-called fatty parts of your book were really funny, and a nice break from the seriousness of the battle."

Maeve flipped the top of her laptop closed.

"Ugh," she said. "I just don't even want to think about it anymore. I'm having the same argument with myself at every section."

"As you wish," I said, holding up the Parilla bag. "Lunch is served."

Ben stood at Maeve's side as she levered herself up from her chair, just in case she needed to steady herself. Mobility assistance dogs tend to be on the larger end of the dog size spectrum, but Ben was a big boy by aussie standards. Maeve, on the other hand, was tiny. She claimed to be five-foot, but she never offered any proof, and so I remained skeptical. She and Ben were perfect for each other.

This time it was Rush and Simon who charged ahead to the kitchen, me in the middle, and Maeve and Ben bringing up the rear. We settled around the table, Maeve in her customary chair with Ben at her feet, and me across from her. Rush lay down next to me, but Simon spotted Ben's cushy dog bed next to the fridge and decided to curl up there, though he kept his eyes on us the entire time.

I slid Maeve's food across the table to her.

"Wrap of Kahn still your favorite?" I asked.

"You bet," Maeve said as I arranged my own food in front of me. "Thanks. This is just what I needed today."

Judging from her tone, it wasn't just the edits that were bothering her. I knew she'd had a meeting with her lawyer earlier. Did Frank come up with some new scheme to drag the court proceedings out even longer? It was a slimy thing to do in any case; but the fact that Frank's infidelity was the catalyst for the divorce made his behavior extra gross.

Maeve didn't volunteer any information, however, and after the conversation from that morning, I didn't want to push her. We ate in silence for a few minutes as the dogs snoozed around us. This wasn't so bad. I could get used to this … right?

"How was the interview?" Maeve asked, loading some stray bits of corn salsa onto her fork. I wiped my hands on my napkin. My Bombay Bomb burrito was tasty, but messy.

"It's a beautiful facility," I said.

"Yeah, I've seen pictures."

"And the people seemed nice, for the most part. And the salary and benefits are above average for the industry."

"But," Maeve prompted.

I hesitated. I didn't want to talk about my fear of permanency, of my reluctance to settle down. I didn't want Maeve to feel she was a burden, because she absolutely wasn't.

Maeve was my hero for most of my life. I wanted to be able to make her life as easy as possible, and give Frank a swift kick in the rear in the process, LIMA be damned. I wanted to be there for her, as she had for me all those years I'd spent traveling, when our parents pretty much disowned me.

The problem was, I still wanted to be able to wake up in a different state from one morning to the next. I loved being able to spend a weekend at a Suzanne Clothier workshop in New York, and then scoot over to Wisconsin to take in a Patricia McConnell seminar, and from there to pack up and take the dogs hiking in the Blue Ridge Mountains. I loved the freedom of spending a month or two working as a humane society adoption counselor in Iowa, of doing a stint at an emergency vet clinic in California over a holiday week-end, of teaching a few rounds of puppy classes in Pennsylvania.

The Cascade Canine Club was, indeed, a dream job. But even with the promised variety of classes and the opportunity to put my years of study and experience to good use, I worried about feeling restricted. Of getting bored. Boredom never really sat well with me. I wasn't good at it.

I looked into Maeve's warm, hazel eyes and knew there was no way I could tell her any of this without hurting her.

"There's this guy," I said instead, and Maeve's eyes sparkled.

"Ooh," she said. "Do tell."

"Ew," I said. "Not that kind of guy. He's like, thirty years older than me. And married, I think. I'm pretty sure I saw a ring."

Maeve took another bite of her wrap as she waited for me to continue.

"He's the trainer I'm going to be replacing," I said. "And he's definitely not going to go quietly. He barged into my interview and started arguing with everyone about how unfair it was that he was being fired."

"Awkward."

"Understatement. Plus, he had this poor rottie wearing a shock collar."

Maeve made a soft, concerned noise through her mouthful of food.

"Now, there are plenty of people out there who use electric collars appropriately," I continued. "Though, they're not a device I personally use or recommend. This was not, in any way, acceptable use of the tool. The dog was clearly stressed and was showing obvious signs of discomfort. Bryan totally ignored everything the dog was trying to tell him until he finally growled. And then he shocked him."

I picked up a fallen piece of bamboo shoot and popped it into my mouth.

"Poor thing," Maeve said, looking distressed enough that I almost regretted telling her the story. She was so softhearted when it came to animals or children.

When I first brought up the idea of getting her a service dog, she nearly declined, worried that the work would be too hard on the dog; the training too emotionally taxing. Even when I assured her that a mentally and physically sound dog would suffer no ill-effects either from the training or the duties of a mobility assistance dog, she remained concerned right up until the day I introduced her to Gentle Ben, then a nine-month-old puppy in the midst of his training. She finally relented when she saw his enthusiasm for the work, along with his delight in any new behavior I taught him.

"It was hard to watch," I said.

"Bryan Reed, right? I think I remember reading a few articles about him, back in the day," Maeve said.

"That's him," I said.

Maeve nodded.

"Yes, he was somewhat of a local celebrity back when we first moved here. He claimed that no dog was too much for him to handle, that he could teach any dog to be completely reliable in any situation, and off leash, too. He was so charismatic. There was never any mention of shocking anything."

"It's usually not something people lead with."

Maeve began packing up the remnants of her wrap. She ate maybe a third of hers. I managed half of mine. The things were monstrous.

"What was he even doing there?" she asked. "Didn't you just say he'd been fired?"

"Maybe fired is too strong a word," I said. "I think they relieved him of his position as a trainer; but haven't banned him from the club altogether. He and the president are good friends. Or at least, they were."

"So, it's likely you'll encounter him again," Maeve said.

"Probably."

"Well, I can see why that would make for an uncomfortable working environment. Are you going to keep looking?"

I thought about that for a moment, buying time by very carefully re-wrapping my burrito, taking Maeve's leftovers to the fridge, and wiping down the table.

"Nell," Maeve said, as I was in the middle of transferring our knives and forks to the sink. "Remember what I said about not needing a maid? Sit down."

I sat. Maeve folded her hands on the table in front of her.

"It's not just this Bryan guy that's bothering you, is it?"

I sighed.

"This is the first time I've ever looked for a long-term job," I said, choosing my words carefully. "It's not like I can just pack up and leave if it doesn't work out."

"You can," Maeve said, softly. "You absolutely can. I don't want you to feel like you're trapped here."

"I don't," I said quickly, almost before she had a chance to finish.

Maeve raised an eyebrow.

"Really, I don't," I insisted. Was I lying? I wasn't sure. I ploughed ahead, needing to convince myself as much as Maeve. "I want to be here. I miss you and the kids. I'd like to be able to go to Julianne's soccer games and Liam's chorus recitals, to pick them up from school, to be here for the aftermath of staining your bathtub purple when I dye their hair."

Maeve rolled her eyes, "I'll remind you that you said that when it's time for the clean-up."

"And I want to hang out with you, too. You know I've never been to one of your book signings? I want to be able to give you feedback, live and in person, while I'm reading your rough drafts. And someone needs to give Frank a what for, and since you won't do it, well, then I'm your woman." I flexed my bicep, feeling a little pang as I did so.

Frank had been Maeve's version of an escape from our parents. Acceptable in their eyes at it was, after all, a marriage. Frank had been instrumental in facilitating my own getaway, as well. He and Maeve lent me the money to purchase the Green Machine. None of which excused what Frank did to Maeve a few months ago, or what he was continuing to do with his ridiculous custody bid.

"Let's leave Frank out of this for now," Maeve said, reaching across the table to lay a hand on mine. "Nell, I'm so excited to have you here. Even if you do decide to turn my children crazy colors and leave a path of destruction in your wake. But I don't want you to feel obligated. I can handle things on my own."

Of that I had no doubt. Maeve would never admit to needing help, and I knew that through sheer determination she'd make any situation work. But her working herself to death wasn't in anyone's best interest. She deserved to be able to relax and share the workload. It would be up to me to convince her that this was my idea, that this was something I wanted. I squeezed her hand.

"It's just a little bit of an adjustment is all," I said. "But, I'm almost thirty. I need to settle down, get a real job, live in a house. What better place to do it than right here?"

I pushed my chair back and got to my feet. Rush and Simon were instantly at my side, ready for action.

"I'm going to take the job," I announced to the room.

Maeve smiled. Gentle Ben *rooed*. Simon thumped his tail, and, not to be outdone by them all, Rush uttered his scream-bark of joy.

Chapter 8

A few days later I sat in one of the upstairs offices of the main training building, putting together informational handouts as I listened to the barks, bangs, and shouts of the flyball practice taking place downstairs. Immediately after I'd called her to formally accept the job, Clarice had asked me if I'd be willing to take on a basic pet manners class.

I was excited to start teaching classes again. Clarice approved my curriculum that morning. I lost no time emailing the six people signed up for the class, introducing myself, and reminding them not to bring their dogs to the first session.

Now, ensconced in the office I shared with Felicia and Deanna, I was busy making sure everything was in order. Samples of various options for training treats were arranged on the left side of the desk, and a box of clickers sat on the right. Next to my purse lay the brand-new keyring, containing keys for most of the buildings on the grounds in addition to a keychain emblazoned with the words *Cascade Canine Club* in bold script above the club's logo of a dog's paw entwined with a human hand.

Rush and Simon lay curled up together on a thick, round

dog bed under the desk at my feet. They looked like a canine interpretation of a yin-yang, the bright red of Rush's coat contrasting with Simon's rich golden sable. Simon's pointed little muzzle rested on Rush's fluffy behind, and Rush's speckled nose was balanced on Simon's bony hip.

Largely ignoring the noise from below, they both lifted their heads and pricked their ears when a particularly shrill stream of barking rose above the cacophony.

"Sounds like quite the party," I murmured. Seeing I wasn't interested in or worried about the sounds, they resumed their positions.

Flyball is a wild, action-packed relay sport. Teams of dogs race each other over a series of hurdles to a tennis ball concealed in a box. The dog hits a button on the box, releasing the ball, which they then grab and run back over the hurdles. The excitement level is always high, and many dogs expressed their enthusiasm by barking: while they wait their turn to run, during their run, and in celebration at the end of their run.

The chaos was mainly why I never did much training or competing in the sport. The noise and frenetic energy just wasn't my cup of tea, though it was certainly fun to watch. In small doses.

The pandemonium was likely the reason that I wasn't aware of Bryan Reed's presence until his voice boomed from behind me.

"Nell McLinton, CPDT-KSA, CBCC-KA," he said, pausing after each letter of my certifications. I whirled around, my ponytail whisking against the back of the chair. He leaned against the doorframe, arms crossed, watching me. His icy blue eyes were flat and cold and calculating. I shivered in spite of myself. Rush and Simon, no doubt picking up on the creep factor, leapt to their feet. Simon let out a warning bark.

"Lie down," I said quietly. They did, but remained on alert.

"Hello, Bryan," I said, forcing a smile. "What can I do for you?"

He reached out a finger, tapping the nameplate affixed to the wall next to the door. Mine was beneath Felicia's and Deanna's.

"Load of gibberish, if you ask me."

I assumed he was referring to my credentials, the alphabet soup of letters that followed my name. My certifications were a testament to my years devoted studying, watching, listening, learning, and practicing the science of canine behavior. I was proud of what those letters signified, and I wasn't going to stand by and let him mock me for it.

"I can get you the Certification Council for Professional Dog Trainers website, if you'd like," I said, still smiling. "I bet it could clear up any confusion for you."

He ignored my offer, peering around me to look at the dogs.

"Little herding dogs," he sneered. "Thought so."

"I'm sorry?" I said, caught off guard by the abrupt change of topic.

His hand moved through the air dismissively.

"Australian shepherd and a, what's the other one, some kind of collie mix? Not much challenge in that, is there?"

"Not like, say, a Rottweiler?" I deadpanned.

He shrugged. "As an example, sure."

"I think none of us would ever progress far as trainers if we defined ourselves by the breeds we've chosen to live with," I said. "I'm sure you've trained your fair share of herding dogs."

"Of course," he puffed out his chest. "I've trained hundreds —"

"And," I broke in, as I couldn't think of anything I was less interested in than his boasting, "though I choose not to live with them, I've trained plenty of Rottweilers, cane corso, American bulldogs, and pit bulls. Wouldn't you agree that every breed presents its own unique behavior challenges, which are, in turn, balanced out with qualities that prove useful in training?"

He didn't respond right away, at least not in words. His lips thinned, his eyes narrowed, and his hands clenched into fists.

"So that's how you have them all fooled," he said, his voice low but menacing. "Spouting off with your big words … you with your fancy titles, your treats and your gimmicks." He punctuated that last word with a poke at my box of clickers, sending it shooting dangerously close to the edge of the desk.

I placed a hand on the clicker box, stopping its forward trajectory, and pushed myself to my feet in one smooth motion. I wanted us on equal footing.

"Marker training isn't a gimmick," I said, a lot more calmly than I was feeling at the moment. I slid the box back to the center of the desk. "And I haven't fooled anyone. I'm not responsible for the club taking training in another direction, Bryan. All I did was answer an ad."

I wasn't expecting him to be cowed by that, not really, but I hoped it would hit home. He had to realize he was wasting his time trying to intimidate me and move onto someone else. Someone with a little more clout than I. A board member, maybe.

Unfortunately, it didn't quite work out that way.

Bryan slammed his hand down onto the desk. I jumped and took an involuntary step back. The reaction was just so out of proportion to the situation. Simon growled, low in his throat, but he and Rush both held their positions.

"Don't you talk down to me," he spoke through clenched teeth, his voice rumbling up from his chest, and thumped the desk again. "I've been doing this for longer than you've been alive! You don't think I've seen fads like your click and treat training come and go time and again over the years?"

Spare me. I was always up for a training methodology

debate. I loved hearing how others liked to train and why. But calling something faddy and touting one's vast years of experience without offering anything to back it up was kind of a cop out. Calling Bryan on that didn't seem like the wisest course of action.

I was still trying to formulate my response when a voice called out, "Everything okay up here?"

I tilted my head slightly, looking over Bryan's shoulder to find the source of the unfamiliar male voice. And wow. Where were they hiding Mr. Tall, Bald, and Beautiful during my interview? The speaker stood a few inches taller than Bryan and had the lean, toned body of a swimmer. His shaved head only accentuated his perfectly symmetrical features, and his eyes were a striking shade of gray. As I stood gawking, Bryan backed away from my desk and turned around.

"Everything's just fine, Calvin," he said. "Did you hear they hired my position right out from under me? And replaced me with one of those clicker Nazis?"

Nazi?

"Sorry about that, man." Calvin was juggling an armload of tennis balls, but he still managed to free one hand to give Bryan a sympathetic slap on the shoulder. "Hey, do you have a sec to help me out downstairs? We're having some issues with one of the boxes not releasing."

Bryan shook his head.

"I don't know what you people would do without me," he said to Calvin as he left the room. "Someone should remind Clarice of everything I do around here."

"Preaching to the choir," Calvin said as Bryan passed.

I dropped back into my seat as some of my confidence dissipated. What if the rest of the members of the club felt the same? Was I going to have this trouble with everyone?

Calvin leaned slightly into the room as he turned to follow Bryan. I braced myself. Calvin grinned, teeth flashing white against his dark skin, and winked before disappearing from sight.

I looked down at the dogs, still holding their downs, their eyes laser focused on me, ready for action.

"Anyone want to fill me in on what just happened?" I asked them. Rush tilted his head to one side, and Simon perked his ears.

"Alright, alright," I said. "Stand down."

They both relaxed into more comfortable positions. I sighed and checked the time. My class was due to start in half an hour. I made sure my handouts were in order and grabbed a handful of clickers. Each plastic box was a different color and had a raised yellow button on the underside. I attached each one to a sturdy elastic bracelet, which would make it easier to manage while also holding a leash and treats.

From the sound of it, flyball practice was still going strong downstairs. I decided to take the dogs for a quick spin around one of the back paddocks before setting up for class. All I had to do was shift in my chair and Rush and Simon were instantly on their feet. I retrieved two slim leather leads, supple and soft after years of use, and peered out into the hall to make sure the coast was clear.

Satisfied that Bryan wasn't skulking about, the dogs and I headed for the staircase. At the base of the stairs, a short hall led to an *Employees Only* exit opening directly to a large, fenced paddock. Before heading down the hall, we paused for a minute or two to observe practice.

Two lanes, each containing four hurdles and a spring-loaded box, were set up in the center of the room, with a significant distance in between. Two teams, made up of four dog and handler pairs, ran opposite each other. The rest of the participants watched along the sidelines. Felicia stationed herself between the two lanes, overseeing the activity.

Calvin seemed to be part of a team consisting of a Jack

Russell terrier, a chocolate lab, and tall, shaggy-coated terrier mix. After seeing how friendly he and Bryan were, I wasn't surprised to see Calvin's dog, a Belgian Malinois, wearing an electric collar.

It was clear after just a few moments, though, that Calvin's approach was the exact opposite of Bryan's. As he waited his team's turn, Calvin kept his dog engaged with a jute tug toy. When the terrier came over to investigate, causing the Malinois to lose focus, Calvin simply moved a few feet away and used the toy to regain his dog's attention. Even though I could see the remote poking out of Calvin's pocket, in easy reach, it obviously wasn't his default response to unwanted behavior. Intrigued, I decided to stay a little longer.

Felicia signaled for the next two teams to line up. Calvin's team stationed themselves at the lane farthest from me. The other team was comprised of a rat terrier, a black, gray, and orange speckled cattle dog, a flat-coated retriever, and a beautiful black tri aussie. The aussie was handled by a tall, slim man wearing a bright blue shirt dotted with neon pink flamingos.

I was cheering for Flamingo Guy's team on principle (he had an aussie, after all), but Calvin's team won by a fraction of a second. As the teams shuffled and the boxes were reset, I signaled to my dogs and we slipped out the back door.

I unclasped the leashes and lobbed a stray tennis ball into the air. Simon pushed off from the ground, jaws closing around the ball when it was still a good four feet above the grass.

"Whoo Hoo!" cheered a voice to my left as Simon landed neatly. Rush lunged for him, and the game of keep-away was ON.

"Oh, hey, I'm sorry," I said, turning toward the young couple who were, apparently, sharing the yard. They'd been leaning against the building, the girl snuggled under the guy's arm, talking quietly together. Between us stood a metal trash can and pooper scooper. "I didn't know anyone else was out here."

"Don't worry about it," the girl said, shrugging out from beneath the guy. She looked to be in her late teens or early twenties. "I wasn't really thinking about visibility when I chose our spot. I just wanted the sunlight."

She shook back her thick blond hair. It hung nearly to her waist in meticulously styled waves. The guy stood about a head taller than she did, and his own carefully coiffed hair was the same shade as hers. They reminded me of Ken and Barbie. I moved to stand next to them in the sun.

"You must be Nell McLinton," the girl said.

"I must be," I confirmed.

"I'm Stacey Callahan. This is my fiancé, Jeff. I'll be your teaching assistant in your pet manners class."

"Oh, right," I said, shaking hands with each of them in turn. "Clarice said something about that in her email. Sorry, it's been a busy few days."

"I'll bet," she said. Jeff leaned forward and gave her a quick peck on the cheek.

"Hey, babe, I gotta get going," he said. "I'll see you after class?"

"Yup," Stacey said, returning the kiss.

"You're sure you'll be ready?"

"Yes," Stacey said, sounding a little annoyed. "I told you I would be."

Simon pranced up to me with the ball, and I threw it to the far end of the pen, giving Jeff plenty of time to exit the gate without being crowded by the dogs.

"He's not a fan of waiting around," Stacey said, as we watched him leave. "Last class I assisted in ended in a dog fight and it took a while to get things sorted out."

Yeesh. I wondered who'd been the unlucky one teaching the class. Dog fights in that kind of situation were the worst.

"Well, I promise I'll have you out of here on time," I assured her.

The dogs flew past us, Simon still in possession of the ball, but Rush not even close to giving up the chase. Their feet churned up bits of grass and dirt, which sprayed over our shoes. I opened my mouth to apologize again, but Stacey only laughed.

"Wow, they sure are fast," she said. "They'd run circles around my guy for sure."

I looked around. Rush and Simon were the only two dogs in the yard.

"He's at home," Stacey said. "I'm only here for a quick meeting and your class today. I didn't want Bruiser to be a distraction."

"What kind of dog is he?" I asked. Standard dog person ice breaker.

"He's a Rottweiler."

"Ah," I said. "Just like Bryan's."

Her expression darkened, but it was so fleeting that I wasn't entirely sure if I'd actually seen it, or if it was just an illusion from a cloud passing over the sun for a moment.

"Yup," she said, flashing me a smile. "Just like Bryan. He actually recommended the breeder. My boy is, I think, a cousin of Diesel?" She laughed. "I'm not really sure how dog family trees work."

I had to work to keep my smile in place. Had Clarice just assigned me Bryan 2.0 as my assistant?

Chapter 9

Most of the flyball participants were gone by the time Stacey and I brought the dogs back inside. Calvin was helping Felicia stow the hurdles and boxes away, his Malinois holding a down-stay in an out of the way corner. Flamingo Guy was deep in conversation with a willowy, middle-aged woman, who was struggling to control her corgi on leash.

Felicia saw Stacey and me standing on the sidelines and waved us over.

"Hey, I see you two have already met. Clarice told me to make sure I introduced you guys, but practice is always a little insane, and it slipped my mind."

"Don't worry about it," I said. "We've got the important stuff out of the way. I know she has a rottie named Bruiser."

Stacey grinned.

"And I know *she* has an aussie named Rush and a border/whippet named Simon."

"Perfect," Felicia said, laughing.

She glanced down at the dogs. Rush danced in place, whining softly. So many new people to meet, so little time. Simon gazed around the room, not showing much interest in anything until he spotted an unattended tennis ball a few feet away. Then the tip of his tail started wagging.

"Simon is too cute," Felicia said. "Such a unique color. You don't see that too often in this cross."

I tried to catch Felicia's eye. Despite what I'd said about having all the necessary information about Stacey, I did want to know a *little* more about her, especially since there seemed to be some connection with Bryan. But Calvin walked up to her, and I lost my chance.

"Everything's all set," he said.

"Thanks so much for your help," Felicia replied. "Those boxes are such a pain to lug around." She waved a hand in my direction. "By the way, Cal, have you met our new trainer, Nell McLinton? Nell, this is Calvin Overby. He's the training director at the Central Oregon IGP Club."

"Hey," Calvin said, offering his hand. I shook it. His grip was firm and confident, and his eyes … wow. They were even more stunning up close. "Sorry about all that with Bryan. I figured the best way to get him to move along was to agree with him, you know?"

"Oh … of course," I said.

A smile spread over his chiseled features, upping the attractiveness factor even more than I would have thought possible.

"Guess I'm a better actor than I thought."

"You had me fooled."

"Okay, but did you see the wink?"

"I did!" I said, laughing. "It was a little ambiguous, though, you have to admit."

Calvin looked as though he were about to say more but was interrupted by Felicia.

"Hold on. What happened with Bryan?"

"Remember his little scene at my interview? More of that. A little angrier, though."

"Gosh, I'm sorry," Felicia said. "Clarice told me to watch

out for him, but I got distracted with everything that was happening at practice."

I looked around for Stacey, to gauge her reaction to the conversation, and found she was arranging chairs in a semi-circle in the middle of the room. Just as I'd planned on doing, though I hadn't said anything to her about it. Kyle materialized out of nowhere and was helping. The two seemed to be chatting companionably.

"You people should just ban the guy already," Calvin said. "It's not like he's going to change."

"It's Clarice's decision," Felicia said, simply. "Besides, as soon as we ban him here, you know he's going to be spending more time out with you guys. He thinks that fat old dog is a Schutzhund superstar."

I'd never trained in Schutzhund, but was familiar enough with the intense, three phase (obedience, protection, and tracking) sport with the ever-evolving name to realize that Diesel likely wouldn't have much success.

"It's IGP, now," Calvin said. "Internationale Gebrauchshud Pruefung."

I was most definitely not a German speaker, but his accent sounded pretty convincing to me.

"Potato, Potahto," Felicia said, unimpressed. "He'll still be your problem, whatever you're calling the sport nowadays."

Calvin shook his head, crossing his arms.

"Not if I have anything to say about it," he said, and I blinked in surprise. "I can have him banned at our club just as easily. He needs to be convinced that it's in his best interest to retire."

Huh. Maybe Calvin and Bryan weren't as friendly as I'd thought.

"Who's getting banned?" We all turned in the direction of Flamingo Guy, who was making his way over to us. The woman with the corgi had gone.

Rush had made eye contact with him, likely the instant he'd decided to head our way, though I'd been too engrossed in the conversation to notice. His bobtail wiggled faster and faster as Flamingo Guy closed the distance between us.

"Hello, gorgeous!" Flamingo Guy exclaimed, spreading his arms wide in a clear invitation. Because of Rush's tendency toward over-exuberance, I generally didn't allow him to greet anyone unless he managed to demonstrate a modicum of self-control. We all make bad decisions sometimes, though, and I dropped the leash. Rush uttered an ear shattering shriek of pure joy and flew across the rubber matted floor straight into Flamingo Guy's arms.

I kept an eye on Calvin's dog, ready to call Rush back if things got too distracting for him. Malinois are, by nature, primed to react to everything in their environment. The dog tensed and whined softly under his breath but held position. Calvin followed my gaze, his arms folded over his chest, far away from the remote in his pocket.

"Don't worry about Axel," he said. "His stays are solid."

"I'm not worried," I said. "I just didn't want to be too obnoxious."

I returned my focus to Rush, who was busy soaking up the attention like a sponge. Flamingo Guy ran his hands over Rush's body in quick, practiced movements, no doubt making note of Rush's structure and condition.

"That's Jared Wesson," Felicia said. "He's been in aussies for years."

Jared looked up at the sound of his name and grinned at the sight of the three of us watching him. He led Rush back to the group and handed the leash to me.

"I love this dog," he proclaimed, and I caught the hint of a southern drawl in his accent. "Where'd you get him?"

"From a breeder in Wisconsin," I said.

"Oh, Deb at Driftwood? Right on Lake Michigan?"

"Yes, actually," I said, a little surprised. Deb was well-respected in the breed, of course, but still. Wisconsin's a long way from Oregon.

Jared leaned over and ruffled his fingers through Rush's neck hair.

"He's just her type, isn't he? 'Course, I guess he didn't read the part of the standard about aussies being aloof toward strangers."

"No, he most certainly did not."

As if to prove his point, Rush whined faintly and started to head back in Jared's direction, though he sank back into a sit at a quiet reminder from me.

Jared chuckled.

"God, I love Deb," he said. "Her dogs are the best. Last I saw her was at Nationals. She beat the pants off me."

"That must have been a sight," Calvin remarked.

Jared waggled his eyebrows at him and grinned.

"Oh, honey, you have no idea."

Everyone packed up and left after that, leaving Stacey, Kyle, and me on our own. I settled Simon and Rush in down-stays against the wall and ran upstairs to get my supplies.

"Thanks for setting up the chairs," I said to Stacey upon returning. In those few minutes, Kyle had disappeared. "That's exactly how I wanted them."

"I figured, when Clarice said you weren't having dogs at the first class," Stacey said. She peered into my box of clickers.

"Oh, is this going to be a clicker class? Cool!"

I'd been mildly stressing about what her reaction to that news would be, and relaxed slightly at her seeming enthusiasm.

"I've always wanted to learn this," Stacey continued. "I know Felicia and Deanna use them sometimes, but I don't usually help out in those classes."

"Well, here," I said. "Take one. Or a few. I've got plenty."

She selected a purple one and slipped it into her pocket.

"Learning is super easy," I said. "Basically, the click is telling the dog that they've done something right."

"That's it?" Stacey sounded a little disappointed.

I laughed.

"It's not magic," I said. "It's just a way to be clearer in communicating. Think about it. How do you tell Bruiser that he's done something good?"

"I, um," Stacey paused, blushing. "I tell him he's the best boo-boo or that he's a good boy. Sometimes I pet him or give him a treat."

"Love it," I said. "If you were training me, all of that would be fantastic. But remember, dogs are nonverbal, and they do best with consistency. With the clicker, your signal of a job well done will be near instantaneous. To be honest, you don't even need the clicker, really. You can use a marker word to accomplish the same thing. I just like that the clicker makes a unique noise that Bruiser is only ever going to associate with that one thing."

"Does it really make that much of a difference, though?"

"Well, it's hard to ask the dogs," I said, smiling. "From my observations, the dogs seem to appreciate the clarity and speed of communication. But don't take my word for it. Give it a try and see what you think."

People started trickling in, and Stacey and I got to work collecting payment and vet records, helping everyone to find a seat, and giving them each a handout and a clicker. For those first few minutes, the room was filled with the sounds of murmured conversation, shuffling papers, and stray clicks. One thing I've always found to be universal … humans can't resist clicking the clicker initially. First classes are always filled with the sounds of people testing out their clickers. Just one of the reasons it's best to leave the dogs at home to start.

I called to Simon, and everyone settled down as he zoomed over and placed himself in heel position. Usually, I let the class participants decide which dog I'd use for my demo, but I felt that Rush would benefit from practicing some self-discipline, so I left him to his down-stay and deemed Simon my assistant for the day.

"How many of you are familiar with clicker training?" I asked, and was met with six blank stares. Someone clicked their clicker.

"Okay," I said, holding up my wrist, from which dangled my clicker. "Now, the clicker is just a tool. And like any tool, it has to be used properly to be effective. And properly means that you only use the clicker for one thing: to tell your dog they've done right and that a reward is coming. It's not to be used to call your dog to you, or to interrupt bad behavior."

"Not very versatile, is it?"

Oh joy. Bryan was back.

My class turned in their seats, and I looked over their heads to see Bryan leaning against the far wall, arms crossed over his chest. Diesel sat at his side, shock collar in place. I plastered on a wide smile.

"It might seem that way, at first," I said. "But, really, marking and rewarding good behavior can be used to train an infinite number of things. This method is used to train performance dogs, service dogs, and sport dogs. It's used to train wild animals at zoos and rehab facilities to allow medical treatment. It's kind of hard to fit a prong collar or shock collar on a tiger or killer whale. But, with this method of training, handlers are able to motivate these animals to remain still and present various body parts for preventative care and treatment."

About half the class wore expressions of wonder. The other half still looked skeptical. So, about average. Bryan remained silent, so I turned to my secret weapon. Simon.

Chapter 10

The action-packed performance (Simon's favorite tricks tended to defy gravity) seemed to win over the skeptics. Members of the class turned excitedly toward each other, looking at their clickers with new enthusiasm.

"Well done," I said to Simon, who sat at my side, looking supremely pleased with himself.

Bryan chose that moment to push himself away from the wall.

"Sure, trick training is fun to watch," he said. "But how useful is having a dog do a backflip to everyday life? Especially if you have to carry a clicker and treats around with you everywhere?"

That's a bit rich coming from a guy who carried the remote control to a shock collar around with him everywhere. I refrained from rolling my eyes with difficulty. One of us, at least, should try to remain professional. Bryan heckling me during my very first class was eroding any sympathy I'd felt for him earlier. Had he always been like this? How had the Club tolerated it for so long?

Taking care to keep my smile in place, I pointed in Rush's direction.

"See that guy over there?" I asked the class.

Everyone turned away from Bryan. Rush, though thrilled to suddenly be the center of attention, held his position.

"Has he been there the whole time?" a woman asked.

"He certainly has," I said. "And his stay was trained the exact same way as Simon's tricks. Once a behavior is established, you can go ahead and chuck your clicker into the middle of Crater Lake, if you want. But don't really, though. Bad for the environment."

The class chuckled. No one was looking at Bryan anymore. But I was. And his expression was murderous.

———

"Well, you've convinced me," Stacey said, once the last person left and Deanna's competition obedience class started filtering in. Adrienne flipped me a quick wave in between working to keep the attention of a petite gray and white husky who seemed to want to explore every corner of the room.

"First thing I'm going to do once I get home is see what Bruiser thinks of the clicker."

"Have fun," I said, returning a wave from Jared as well. He had a different dog with him, a sturdy looking red merle male. I added, "And fair warning, it's addictive."

"Turning dogs into treat-crazed clicker junkies. Now there's something to be proud of."

Really? Did Bryan not have anything better to do than mock my every word? If he put as much effort into training his dog, he'd likely be able to ditch the shock collar. I bit that remark back just in time, choosing instead to close my eyes and silently count to ten.

"She doesn't even deny it," Bryan continued. "Once the

novelty wears off, you think your pet training clients are going to like turning their dogs into living, breathing slot machines?"

I took a deep breath before opening my eyes and turning to face Bryan.

"When I said addictive, I was talking about the *people*," I said. "I realize it's a tough concept for you to grasp, but there are people out there who enjoy being able to train their dogs without utilizing pain and intimidation to ensure compliance."

Bryan stomped forward, pressing a button on the remote in his hand when Diesel didn't automatically follow. The Rottweiler jumped and bolted forward, placing himself in heel position and looking up at his owner nervously. I winced in sympathy for the poor dog. Bryan loomed over me, making the most of his height advantage, pointing a meaty finger in my face.

"You listen to me, missy."

Missy?

"No. *You* listen to me." I took a step forward, closing the gap between us and glaring into eyes so full of rage that an eruption seemed imminent.

Deanna, as well as several members of her class, stopped what they were doing to stare. I caught a glimpse of Kyle, a can of paint dangling from one hand, standing near the door, wide-eyed. We were making a scene, but after dealing with this all day, I was beyond caring.

"I get that you're having a hard time with this. Really, I do. But that does not give you the right to harass me everywhere I turn. It absolutely doesn't give you the right to interrupt and attempt to undermine me while I'm teaching. I've said it before, and I'll say it again. I had nothing to do with your removal from this position. Any problems you have, you need to take up with a board member."

Right on cue, Adrienne abandoned all pretense of working with her dog and allowed the overgrown puppy to do what she did best; pull her toward us. Diesel growled as the husky beelined in his direction. Bryan shocked him.

"I wish you'd stop that," I said through gritted teeth.

"Yeah, I'll just bet you do. Here's a lesson for you, girlie. Dog training isn't all unicorns and rainbows."

"Who said it was? You're acting like minimizing the use of aversives is some unrealistic pipe dream. News flash, it's not!"

"Hey, hey! You guys maybe wanna take this somewhere else?" Adrienne said, pausing a few feet away and reeling her dog in closer to her.

"No, I don't!" I whirled in her direction. She took a step back. "This has been going on all day and I'm sick of it! It's not even about methodology with him; it's about me being hired for a position he thinks should be his!"

"Damn right it should be mine!" And there it was. The rage eruption. "Have you seen what she's doing out there? Throwing around treats and playing with her little plastic toys."

Bryan used the sturdy antennae of his remote control to flick the clicker hanging around my wrist. I jerked my hand away.

Failing to make the husky go away with his aborted growl, Diesel decided that the next best option was to leave. He started to back up. Bryan shocked him again without even repositioning his hand. Diesel froze in place, his wide eyes full of a bewildered, helpless fear that turned my stomach.

Without pausing to think about what I was doing or considering the consequences, I grabbed the remote and hurled it across the room. It hit the wall with enough force that it shattered. No one, human or dog, made a sound. I could not believe I just did that.

"I'm sorry," I said, nearly paralyzed with shock. "I'm sorry, I'll replace it."

Still, no one spoke. Even Bryan was dumb struck. Well, that was something, at least. I started to back away.

"I'll replace it," I said again.

Adrienne reached out, I think to pat my shoulder, but I shrugged out from under her.

"Would you get me the details of make, model, and cost?" I asked her, not quite able to meet Bryan's eyes.

"Don't worry about it, Nell, we'll figure it out," she said.

"Just let me know," I said. "I'm going to … I have to get some work done."

I grabbed my box of clickers and fled up the stairs, calling to Rush and Simon as I went. Once I reached the top, I dumped the box of clickers onto the table next to the stairs and ushered the dogs ahead of me into the office.

"Holy shih tzus," I breathed, leaning back against the door. I shook my head, trying to clear it. I'd never done anything like that before in my life. I was so fired.

Rush and Simon both stared at me with identical worried expressions.

"Hey, guys, it's okay," I said, speaking softly and quietly. I slid down the door's surface, landing in a crouch. The dogs crowded around me, each trying to comfort me in his own way. Rush pressed himself against me and tucked his muzzle under my chin. Simon leaned close and snuffled my ear.

We didn't move for a few minutes. Finally, I got up and settled myself in the desk chair. Assuming I still had a job, I had work to do before next week's class. I put my earbuds in and cranked up the volume on the loudest, hardest rock station on Pandora I could find. I wanted to drown out any sounds of the class below, any voices from the offices on either side, any knock at the door.

———

I wasn't sure how long I spent in my makeshift sensory deprivation chamber pounding away at my laptop. By the time I finally looked up, I could see that it was starting to get dark. I turned off the music and pulled off my earbuds. There was a missed call alert on my phone screen, and a text, both from Adrienne. The text was reassuring, saying that I wasn't the first person be provoked into a confrontation with Bryan, and that everything would work out.

I shoved the phone in my pocket and blew out a frustrated breath. Part of me was grateful for the support, but I was mainly still just angry about losing control like that. It most definitely wasn't the least intrusive way of handling the situation.

Automatically looking down to check on the dogs, I was surprised to find that they weren't curled up together on the dog bed as expected.

They crouched at the door, their noses pushed into the space between the bottom of the door and floor. Rush's hindquarters were quivering. Simon held his tail in a stiff half circle over his back.

"What's up, guys?"

They turned back to look at me, and then fixed their attention on the door once more.

I listened carefully. No sounds came from the training area downstairs. Cautiously, I opened the door a crack.

"Hello?" I called into the empty space. "Anyone out there?"

No one answered. I opened the door wider and let the dogs exit the room. They raced each other to the top of the stairs and paused, looking back at me.

"Go on," I said, granting them permission to run ahead. They disappeared.

I followed at a slightly more sedate pace, stopping short at a familiar clicking sound, followed by the crunch of plastic beneath my foot. I looked down and saw that my box of clickers had somehow been overturned at the head of the stair-case. Multicolored clickers were scattered everywhere. Was this Bryan's doing? It seemed a little petty, but then again, Bryan had proven himself to be nothing if not petty.

Gently moving clickers out of the way with the tip of my sneaker, I made my way to the top of the stairs. Clickers littered the first few steps. But that wasn't what made me press both hands to my mouth to muffle a scream as I peered down to the landing.

Bryan was crumpled at the foot of the stairs, clickers strewn all around him. His head lay in the middle of a large pool of blood. He wasn't moving.

Chapter 11

"Omigod!" I gasped from behind my hands. Rush and Simon circled Bryan's body, sniffing intently. My stomach lurched at the sight of one of Rush's white paws in that red, red puddle.

"Get back!" I commanded, finally recovering my wits.

Both dogs jumped away, startled. I didn't normally speak so sharply to them.

"Lie down," I said, working hard to sound calm as I raced down the stairs.

At one point halfway down, I tripped over a random clicker and nearly ended up in a heap next to Bryan. I caught myself just in time and managed to get to the bottom of the stairs in one piece.

"Bryan!" I called out, dropping to my knees next to him. I looked around for Diesel, but the rottie was nowhere in sight. Bryan was alone in the room.

His eyes were wide and staring. With a shaking hand, I felt for a pulse, first at his wrist, then his neck. I didn't think I could feel anything, and it didn't seem like he was breathing. But what if I was wrong? He was still warm.

I fished my phone from my pocket and dialed 911, hitting

the speaker icon before letting it fall to the floor. The dispatcher answered as I started chest compressions.

"Yes, I'm at the Cascade Canine Club facility," I said, realizing too late that I didn't know the exact address. "Someone's fallen down the stairs and he's ... I think he's ...." I couldn't say the word.

The dispatcher, of course, was used to this sort of thing, and understood what I was trying to say. She asked if I was sure, and I told her that I wasn't, not entirely. She asked if I knew CPR and if I felt comfortable administering it. Comfortable was a strong word, but my certification was current.

"Is anybody else here?" I shouted between rescue breaths. No one responded. I continued CPR, each minute feeling like an hour. Sweat beaded over my forehead and trickled down my back. I was winded, as though I'd attempted to sprint up Pilot Butte. My arms began to feel like Jell-O, but I kept going, telling myself I could get through one more round of compressions. Two more breaths. I did it over and over again, until at last, the paramedics arrived. And told me I could stop. Bryan was gone.

———

Once the police cruisers and ambulance showed up, the training building was suddenly full of people. Felicia had been teaching an agility class next door, and the entire class spilled out into the parking lot. The police quickly set up barricades, and the class participants crowded around them.

Through the open door, I saw pretty much everyone who had been at my interview. Calvin and Jared were there, plus about six or seven other people I didn't recognize. *Big class,* I mused idly from where I crouched against the wall next to Rush and Simon.

"Excuse me, who's in charge, here? Would you let me through, please?"

I craned my neck to see Clarice flagging down the police officer patrolling the barricades. She hadn't been part of the initial crowd from the agility class.

"Ma'am, I'm going to have to ask you to stay back," one of the officers, probably young enough to be her grandson, said, motioning for her to keep her distance.

"I own the place," she responded, peering around him to see inside.

The police were in the process of meticulously documenting the scene. Bryan's body was covered with a sheet. One unlucky soul worked the tedious task of recording the precise location of each clicker.

I was instructed to keep out of the way, but also to stay close and keep the dogs quiet. An evidence technician took pictures of the dogs, particularly their feet. Rush had gotten close enough to step in the blood. Simon hadn't.

They did the same to me, photographing my face, hands, and clothes before taking a cheek swab, in case any DNA was found at the scene. Since I'd been administering CPR for nearly ten minutes, all told, my DNA was probably all over the place.

"Not because we suspect anything," Detective Rodriguez assured me in his lightly accented voice. "But just so we can quickly categorize anything we find."

Yeah, right. I'd heard some of the hushed conversation between him and the crime scene techs ... how some of the wounds on Bryan's head didn't seem to fit with an accidental fall. I noticed the way the detective was always watching me, even when occupied with other tasks. He didn't even let me use the restroom when I'd asked. Hopefully that didn't last too long. The situation was becoming somewhat dire.

Clarice was still causing some polite commotion at the

barricades, insisting they tell her was happening. Detective Rodriguez walked over to assist the officer outside. A small group gathered around him, including Adrienne and Calvin. A flash of movement in my peripheral vision caught my attention. I looked across the room in time to see a man stumble through the side door. I heard a snarl and spied a bulky black and tan mass lunge forward before the guy managed to slam the door behind him. Was that Diesel? It was bothering me that the big dog didn't seem to be anywhere in sight.

A quick glance around the room found most of the police occupied with the growing crowd at the barricades. The other two or three deep in talk with the crime scene techs. I returned my attention to the new arrival, watching as he adjusted the gray messenger bag over his shoulder and ran a hand through a mop of dark, curly hair. He was of average height and heavyset, dressed casually in jeans and a zippered green hoodie. Definitely not a police uniform. I leaned forward, looking for the tell-tale light flashing off a badge. Nothing. I was pretty sure that, whoever he was, he wasn't supposed to be there.

Still, no one else in the room seemed to notice him, save me and the dogs. Rush's bobtail wagged madly, and he trembled with the effort of holding his down-stay. The man caught my eye and gave a small wave. Could he be from Felicia's agility class? As he drew closer the lack of standard dog class paraphernalia-- leash, treat pouch, and poop bags-- became starkly apparent.

"Hi," he said, jogging the last few steps to close the distance between us. "Cute dogs. Not like that one out back. I thought I was gonna be dinner for a second."

He spoke quickly, and his accent was very decidedly East coast; New York, I guessed. He reached down toward Rush. His movements were sharp and jerky, as though he wasn't used to being around animals. Bending at the waist, he hovered directly over the dogs, reaching straight for the top of Rush's head. Rookie move. Not that Rush was bothered. Attention was attention to him, no matter who it came from, or how it was delivered. Simon, on the other hand, pushed himself up to a sit and stared haughtily down his long nose at the newcomer.

I rested a hand reassuringly on Simon's shoulders and he slid back into a down.

"Probably best not to touch the dogs right now," I said, ignoring Rush's whine of disappointment as the man straightened and obediently stepped back. "I'm pretty sure they're being considered evidence."

"Really?" the man said, his tone hushed. Dark brown eyes surveyed the room from behind black-framed glasses. His thumb brushed against the screen of the smartphone he held in his hand, opening a writing app. He wore a medical alert bracelet on his left wrist, though I was too far away to read it. He looked to be in his early thirties.

"Evidence of what?" he asked

I pretended not to hear the question, and threw out a few of my own.

"Did you say there was a dog out there? Was it a Rottweiler?"

"A what?"

I narrowed my eyes. Anyone who had any reason to be at the club would surely know what a Rottweiler was. They've been ranked in the top ten most popular breeds in the country for at least the last few decades.

"Big, short-haired, black and tan," I said.

"Yeah, that's him," the guy said eagerly. "He was on the other side of the yard, watching the people in the parking lot. But the second I got inside the fence he came for me, barking like crazy. If I'd gotten to the door a second later, I wouldn't be standing here talking to you, and Cujo would be enjoying a Jewish deli."

Diesel. It had to be. It was a perfectly appropriate place for him to be. Still, it seemed strange. Bryan never seemed to let the dog out of his sight. While I was pondering that, another thought occurred to me. The outer gates were kept padlocked as a safety precaution. Certain club members had keys, but Clarice didn't give them out to just anyone. Definitely not nosey, non-dog owning strangers.

"How did you even get in the fence?" I asked, eyes still narrowed. The fences weren't particularly high, to be sure, but the guy wasn't exactly Jackie Chan. He grinned, eyes twinkling.

"I'm more agile than I look," he assured me. I couldn't help but smile back. He shifted his phone to his left hand and held out his right.

"I'm Daniel Friedman," he said, as we shook hands. "I'm with the Central Oregon Chronicle. Can I quote you on the dogs being evidence?"

A journalist. Of course. I was about to tell him where he could shove his quote, but Detective Rodriguez didn't give me the chance.

"Mr. Friedman!" he thundered as he strode over to us.

"Busted," Daniel muttered under his breath. He tucked his phone away.

"Hey, Detective," he said aloud. "Fancy meeting you here! Could I get a statement from you? Does it look like an accidental —"

"Out!" Detective Rodriguez said, pointing. "You'll get your statement when we hold a press conference, just like everyone else."

He beckoned one of the uniformed officers over to escort Daniel Friedman out the front door. Once the reporter was safely behind the barricades, the detective turned back to me.

"He came in through the side door," I said. "In case you were interested."

Detective Rodriguez raised his eyebrows.

"I didn't think anyone would want to try and get past that huge dog out there," he remarked. He looked away briefly as a metallic clatter sounded from across the room. The paramedics transferred Bryan to a black body bag and were preparing to roll the gurney out of the building. I swallowed hard.

"The dog belongs ... belonged ... to Bryan," I said, blinking furiously as my eyes filled with tears. Training methods aside, Bryan had clearly loved Diesel. I wondered what would happen to the dog now. I didn't even know if Bryan had any other family.

Detective Rodriguez nodded.

"Yes," he said. "Your club president informed me. She said he'd be well cared for. In the meantime, would you please accompany me to the station?"

His tone was perfectly pleasant, but his body language indicated that I really didn't have any choice in the matter. Fantastic.

Chapter 12

Detective Rodriguez refused to let me drive myself to the police station. Which didn't exactly fill me with reassurance about the situation. At least he allowed me to get the dogs settled in the Green Machine before we left. Because it was after dark and rapidly cooling off, I felt comfortable leaving Rush, his left front paw once again pristine and white thanks to some hydrogen peroxide, and Simon in their home on wheels. Especially with so many people still in and out of the buildings.

The detective's unmarked car was neat and clean. Without hesitation, he directed me to the front passenger seat. I wanted to ask if I was being charged with anything but couldn't decide if that would make me seem suspicious. It seemed safer to keep quiet, so I used the time to send a hurried text to Maeve, letting her know that I'd likely be late. I also warned her not to listen to the news.

Once at the station, a female officer conducted a thorough search of my person, finally allowing me to use the bathroom after she'd finished. Then she led to a small, windowless room containing only a table with a chair on either side. Detective Rodriguez occupied one of them. As I entered the room, he motioned for me to take the other. He waited, hands folded on the tabletop, while I situated myself.

"Would you please state your name for the record?" he asked at last.

"Nell McLinton."

"And you've been employed by the Cascade Canine Club for how long?"

"Just a few days," I said. "I taught my first class this afternoon."

Detective Rodriguez made a note on the pad in front of him, solemn and professional.

"There was some controversy surrounding your employ-ment, correct?"

"I ... not really," I said. "Just with one person."

"The deceased."

I blanched at the reference to Bryan, but nodded.

"How, exactly, did Mr. Reed make his feelings known?"

I sat up a little straighter in my chair. Detective Rodriguez's tone made it seem as though the question was significant. I figured that they must have found something suspicious about the scene just based on the way they'd shut everything down; the care taken with potential evidence. How the detective had been unwilling to let me out of his sight. Was he trying to establish a motive?

"Mr. Reed interrupted my interview on Friday," I said, figuring there was nothing to be gained by lying about it. "And he has been antagonistic in every interaction since then. Ask any one of the training board members."

"I have," Detective Rodriguez assured me. "And I heard from several witnesses that there was an altercation between the two of you this afternoon."

I nodded.

"Could you elaborate, please, Ms. McLinton?"

Holy shih tzus. This didn't seem to be heading in a good direction at all. Did I need a lawyer?

"Mr. Reed disagreed with my training methodology," I said slowly. "He was clearly bothered that I was hired to a position he saw as his."

"The two of you were seen arguing quite heatedly."

I tried to catch Detective Rodriguez's eye, hoping maybe there'd be a hint of what he might be thinking, of where this conversation might be going. He made brief eye contact, but his features betrayed nothing. He tapped his pen twice on the scarred surface of the table.

"There were also reports that you destroyed a piece of Mr. Reed's property."

"I —" I stopped as suddenly as I'd started, feeling that I would look bad no matter how I responded.

"And that you were the only other person in the building at the time of the murder."

Murder. It was the first time he actually used the word. I swallowed hard.

"I didn't see anything," I said. "He'd already fallen when I came out of my office."

Detective Rodriguez gave a slight nod.

"You're sure?"

"Of course," I said.

"You didn't have any interaction with him at all after the scene in the training arena?"

"No," I said, firmly.

Detective Rodriguez's pen scratched across his notepad. Our eyes met again, and he held my gaze for a few seconds. I was expecting the cold, hard stare of someone determined to get to the truth. I was thrown by the kindness in the detective's dark eyes. Rather than reassuring me, the change in his demeanor piqued my suspicion, and I steeled myself for his next question.

"It must be a bit of a relief," he said, quietly. "Now that he's gone."

Tears burned at the corners of my eyes. The lump in my throat threatened to choke me, and it was all I could do to manage to whisper past it.

"I didn't want him dead," I said. "I tried to help. From the moment I found him, until the paramedics arrived." A tear slid down my cheek as I recalled the feeling of hopelessness and despair as the minutes ticked by while I tried to revive Bryan. It was the first time I'd ever had to administer CPR to a human. I never imagined that those actions would wind up getting me blamed for his death.

"Accidents happen," Detective Rodriguez said, handing me a tissue. "No one is disputing your efforts after the fact. What I'm concerned with is what happened before."

I balled the tissue in my fist.

"All I know," I said, concentrating on each word, "is that he was perfectly fine when I left the training area. I worked in my office for about an hour and a half. I had loud music playing. When I came out, I saw him at the bottom of the stairs. I can't tell you what happened in between."

"Can't?" Detective Rodriguez repeated. The unsaid *or won't* hung in the air.

I took a deep breath.

"Are we at the point where I need to ask for a lawyer?" I asked.

———

The interview ended soon after I questioned my need for an attorney. I was told I was free to go, and that Detective Rodriguez would be in touch. I confirmed my contact information with him before walking calmly out of the station. Once I was sure I was a safe distance from the security cameras, I leaned against the brick wall and took several long, slow breaths, attempting to steady myself.

My first thought was to load everything up into the Green Machine and hit the road. If the events of the past few days were any indication, I absolutely wasn't meant to settle down. I hadn't been to Canada in a while. Maybe it was time to revisit. Heck, maybe I'd drive all the way up to Alaska. That was one feat I had yet to accomplish. Nothing like a murder accusation to inspire new travel goals.

I spent a pleasant thirty seconds fantasizing before reality kicked in. If there was one thing guaranteed to make me look guilty, it would be running away. And it's not like a lady with rainbow hair, a giant green van, and two distinctive looking dogs could easily disappear. I'd be caught and dragged back to Oregon in days.

And then there was Maeve, Julianne, and Liam.

No, I'd have to stay put. At least until the whole custody thing had been sorted out. But I still had absolutely no idea of what to do next. Did I even have a job anymore? After the shock collar remote destruction alone, I expected to be fired. There was no way they'd still keep me on staff after everything else. And then what? Bend wasn't exactly a booming metropolis. I imagined word would travel fast. Would I even be employable in the animal field at all after this?

Perhaps making a break for Alaska wasn't such a bad idea after all. I pulled out my phone, halfway wondering if I could convince Maeve and the kids to join me on an adventure.

"It's Nell McLinton, right?" a voice interrupted me.

I looked up to find the reporter from the dog club standing just a few feet away under a streetlight. I thought back, trying to remember his name.

"Daniel Friedman," I said at last. "But I don't recall giving you *my* name."

He took a few steps closer.

"It's Dan, actually," he said. "The only one who ever calls me Daniel is my mother."

"Okay, then, *Dan*. How did you find out my name?"

"A journalist never reveals his source," Dan said, grinning. I crossed my arms and glared at him. He spread his hands in a gesture of surrender.

"Hey, it's not like you don't stand out, you know? It wasn't exactly difficult."

Hmph. I had to give him that, I supposed. All he likely had to do was hang around the dog club after I left with the police.

"Is everything all right?" he asked. "People were a little worried when they saw you leaving with the cops."

"Super-duper," I replied, fully cognizant that anything I said was likely to wind up in the newspaper.

"So, are they suspecting foul play?"

I shrugged.

"Couldn't tell you."

"Seems like a lot of effort to haul you down to the station just to take a statement about an accident."

"Pro tip, Dan. If you have a question about police procedure, I'd recommend, you know, talking to the police."

The text alert sounded on my phone. I looked down to see at least a dozen frantic messages from Maeve. She must have watched the news even after I'd warned her not to.

I'm fine, I tapped out, not even reading what she'd sent. *Be back soon*.

"I could give you a ride back to your van, if you'd like," Dan offered, glancing toward my phone.

Yeah ... no.

"Thanks, but I'm good," I said, angling the screen away from him. "You'll have to get your scoop somewhere else."

I opened the Lyft app on my phone and requested a ride. Dan's smile faltered a little.

"I'm not just about the story, you know," he said.

"Sure, you're not," I said, rolling my eyes. I didn't think he'd catch it in the dark, but for a moment, his smile disappeared entirely. I would have felt bad about it, except he was blatantly trying to get information on an active investigation for publication. Not cool.

His phone chimed. After glancing down at it, he chuckled.

"Did you just order a Lyft?" he asked.

"Maybe."

He turned the screen to me.

"At your service, then. Unless you want to wait and match with someone else."

"You're a reporter and a Lyft driver?" I asked dubiously.

He shrugged.

"Man cannot live by writing alone."

I looked away as I felt the corners of my lips twitching in a smile at the adapted quote. I didn't really want to encourage him to keep trying to get information out of me, which I figured was the reason behind the offer of a ride. But the dogs were waiting in the van and Maeve was at home freaking out. Might as well put my big girl panties on and deal with it.

"Fine," I said.

His finger hovered over his phone's screen.

"You could just cancel," he said, "I could give you a ride like I suggested before. For free."

"How about I pay you," I said, "And you don't ask any more questions about Bryan Reed, or the case in general."

"Fair," he said, and swiped his thumb across the phone's screen.

Chapter 13

"So, here's the thing I don't get," Dan said, once we were both strapped into his Subaru and on our way. "Everyone I talked to said that you and Bryan Reed were having a major argument about your training methods."

"Didn't we literally just agree not to talk about this?"

"This isn't about what happened to him," Dan insisted, looking away from the road briefly to make eye contact. "I'm honestly curious about what there is to argue about in dog training. Sit, stay, come, right? Seems pretty simple."

"I'm guessing you've never had a dog," I said drily.

Dan shook his head. "No. Well, we had one, once, when I was a kid. His name was Elmer, and he was a beagle. He was a nightmare, completely unmanageable. My parents couldn't deal with it, and finally gave him away. My Grandma used to say our people weren't dog people anyway, you know? She pretty much screamed it, actually. In Yiddish. But, to be fair, it was her famous brisket that Elmer liked to steal especially."

I laughed in spite of myself.

"Scent hounds are a challenge," I said. "And you're partly

right about the training thing. Sit, stay, come is the goal. Where
the conflict comes is in how you get there."

"Meaning?"

"Like, you know how way back in the day it was pretty
normal for people to beat their kids? Which then progressed to
less intense beatings, like a spanking. And then we, as a society,
began to understand more about how humans think and learn.
Corporal punishment has largely been phased out."

"For some," Dan said. "But there's still plenty of people out
there who think a good smack upside the head is the best way
to get the message across."

I blinked.

"Not me," Dan said, quickly. "I don't even have kids. But,
you know. People. They're out there."

"That's exactly my point," I said. "Dog training is no
different. And dogs truly are amazing. They're so adaptable, so
good at reading people and figuring out what we want, that
many of them will learn no matter how they're trained."

"Why the argument, then?"

"Because, while dogs will learn from a variety of training
methods, it doesn't mean that all of those methods are benign.
See, as we've gotten to know more about how people learn and
think, similar findings have been made about dog behavior.
Behaviorists have discovered is that certain types of punishment really do have a detrimental effect on the psyches of
dogs. What they've also figured out, is that dogs can and do
learn remarkably well through management and positive reinforcement."

"I'm not quite following," Dan said. "So, you're saying that
dogs can be taught equally well whether or not they're trained
with punishment or positive reinforcement?"

"Well, they'll generally learn, let's just say that."

"But the positive stuff is healthier for them mentally."

"Confirmed by science. There was actually one study that tested cortisol, that's the stress hormone," I added as Dan opened his mouth to ask the question, "anyway, they tested the cortisol levels of dogs during training with a variety of devices. They found that the very act of placing a shock collar on a dog … not even using it, but just placing it on a dog, increased their stress levels significantly."

"Really?"

"Really. And that doesn't necessarily mean that an electric collar should never, ever be used. But it does indicate that people should think really hard if that particular tool is necessary for what they're trying to teach."

"Why the arguments, then?"

I threw up my hands.

"Why do people argue about anything? Everyone is convinced that their way is the best way. It's human nature. It all really just boils down to choice. I've made a conscious choice to train the way I do, to minimize the use of aversives and intimidation because that's what resonates with my personal values. That doesn't mean that people who feel differently are wrong or bad. The major issue I had with Bryan wasn't that he was *using* a shock collar. It was the *way* he used it. Completely unprofessional and inappropriate." I paused for breath, noticing Dan's sideways glance and the smile playing around his lips.

"Sorry," I said.

"Don't apologize. People should be passionate about their work."

We'd turned onto the long, twisting drive leading to the Club. Neither of us spoke for a few minutes as the Subaru chugged up the steep hill.

"Bryan must have been a real pain in the tuchus," Dan remarked, slowing down at a particularly sharp curve.

I nodded, admiring the way the moonlight illuminated the spacious paddocks and neatly maintained buildings. It really was the most beautiful training facility I'd ever seen.

"Bryan was the one bad thing about this job," I murmured absently. It took a few seconds before I realized who I was talking to. I whipped my head in Dan's direction.

"Strike that from the record!" I ordered.

"Consider it stricken," Dan said.

I narrowed my eyes. He lifted his hand from the gearshift and held up three fingers in the familiar salute.

"Scout's honor," he said.

I wasn't convinced, but at this point, what other options did I have, other than taking his word for it?

We pulled into the parking lot. Police tape still surrounded the main training building, but the area where I parked the Green Machine was untouched. Dan headed for it without any direction from me. I couldn't give him too much credit, though. My van was the only vehicle in the lot.

I sent my payment as he pulled into the space next to the van. I could hear the dogs barking next to us and was eager to get to them.

"Thanks for the ride," I said.

"It was my pleasure," he said, giving a small bow. "Do you want me to hang out for a bit? It's kind of desolate out here."

"No," I said, almost before he'd finished. "I'm good."

I watched until his headlights disappeared before switching on my phone's flashlight and unlocking the van. Simon and Rush burst out of the back and danced around me, Simon uttering high pitched barks of excitement while Rush screamed. Both seemed unsettled, expressing their anxiety by frantically jumping all over me.

I spoke soothingly to them, stroking them both under their chins. They settled after a minute or two and trotted off to water some trees. I busied myself shaking out crumpled blankets and filling bowls with food. It was past their dinner time. The parking lot was well-lit by several floodlights. Beyond the reach of the lights, everything was dark and silent. I shivered. I wouldn't have admitted it to Dan, of course, but it was a little creepy. The wind rustled the sagebrush behind me, and I flinched away, heart racing.

Simon, as usual, finished his meal first. He drifted a few feet away, nose to the ground, while I wiped out his bowl and waited for Rush. Rush and I both jumped when he uttered a staccato series of deep alert barks. Simon only barked like that to announce the presence of humans he deemed suspicious.

"Over here, guys!" I ordered automatically. Rush and Simon planted themselves at my feet as I snapped their leashes on. I strained to see in the gloom outside the parking lot, but picked out a sphere of light floating in the distance. My hand clenched around the ends of the leashes.

"Hello?" I called into the night, pleased that my voice sounded steadier and more confident than I felt. My keys dangled from the Green Machine's ignition. Mentally I mapped out how I'd shove the dogs into the vehicle and escape if needed.

"It's just me!" a familiar voice responded. It took me a second, but I recognized Clarice's voice just as she stepped into the light. In one hand she held the ends of three leashes attached to three regal looking salukis. In the other, she held a large flashlight.

"Oh, Nell," she said with relief. "I saw the lights coming down the drive from the house, and with everything going on, decided I'd better come and investigate. I'm glad I didn't just call the police!"

"I appreciate that, even though it was probably the safer option," I said. "I imagine they've had enough of me for one day."

Clarice closed most of the distance between us, stopping a polite five to six feet away in order to give the dogs plenty of space. Rush's stubby tail wiggled frantically, while the hair stood up between Simon's shoulder blades and he growled softly.

"That's about enough of that," I told him quietly, and he relaxed, his attitude shifting to match the haughty disinterest of the salukis.

I took a moment to appreciate the refined beauty of Clarice's dogs. All three were tall, long-legged, and lean. They moved with effortless grace, the wispy feathering on their legs, tails, and ears fluttering in the light breeze.

"Your dogs are absolutely stunning," I said.

"Thank you," Clarice said. "The larger gold boy is Ra. His daughter, Ma'at is the red. And the black and silver is Inanna. She's the baby of the family. Just a year old."

I smiled at the Egyptian mythology names. I probably would have chosen similarly for such regal creatures.

"I'd love to see them in the daylight sometime," I said.

"Oh, we'll get to that soon. They love showing off."

I raised an eyebrow. Did that mean I still had a job? The best thing probably would have been to just not say anything more, but that's never been my strong suit.

"My sympathies for your loss," I said. "I know that you and Bryan were close."

Clarice looked away, suddenly hyper-focused on the dogs. Ra sniffed the air, catching the scent of something. Coyote, skunk, owl? Or maybe he was just interested in my dogs. Either way, he hadn't moved other than to lift his narrow, pointed muzzle skyward. Clarice gave a sharp tug on the leash, and Ra shot her an annoyed look, clearly unused to such treatment.

"The police told me we'll be able to hold classes again in a few days," she said, her voice sounding oddly muffled. "We'll start out with a meeting for board members and trainers to make sure we're all on the same page. I'll email you when I know more, okay?"

"Okay," I echoed, but she'd already turned around, ushering the salukis ahead of her out of the parking lot. I watched the light of her flashlight for a while, bobbing in the dark as she made her way up the hill toward the house.

Chapter 14

"Nell! Thank God! I was so worried!"

I just barely cleared the doorway before Maeve flung her arms around me, her cane clattering to the floor. Her grip was surprisingly strong.

"I told you not to watch the news," I said, motioning for Julianne to retrieve Maeve's cane from where it had rolled down the hallway. Normally, that was one of Gentle Ben's favorite tasks, but he sensed that Maeve was unsteady and plastered himself to her side.

"It popped up on my Facebook feed," Maeve mumbled against my shoulder. "The article said a trainer at the Club had been murdered, but they didn't give a name."

"They actually said murdered?"

"Suspicious death, I think," Julianne piped up. Her eyes were red-rimmed.

"I texted you that I was fine as soon as I could," I said.

Maeve pulled back, dropping one hand to Gentle Ben's shoulders to steady herself. Julianne handed her cane back to her.

"Cryptic and abrupt," Maeve said. "And then you went MIA immediately after."

"Well, I thought it best to turn my phone off during the police interrogation."

Maeve's and Julianne's eyes widened.

"You got arrested?" Liam exclaimed.

"More like just rigorously questioned," I said. "Now, come on, guys. Let's move this party to the living room so your mom can sit down."

I herded everyone ahead of me out of the hallway and into the living room. Maeve sank down onto the sofa. Gentle Ben settled himself beside her. Liam sat on her other side. Maeve placed one arm comfortingly around his shoulders.

I parked myself in an overstuffed armchair. Simon and Rush made to jump up with me, and I was just about to signal to them to go ahead when I caught sight of Julianne. She'd been very quiet since I entered the house, which was unusual for her. She stood, slightly away from the rest of us, her hands clenched into fists at her side, eyes bright with unshed tears.

I scooched to the side and patted the seat next to me. Julianne wedged herself between me and the arm of the chair. I gave a gentle tug of her ponytail, and she smiled shakily before leaning back slightly, cuddling up close.

Then it hit me. Anything I did, or anything that happened to me, wasn't going to only affect me anymore. For better or for worse, the four of us were all in this together.

———

The next morning was gorgeous. Clear and cold, the ghost of the moon still visible in the weak light of an early sunrise. I cranked up the heat in the Green Machine as I followed Julianne's instructions to a nearby hiking trail. The three dogs sat at attention in the back, my two with unabashed excitement, and Gentle Ben seemingly torn between excitement and mild anxiety over leaving Maeve.

I frowned slightly as I watched him in the rearview mirror.

"He always does this for the first few minutes," Julianne piped up from the passenger seat. "It's like he's not sure he's supposed to be having fun without Mom, but he eventually gets over it. I take him for walks, just me and him, all the time. Mom says it's not healthy for him to be cooped up with her all day while she's writing."

"Exercise is always good for aussies," I agreed.

"Turn here," Julianne said suddenly, and I had to hit the brakes harder than I'd intended to make the odd, sharp turn onto a dirt road. We passed a large horse farm and a few grand, showy houses before the residential area gave way to miles of juniper trees, sagebrush, and random stretches of barbed wire that seemed to lead nowhere.

The parking lot at the trailhead was huge and beautifully maintained. I attached small tab leashes, basically just a handle to grab if necessary, to Simon and Rush's harnesses, while Julianne folded Ben's leash in one gloved hand. The dogs heeled next to us as we left the parking area and crossed the dirt road to the trail. There they paused, Ben's tongue lolling, Simon in his classic border collie crouch, eyes fixed on mine, and Rush quite literally vibrating with excitement until I gave the go ahead with a quiet,

"Okay."

The dogs exploded forward. Julianne and I followed at a slower pace, carefully picking our way around rocks that didn't even register as obstacles for the dogs.

"So, how's things, Jules?" I asked, after we'd been walking for a bit.

She shrugged, watching as the dogs zoomed past in a furious game of chase. Rush was in the lead, with Simon at his heels. Gentle Ben followed a few paces behind. I wondered what was bothering her. Was it Maeve? She'd seemed pretty frail lately. Or the divorce? I gave Julianne a playful bump in the shoulder.

"Come on," I said. "You can tell me anything. You know that."

Julianne kicked at a small stone and it skittered a few feet ahead, bouncing along the frozen ground.

"Mom's worried about you," she said, finally.

"I'm fine," I said, waving a hand nonchalantly. Nothing to worry about here, no ma'am.

"Aunt Nell. It's been less than a week, and you're already being investigated for a murder."

"Just questioned," I pointed out. "They didn't even tell me not to leave the area. That's rule number one for a person of interest." But even as I said the words, my stomach flip flopped. Because, true enough, Detective Rodriguez hadn't explicitly said not to leave the area, but his demeanor during the questioning also made it clear that he was taking this seriously.

"Who do you think did it?" she asked.

"That's the million-dollar question, isn't it?" I said, side-stepping to avoid the tornado of teeth and hair that was Rush and Simon wrestling in the middle of the trail. "There were plenty of people around that day, to be sure, and between you and me, Bryan really wasn't the most popular guy."

We walked in silence for a little while longer, laughing at the dogs' antics. Julianne pointed out a deer in the distance, and we made sure to keep the dogs close until it was out of sight. Deer in Central Oregon are no joke. If they feel crowded or threatened, they don't hesitate to attack. Those hooves pack a mighty wallop. On the few occasions I did some relief work at the local emergency animal hospital, I saw firsthand the damage that could be done to a dog.

I paused to admire a skein of neon green colored moss

hanging from one of the juniper trees. Julianne walked a little way ahead, shading her eyes with one hand as she looked out across the distance.

"What was it like?" she asked, suddenly.

"What was what like?" I responded, pulling out my phone and snapping a photo of the moss.

"Finding him when you were all alone like that." Julianne shuddered. "I've been trying to imagine it, and I can't."

I slipped my phone into my pocket. Ben came prancing up to me with a stick in his mouth. I held out my hand and he gently surrendered the stick before backing up a few paces in anticipation, bounding after it with delight when I finally threw it. Simon began sprinting in pursuit, but I immediately called him off, allowing Ben to have his fun without having to deal with Simon trying to steal the stick from him.

"It was disturbing," I said, finally, after thinking about it for a minute or so. "I was pretty sure there wasn't anything I could do for him, but I couldn't be sure, so I tried my hardest to do what I could until the paramedics got there." The image of Bryan at the bottom of the stairs in a pool of blood planted itself in my mind, and it took some doing to force it away.

"Weren't you worried that the killer was still there?"

I shook my head.

"Honestly, Jules, the thought never entered my mind. I didn't even realize it was a murder. I just thought it was all a horrible accident."

A shiver coursed through my entire body at the thought that the person who murdered Bryan might have been watching as I tried to save his life. I drew in a deep breath, attempting to stay calm. I remembered how my voice echoed through the empty building as I called for help; how utterly alone and isolated I felt the entire time. I surely would have known if someone was there. There weren't that many places to hide. Right?

Julianne brought me back to reality by tapping my elbow. She gestured down the trail, where a group of people were approaching. The comfort and safety of everyone sharing the trail was always at the forefront of my mind when hiking, so Julianne and I immediately leashed up the dogs and kept them close.

It's impossible to predict if people are nervous around dogs, or just not interested in being greeted by them; often until it's too late. Even though all three dogs were well trained enough to stay in heel position without leashes, the leashes sent a good visual cue to anyone approaching that the dogs were under control and wouldn't be a nuisance.

Everyone smiled politely at each other as we passed, with one woman in the group commenting on how gorgeous Gentle Ben was. She wasn't lying. His size and coloring really made for a striking combination.

I caught a snippet of conversation as they passed, and it stopped me cold.

"That's her, isn't it? From the article in the *Central Oregon Chronicle*."

"Hard to miss that hair," another person said.

"She doesn't look like a murderer," said the third person, and that's the last I heard before they moved out of range.

I turned to Julianne, my mouth hanging open. She grabbed my phone from where it dangled uselessly from my hand.

"What's the passcode?" she asked.

I could only stare at her. She lightly thumped my elbow.

"Aunt Nell. Passcode."

My brain started working again, barely, and I swiped a finger over the screen, unlocking the phone. Julianne lost no time pulling up the *Chronicle's* webpage. Her eyes widened, and she wordlessly handed the phone back. I recognized the photo of me and the dogs as one Maeve took in the back-yard. It was the one I sent Adrienne to post on the Club's website with my bio. A big, black line of text over the photo read,

Is Bend's Newest Dog Trainer out to Permanently Eliminate the Competition?

And, in smaller letters, just before the article, was the name of the author. Daniel S. Friedman.

————

I barged through the door of the Central Oregon Chronicle, even angrier after reading the entire article. I expected a room full of chain-smoking reporters pounding away at computers in a large, disorganized pool, shouting for assistants to contact sources or hurry up with research. And yeah, I was aware that it hadn't been legal to smoke in a public building in more than a decade, but that was the image stuck in my head. Too many movies, I guess.

What greeted me instead was a single desk manned by a somewhat matronly older woman. Behind her were several rows of cubicles, strategically designed, it seemed, to prevent the journalists from being observed. It was eerily quiet; the only indication of anyone else in the room was the telltale clacking of several keyboards. Expecting to be able to march straight up to Dan, I stopped short and staggered as the sudden cessation of movement unbalanced me. The receptionist looked up from her computer as I tripped through the doorway.

"Good morning, Miss …" she trailed off, seemingly realizing who I was. And why wouldn't she recognize me? There was a stack of the current edition of the paper right next to her.

"I'd like to speak to Daniel Friedman, please," I said primly, trying to smooth my hair and pretend like I hadn't nearly sprawled face-first on top of her desk.

"Of ... of course," she stammered, and got to her feet. "Wait here a moment, please. May I get you something to drink?"

"No, just Mr. Friedman will be fine," I said. Once her back was turned, I swiped one of the papers off the pile. Since I'd made the front page, I figured I was entitled. I watched as she made her way to one of the cubicles in the center of the room and bent down to speak its occupant.

Dan's curly topped head popped up almost immediately, and he followed the receptionist back to her desk casually, his hands stuffed in his pockets. Other heads appeared over the cubicle walls, obviously sensing that what was happening right in front of them was, for the moment, more interesting than the stories they were working on.

"What can I do for you, Nell?" he asked, coming to a halt a few feet in front of me. The receptionist reclaimed her seat and began typing away at her computer, studiously ignoring us.

I glared at Dan, holding up the copy of the paper I'd pilfered, and he at least had the grace to look somewhat sheepish.

"What the hell is this?" I hissed through my teeth, mindful of the handful of other journalists in the room.

His eyes were the picture of innocence.

"Hey, I gave you the chance to tell your side."

"My *side*?" It came out louder than I'd intended, but *seriously*? A man was dead. It wasn't like this was some kind of petty dispute. Dan's eyes widened, and he quickly closed the distance between us.

"Let's talk out here," he said, gesturing toward the hallway. He placed a hand on my shoulder to guide me, but I shrugged out from beneath him.

"Look," he said, once the door had closed behind us. "My editor needed something to print for this morning. All my source at the police department could tell me was that it was definitely murder, and you are the person of interest at the moment."

His source at the police department? Who? I was willing to bet it wasn't Detective Rodriguez. And I was *the* person of interest? As in the only one? Super. That wasn't terrifying at all. I couldn't let him see that he'd rattled me, though. I pushed the thought to the back of my mind and forced myself to concentrate on the article.

"What about this?" I thrust the paper in front of his face, my finger jabbing the line that read, *and, as the Chronicle can exclusively report, Ms. McLinton has admitted to having an adversarial relationship with the victim, and that his very existence was an inconvenience to her.*

"Off the record, you said. Scout's honor, you said."

Dan glanced at the part I'd indicated and then stepped back, shrugging, his hands once again in his pockets.

"Well, the thing is, I never was a scout," he said.

I wanted to fling the paper in his face. Instead, I rolled it into a slim tube and clenched it tightly in my right hand.

"So, basic journalistic integrity's not your thing, then," I said. "Good to know."

Just before reaching the door, I looked down, realizing that the newspaper was still clutched in my hand. I tossed it in Dan's direction. It hit the floor just in front of him, the pages unfurling and swirling around his feet. I gave a curt nod of satisfaction and continued on my way.

The farther I got from the *Chronicle* building, though, the more anxiety settled in. This was bad. If running away wasn't a viable choice, then my only remaining option was to stay and find a way to prove my innocence.

Chapter 15

"This is fine," I said to the dogs, back inside the Green Machine. "I can solve this. All that time spent listening to true crime podcasts while driving around the country is about to pay off."

My eyes flicked to the right. Mounted on the passenger side dashboard was a photo of a black and white dog with brindle points on the sides of his muzzle. Sebastian, my first ever dog. Below the photo I'd pasted a quote, in swirling black calligraphy. *Try Harder, Be Better*. It was something that one of the hosts of RedHanded often said. I made it my mantra. After the confrontation with Dan, it seemed even more apt.

I straightened in my seat and glanced in the rearview mirror. Both Rush and Simon stared at me attentively, as if offering their assistance. I smiled in spite of myself, briefly imagining taking down the killer with a crazy red aussie and scrawny little border/whippet. If we pulled it off, maybe the RedHanded hosts would cover the case. We'd be famous. I shifted my gaze back to the road, but not before catching sight of the clock out of the corner of my eye.

"Shih tzus," I muttered. Unless the Green Machine suddenly sprouted wings and a jet propulsion engine, I was about to be late for my meeting with the board members of the Club. Luckily, the snow and ice from the previous week had long since melted, and I could risk speeding a little. By the time I pulled into the parking lot, I was only five minutes late. Still not the greatest, considering what was at stake.

The parking lot was fairly full, and I couldn't find a shady spot for the van. It was a typical March day in Central Oregon -- sunny, growing warmer by the minute, and not a cloud in the sky. It wasn't supposed to get above fifty-five degrees, according to my weather app, but even at that relatively low temperature, I wasn't comfortable leaving the dogs in the direct sunlight.

"All right, guys," I said, attaching their leashes. "You can help me argue my case."

We ran inside the main training building. The police tape was gone, along with any evidence of a murder having taken place. Still, I felt a pang as we passed the area where Bryan's body had lain and had to force my eyes not to linger as we flew up the stairs.

"Sorry I'm late," I gasped as I burst through the doorway of the main meeting room, where I had my interview less than a week before.

"It's not a problem," Clarice said. "I know traffic can be tricky this time of day."

She gestured to an empty seat at the table.

"Is there somewhere I can stash the dogs?" I asked. "It's a little too sunny for them to wait in the car."

"They can stay," Adrienne said, smiling. "I was just saying how weird it was that no one brought a dog today."

"Thanks," I said, and settled Rush and Simon in downstays behind my chair.

Once I sat down and tucked my purse and leashes between

my feet, I managed to get a good look around. Everyone who was at my interview was there, along with a handful of people I didn't recognize.

"Thanks for coming in on such short notice, everyone," Clarice said. She turned to me. "Nell, I believe you're familiar with the training directors and Adrienne. I asked the rest of the board members here because this will be a decision that affects the entire Club."

"Of course," I said, looking from new face to new face, wishing I was on time, at least.

Felicia raised her hand. Clarice nodded at her.

"I move to dispense with the introductions for now," she said. "And let's just get down to business. There'll be time enough to mingle after."

Leave it to Felicia to get right to the point. Why bother taking the time to introduce me if they were just going to fire me anyway? I folded my hands on the table in front of me and lifted my chin, determined to not embarrass myself further even if bad news was coming. But my mind was racing. What if I got blacklisted and couldn't find training work in Central Oregon at all?

"Agreed," Clarice said. "I'm sure we all have questions and concerns about what happened yesterday. Bryan was with us from the beginning, for better or for worse, and he will be sorely missed by all of us."

Her voice quivered on those last few words. There were murmurs of agreement from around the table, and more than a few eyes looked suspiciously bright. Not Adrienne, though. Or Felicia. The latter sat silently, head bowed, and her mouth twisted almost as if she were hiding a smirk. That couldn't be right. When I went back for a second look, her expression had smoothed, and she tilted her head toward Deanna, who was whispering something to her.

"Please," Clarice said, in a much firmer voice, "If you have anything to add, I'll ask you to share with the group. This is an unprecedented situation, and I value all of your opinions."

Deanna and Felicia quieted.

A middle-aged woman with a sleek, blonde bob asked, "Do we have an official cause of death?"

"They haven't released anything to the public, yet," Clarice said. "However, I spoke with Bryan's wife, and she said that the police ruled Bryan's death a homicide. They believe he was struck on the head, though it's unclear if that was the primary cause of death, or if it was the fall down the stairs. We won't know for sure until the autopsy."

"How's Katherine holding up?" Adrienne asked.

"She's doing okay, all things considered," Clarice answered. "She didn't have too much time to speak with me, since she was in the middle of trying to make arrangements. I did let her know to contact the Club if there's anything she needs."

"Let her know that if she needs a place for Diesel until things calm down, I have a few Rottweiler-savvy foster homes I can contact," said a petite woman with golden brown skin and a shining mane of straight black hair.

"Thank you, Linh, I'll be sure to pass that along."

An elderly man, almost completely bald, unfolded the newspaper he was holding and slid it toward the middle of the table. Everyone leaned forward to look, except for me, that is. I didn't need to see it to know it was the *Chronicle*.

"Let's cut to the chase," the man said, in a reedy voice. "What are we going to do about this?"

"It doesn't reflect well on the Club, for sure," the blonde said.

"That someone was murdered here in and of itself doesn't reflect well on the Club," Adrienne said. "We need to make sure, first and foremost, that everyone feels safe here."

"Can we all agree that step one should be to not employ the person of interest?"

Ouch. Right to the quick. I took another look at the elderly man. Though he was somewhat frail and stooped, his liver spotted hands were large and capable-looking. His brown eyes were still clear and sharp, and he held himself with the air of a man who was used to being in charge and taking command of a room.

"Harvey, she hasn't even been charged," Adrienne objected.

"So?" Harvey barked. "Wasn't there an incident of a fight in front of clients? Of destroying training equipment in the middle of a class? That's not the kind of behavior you condone from your trainers, is it, Clarice?"

"Of course not," Clarice said.

"I agree with Harvey," the blonde said. "We don't need that kind of negative publicity."

I couldn't take it anymore.

"Excuse me," I said, standing. All eyes were suddenly fixed on me, and I felt my face grow hot.

"Excuse me," I said again. "But would it be okay if I said a few words?"

For a moment everyone was silent. Harvey surveyed me through narrowed eyes. It didn't seem like an altogether hostile look, though. Maybe he just forgot his glasses.

"Go ahead, Nell," Clarice said.

"Thank you," I said. "I just wanted to say that I understand if you feel the need to fire me for my behavior at the beginning of Deanna's class yesterday. Raising my voice with Bryan in front of clients was unprofessional and rude. And smashing his remote control was unacceptable—"

"Nell. You were provoked. We all saw it," Adrienne interrupted. She turned to the other trainers. "Didn't we?"

Felicia and Deanna nodded.

"Still, it's no excuse," I said.

"Be that as it may," Deanna said, "I think that most of us here can understand your frustration. Bryan was completely out of line and behaving aggressively. We should have stepped in sooner, and not left you to deal with him on your own."

I didn't expect that. For an instant I was struck dumb, losing track of my train of thought. The blonde woman tucked a lock of hair behind one ear.

"If it were just a fight, that would be one thing," she said, her tone fairly dripping condescension. "But things apparently escalated after that."

"Elise!" Adrienne scolded.

"It's okay," I said, before things went any further. "That's what I was getting to next. I accept full responsibility for my part in the fight. I did not like Bryan. He, as many of you witnessed, absolutely did not like me. There was conflict. But I didn't murder him."

"I don't think anyone here was expecting a confession," Harvey grumbled. "But you have to admit, Ms. McLinton, that this all looks mighty suspicious."

"Yes, it does," I said. "And I can only tell you what I know for sure. I was in my office. I didn't see or hear anything. And I most definitely didn't have anything to do with Bryan's death."

"Who, then?" Elise asked.

"I don't know," I said. "All I know is that I wasn't involved. And also ..." I paused, pulling my phone from my pocket and bringing up a screenshot of the class roster. "I wasn't the only one on the property. I may have been the only one working in this building, but Felicia was teaching another class in the agility building. Quite a large class, by the looks of things."

"I hope you're not insinuating that I had anything to do with it!" Felicia exclaimed.

"No more than anyone else who was there," I said, and started to read: "Felicia Yin, Adrienne Santi, Deanna Welton,

Jared Wesson, Calvin Overby, Alexis James, Susan Fourier, David Gorman, Heather Schultz, and Elise Marsh."

The blonde woman startled as I read her name. I didn't remember seeing her in the crowd at the barricades, but admittedly, I wasn't at my best at the time. According to the roster, she was at the class. I set my phone down and looked around the table, making brief eye contact with everyone.

"I know there's nothing I can say today that will make you believe me without a shadow of a doubt," I began, but Adrienne jumped in before I could finish.

"Nell's right. There were at least a dozen other people around that day. We can't really discount any of them. I know I wasn't in class the whole time. No one was. We all popped in and out between runs. It could have been any one of us."

"It wasn't me!" Elise cried.

Clarice held up a hand.

"No one's accusing you," she said to Elise. "But Nell makes a good point. We can't prove it was her any more than we can prove it wasn't any one of those people attending class."

"Or you," Felicia said. "You're here all the time. You own the property."

No one appeared to want to speak after *that* declaration. Everyone suddenly seemed to feel the urge to stare at their hands, shuffle their feet, or check their phones for messages. Deanna bravely broke the silence.

"At this point in time, I don't think being overly reactive is going to do us any good," she said. "Nell is a good trainer. We had a phenomenal response to the first class she taught, and that was only the introductory lesson without dogs. The attendees have been emailing all week to say how enjoyable the class was, how engaging and inspiring Nell's performance with her dog was, and how excited they are to come back next week. Also," Deanna turned to me, "They love your hair."

Several people chuckled, and even I laughed in spite of myself. Harvey sniffed.

"Yes, yes, she's very colorful. But we need to make a decision, here."

Expressions grew solemn, and everyone looked toward Clarice. I held my breath.

Chapter 16

It turned out that the final decision was to make no decision. They'd reserve judgement until more information was released. Which I took to mean they were waiting until I was arrested to fire me. Progress. It gave me some time to figure things out, to try and clear my name.

No problem, I thought as I herded the dogs ahead of me to my shared office. Neither Deanna or Felicia decided to stick around, so I had the place to myself. Okay. I was innocent. I knew that. The police had to come around to that conclusion sooner or later. All things considered, though, I'd prefer sooner.

Simon and Rush curled up together on the dog bed at my feet as I waited for my ancient laptop to boot up. Once it was ready, I pulled up the agility class roster one more time and carefully entered the names into a new document. After a moment of reflection, I added Clarice's name to the list.

Clarice didn't look capable of even raising her voice, let alone murdering someone in such a gruesome fashion. But wasn't that the way it often worked? Clarice had a lot to lose if Bryan decided to go after her business. I placed an asterisk next

to her name, to signal a potential motive and that a more thorough investigation was warranted.

Who else? I perused the list again. Felicia and Adrienne got
asterisks next to their names as well, since they both seemed to
harbor quite a bit of hostility toward Bryan. Felicia was overly
defensive when I brought up that I hadn't been the only one on
the property at the time of the murder.

My cursor next landed on Calvin Overby's name. I had no
idea what to think of him. Well, that wasn't completely true.
He was the most gorgeous guy I'd seen in a long time, and his
dog was striking. So, there was that. However, I couldn't just
ignore the fact that he'd gone from acting like Bryan's best
friend to threatening to get him banned from the IGP Club.
Which was the truth? He got an asterisk as well, simply for
being an enigma. A smoking hot enigma.

Who else was around that day? Should I consider anyone
who attended Deanna's competition obedience class between
my class and Felicia's? A quick look at that roster revealed a
much smaller class than Felicia's, with only Jared, Adrienne,
Calvin, and Susan Fourier listed. Every member of that class
also attended Felicia's agility class immediately afterward.

Who else? Rush disentangled himself from Simon and
placed his head in my lap. I absently rubbed his favorite place
at the base of his muzzle, right between his eyes, as I mentally
ran through names and faces from that day.

There was the assistant from my class, Stacey. I couldn't
remember seeing her leave, though I was around when her
fiancé said he'd pick her up after my class. In the interest of
being thorough, I included her name. And that kid, Kyle, had
been around doing some painting. I typed in his name as well,
though he'd seemed pretty friendly toward Bryan.

Once more, I started from the beginning of the list. I
added an asterisk next to Deanna's name. She wasn't Bryan's

biggest fan either. Elise Marsh had seemed a little suspicious to me during the meeting. I'd never been formerly introduced to her and had no idea what her role in the club was, though it must be a significant one if she was on the board. I got the impression that she didn't like me much. I decided, for the moment, that was enough to earn her an asterisk too.

I ignored the client names for the time being, simply because I didn't know enough about them. I also skimmed past Jared's and Stacey's names. Neither seemed to have any particular affiliation with Bryan, other than Bryan and Stacey sharing the same breed preference. Being a Rottweiler fancier was hardly evidence of a deviant personality.

"Not a bad start, I suppose," I said to the dogs as I sat back in my chair. "Lots of possibilities."

Too many possibilities. I had to find some way to narrow down the list. I pushed away from the desk, quietly asking Rush to lie down. He returned to his place next to Simon with a sigh. It had just occurred to me that Bryan likely had an office around here somewhere. Surely the police had searched it, but all that meant was that no harm could come from me having a look around.

"Hello?" I called, sticking my head out into the hallway. No one answered, and I stepped out of the office. I ticked off doors as I made my way down the hall. Meeting room, Clarice's office, and another office shared by Adrienne, Harvey, and someone named Jackie. Then there was a storage closet, and another office with unfamiliar names on the plaques near the entrance.

I hit pay dirt with the door at the end of the hall. Bryan's name was printed on a faded brass plate. I placed a hand on the knob and gave an experimental twist, pretty sure it would be locked. To my surprise, it opened easily. I quickly stepped inside and pulled the door closed behind me. I wasn't hiding, not exactly, but it seemed best to keep a low profile, considering the circumstances.

I surveyed the space. A metal desk stood in the center of the room, flanked by metal filing cabinets, all the same shade of industrial grey. One of the walls was split by a nondescript wooden door, which turned out to be a closet full of old outdoor clothing and boots. A quick search of the small chamber revealed nothing else of interest. I closed the door, disappointed. You'd think there'd be all kinds of goodies stored in a closet.

A large, round dog bed covered in black dog hair took up one of the corners. The walls were covered with framed newspaper clippings, all touting Bryan's training prowess. Upon closer inspection, the most recent was nearly a decade old.

Out of curiosity, I drew closer to the wall and read a few of the articles. The content didn't really change from one to the other. Seemed like every year or so there was a feature about Bryan, painting him as a bonified miracle worker. The pieces were all light on actual training information and heavy on nonsense like dominance theory, which had long since been disproven by behaviorists. All the dogs Bryan appeared with in the photos had that telltale black box fitted snugly around their necks.

The misinformation would ordinarily have aggravated me, but, standing here in this room that Bryan would never enter again, surrounded by press he'd obviously been proud of, I felt only pity. He was at the twilight of his career. He deserved to have been able to retire quietly, basking in all that he'd accomplished over the forty-some odd years he'd been training.

Would it have made a difference, I wondered? If Bryan had decided to go quietly, to not continue to fight the inevitable, would he still be alive?

Turning away from the articles on the wall, I approached

the desk. The top was neat and clean, and nothing seemed out of place at first glance. A framed photo in the corner displayed a pleasant looking middle-aged woman with soft brown curls and rosy cheeks, sitting in a chair and smiling into the camera. Diesel lay regally alongside the chair, his head cocked to the side in that adorable way that Rottweilers are masters of. That must be Bryan's wife. I wondered what she was like. Judging by what was said during the meeting, at least several of the club members were friendly enough with her to be in contact after the murder.

Finding nothing else of interest on the desktop, I next focused on the file cabinets. About half of the drawers were empty. The other half contained neatly organized files of class descriptions and schedules, brochures, and flyers for various electric collar companies. There were a few handouts on training with shock collars, and almost an entire drawer full of copies of what looked to be the same articles that were hanging on the wall. Boring.

I returned my attention to the desk. There were several drawers alongside the chair space. One, a large bottom drawer, sported a silver lock on its front. I made a beeline for that one first, but as I'd suspected, it was locked.

"Shih tzus," I muttered. So far, I hadn't found any sign of a key in the room. A hasty search of the remaining drawers failed to produce either a key or anything else of interest. Frustrated, I gave the drawer a few more tugs.

A tiny, white corner of what appeared to be paper appeared in the crack between the drawer and the rest of the desk. Leaning closer, I discovered the scrap was a little thicker than normal paper, almost like cardstock or photo paper. Intrigued, I jiggled the drawer again, trying a few different angles, hoping to dislodge the object. It took a few minutes of maneuvering, but finally the paper slid out enough that I could gently pull it the rest of the way.

It was a fetal ultrasound photo. A human fetal ultrasound photo. I stared at the clearly defined nose and forehead and the tiny little fingers. I was so focused I nearly missed the sound of footsteps approaching the door.

Chapter 17

Voices sounded in the hallway; faintly at first, but steadily growing louder. I froze in place, crouched behind the desk, straining to hear.

"Thanks again for agreeing to let me come down on such short notice," an unfamiliar voice said.

"Not at all," Clarice responded. "You have every right to Bryan's things. I called you as soon as the police gave the okay after their search."

Holy shih tzus! I leapt to my feet, slipping the photo into my pocket as I looked wildly around the room for a means of escape. There was only one door, which led out to the hallway; directly in Clarice's path.

Okay. Fleeing was out. Next best thing? Hiding. The desk didn't provide enough cover, and besides, I was sure it would be the first place they'd check out. Even if I could move the file cabinets to squeeze behind them, it would surely take too long, and make way too much noise.

I turned in a desperate circle, considering and then rejecting every corner. The closet! I yanked the door open, wrinkling my nose at the smell of musty old clothes. No time to be fussy, though. I nearly dove inside.

Jamming my feet into the first pair of boots I came across, I clomped to the far corner of the closet. I hastily arranged the hanging coveralls and coats in a way that would hopefully conceal me, yet not look too suspicious. Lucky Bryan had been such a big guy. My feet, even with my shoes on, fit easily inside the large boots. A few coveralls and one gigantic overcoat hung nearly to the floor.

I pulled the closet door closed with a quiet click less than a second before I heard the office door open. I tried to keep as still as possible in the complete darkness, struggling to hear the conversation between Clarice and Bryan's widow.

"Adrienne's on her way with a box for whatever you'd like to take," Clarice was saying. "Did you want the dog bed for Diesel?"

"I don't think I need the bed," Mrs. Reed responded. "We have some nicer ones at home. That one's pretty old. Could we donate it somewhere?"

"I'm sure Linh, our rescue coordinator, will be able to find a place for it," Clarice assured her.

They didn't talk much after that, making it easier for me to hear them moving around the room. File cabinets and desk drawers were opened and closed. At some point, there was a knock at the door.

"Come in," Clarice called.

"Here's a box," Adrienne said.

"Thank you."

"Katherine, I'm so, so sorry for your loss," Adrienne said. There were some scuffling noises, which I assumed was the box being filled with whatever items Mrs. Reed wanted to take. The ultrasound photo seemed to be burning a hole in my pocket. Could it be hers? Bryan had been in his sixties, and I'd assumed Mrs. Reed was around the same age. A pregnancy was unlikely. Not impossible, though. Hadn't there been a woman in her seventies in India who gave birth to twins?

I had to fight the impulse to dig out my phone and start Googling the likelihood of pregnancy in one's sixties.

"Have you seen Nell around?" Adrienne asked, and all thought of geriatric pregnancy vanished.

"I haven't," Clarice said.

"Her dogs are in her office, but I can't find her anywhere."

"Nell," Mrs. Reed repeated. "Is she the one who —"

I nearly passed out. Good greyhounds, what next?

"I'm sure she's around, if her dogs are here," Clarice said. "Perhaps you could take the search elsewhere?"

"Oh, of course. I'm so sorry, Katherine."

"It's alright, dear. Innocent until proven guilty, I always say. I certainly wouldn't expect you to bar the poor girl from the premises."

"I appreciate that," Clarice said. "But all the same, you shouldn't worry about running into her. Adrienne, I'm sure, will see to it that doesn't happen as she continues her search."

"Of course," Adrienne said again, and I heard the door close.

I leaned one shoulder against the wall of the closet and tried not to hyperventilate. If I ever got out of there, I vowed to shut myself in my office and never come out. I hardly even started to recover from that last conversation when I heard the unmistakable sound of the locked drawer being rattled. I leaned forward in anticipation.

"This key is stuck," Mrs. Reed said, sounding slightly out of breath.

"It's an old desk. Try jiggling it a little."

"Got it," Mrs. Reed said after a few moments. I could just barely hear the drawer sliding open through the closet door.

"It's empty!" Disbelief was evident in her voice. "He's always kept a little wooden box in here. I've seen it."

"So have I." Clarice's tone matched Mrs. Reed's.

"Well, it must be around here somewhere."

The sounds of the file cabinet drawers and the remaining desk drawers being opened and closed resumed.

"What about the closet?" Clarice asked.

I held my breath as the footsteps drew nearer. If they found me, how in the world was I going to explain myself? What if they searched me and found the photo? That would be the end, I was sure of it.

The knob turned, and I shrank back against the wall. Part of Mrs. Reed's face was visible through the hanging clothes as she peered into the gloom. Her eyes were red-rimmed and puffy.

"We never did get around to having a light installed in there," Clarice remarked from somewhere behind Mrs. Reed.

"I don't think he would have kept anything important in here, not when he had the locking drawer. As far as I knew, he only stored his old tracking equipment in here. He hasn't done any tracking for years. Not since before Diesel washed out of Schutzhund."

Mrs. Reed stood up onto her tippy toes and reached for the shelf over my head. I squeezed my eyes closed. As if that was going to help anything. She was close enough that I smelled her perfume. It was light and flowery, not at all overpowering. Classy. I listened to the shuffling sounds as she moved things around on that shelf. The sound of my pounding heart filled my ears. Surely, they must be hearing it as well. It was just too, too loud.

I felt, rather than saw Mrs. Reed step back, my eyes still tightly closed. Could they really not hear my heart crashing against my ribs?

"Nothing," she said, finally. Relief washed over me. I screwed up the courage to open my eyes just in time to see her fling a hand forward and give the coats and coveralls in front of me a shove. I'm pretty sure I had a mini stroke. Frozen in place, not even daring to breathe, I counted the seconds as they dragged by, fully expecting to be discovered at any moment.

But Mrs. Reed only sighed and ran a hand over the thick plaid fabric of one of the jackets before closing the door. I sagged against the wall, forcing myself to take slow, deep breaths.

"Perhaps Bryan took it home with him?"

"I don't remember seeing it at the house. But I guess I haven't really been looking for it, either. I assumed it was here, like it always is. I just want to be sure it's safe. There are important things inside."

"We'll find it," Clarice promised. "In the meantime, would you like to take a break and come up to the house for a bit? We can have some coffee."

And then, incredibly, the door closed. I was alone in the dark and the silence.

Chapter 18

I counted to one hundred before cautiously opening the closet door. The room was empty. With my hand clamped protectively over the pocket containing the ultrasound photo, I moved carefully, remaining alert for the sound of anyone approaching. Finally making it to the door, I pushed it open just a sliver, scanning the hallway for any signs of life.

Satisfied the coast was clear, I slipped out of the room and pulled the door securely closed behind me. Jumping Jack Russells, that was close. As I made my way down the hallway, I held my head higher and grew more confident with each step. My mind was still back in the closet, pondering everything I'd heard from Clarice and Mrs. Reed.

So, Bryan had a secret box that he kept locked in his desk. Clarice and Mrs. Reed knew it existed, but neither seemed to know exactly what was inside. Both seemed shocked by its disappearance. Did police take it? Surely, they would have informed Mrs. Reed if they did. Unless … unless she was a suspect, and the box contained some damning evidence! That would explain why she was so determined to find it.

I was so deep in thought that I crashed headlong into Stacey as I rounded the corner.

"Oh!" I gasped as we both reeled back. "I'm so sorry!"

"It's all right," Stacey said, rubbing her shoulder. She'd curled her body protectively. I was momentarily confused until she straightened, revealing the boxy headed, muscular, black and tan dog at her side. Bruiser, I presumed. He tilted his head, gazing at me inquiringly. He was adorable. I looked up, grinning, to voice the thought to Stacey, but was brought up short by her pallid face and red rimmed eyes.

"Hey," I said instead. "Are you okay?"

She sniffed and nodded.

"I'm fine."

"Sure, you are."

She managed a small smile.

"I know it's stupid, but it's just so sad. Like, this was Bryan's favorite place in the world. And then to be attacked like that, just down the hall ..." Stacey trailed off, seemingly just realizing who she was talking to.

And yeah. Awkward. I cleared my throat, deciding to attempt to steer the conversation in another direction.

"Were you two close?" I asked.

Stacey sniffed.

"No," she said. "No, but he ..." she trailed off again, looking away.

Bruiser gave a soft whine and nudged her hand. Stacey's features relaxed as she looked down at him.

"He's a beautiful dog," I said.

Stacey managed a wobbly smile.

"Thanks," she said.

"May I?" I asked, gesturing toward him.

"Of course. Bruiser loves attention."

"Hey, big guy," I said.

Bruiser heaved himself to his feet and ambled over. He

took the treat I offered him politely, and afterward pushed his muzzle into my palm. I scratched behind his ears and ran my hand over his broad head. His stub tail wagged madly, and his tongue lolled. I smiled down at him, forgetting, for a moment, Bryan's death and the club's suspicions. Dogs are great stress relievers that way.

"You didn't —" Stacey cut herself off. There was an uneasy pause. I looked up from Bruiser. Stacey took a deep breath as though she were about to speak again, but couldn't quite find the words.

"I didn't hurt Bryan," I said. "If that's what you were asking."

Stacey blushed.

"There's a rumor going around."

"Perks of being the one to discover the body," I said. "And look, Bryan and I certainly weren't friendly, but I doubt either of us had murder on our minds. I know for sure I didn't."

"You really don't seem the type," Stacey allowed. And I was left to wonder what kind of person was "the type," to commit murder.

Before I could respond and either help or hurt my case, a voice came from the stairwell.

"There you are!"

Stacey and I looked over to find Jeff ascending the stairs.

"I've been looking everywhere," he said as he reached the top.

"Sorry. I was just —" Stacey fumbled with Bruiser's leash, her eyes downcast.

"I don't want any excuses. Let's just go. We've wasted too much time here as it is."

I'm pretty sure I was staring openly. But I couldn't bring myself to look away. This was not the happy, cuddly couple I'd met just a few days ago. Even though I hadn't said anything, Jeff turned toward me.

"I read about you," he said. "In that article. Aren't you supposed to be in jail or something?"

"Jeff, please." Stacey made to place her hand on his arm but froze at his glare.

"Not guilty, actually," I said, silently cursing Dan Friedman. "Not of the murder, anyway. But I am the reason Stacey's late. I ran into her and kept her here, telling her all about how I'm working to prove my innocence. Already got a few clues."

Jeff's eyes narrowed.

"That so?"

I nodded.

"Sure is. Just about to meet with the detectives, actually." I'm not sure why that popped out of my mouth. I certainly didn't have any plans to contact Detective Rodriguez. Jeff's attitude and his mention of the article had aggravated me, though. I liked idea of throwing him off balance a little.

"I'm sorry," Stacey said again. "I'll get my things. Come on, Bruiser."

My brown furrowed in concern as I watched them leave. Was Jeff just having a bad day? Or was there something more sinister going on? Stacey's anxiety appeared to spike once Jeff appeared.

"He doesn't treat her right." A voice sounded from just behind me. I whirled around to find Kyle leaning against the doorframe of one of the offices. Where did he come from? The guy really was a ninja.

"I think it's hard to judge from one interaction," I said slowly.

Kyle was still staring after Stacey and Jeff, though they were no longer in eyesight.

"I never said I was judging from one interaction."

The words hung in the air between us. Kyle continued to stare in the direction Stacey had gone, ignoring me. It seemed to me it was about time to make myself scarce. I only managed a few steps when I heard Kyle say softly from behind me, "She deserves better."

———————

I finally made it back to my office, breathing a sigh of relief as the door closed behind me. Simon and Rush mobbed me, plastering themselves against my shins.

"Hey, guys," I said. "Sorry it took a little longer than expected. This sleuthing business is no joke."

I sat down in my desk chair, shoving my computer aside and pulling the photo from the pocket of my jeans. Was it relevant to the case? Should I hand it over to the police? What if it was, like, thirty years old and that baby was now grown up and independent with babies of his own? Or her own. I certainly couldn't tell the sex of the baby in the photo.

I thought for a moment. Maeve's ultrasound pictures had always come with her name and birthdate, as well as the date of the ultrasound printed on the bottom. There was only a jagged edge where that information should have been. Someone made sure the photo contained no identifying information whatsoever.

Interesting.

I flipped the photo over. A date was stamped across the back. Exactly one week ago. Excitement building, I turned the picture face up again, and took a closer look at the ripped edge of the paper. I could just make out the beginnings of one capital letter. 'A.' I consulted the suspect list I compiled earlier.

Adrienne.

"No way," I breathed. Could the photo be hers? And if it was, why did Bryan have it?

A knock sounded at the door, and I hastily shoved the photo back into my pocket.

"Come in," I said, motioning for the dogs to lie down and stay.

"Hey," Adrienne said, poking her head in the door. "I've been looking for you."

"I've just been here, mostly." My fingers were crossed behind my back, but what Adrienne couldn't see wouldn't hurt her. Probably.

"I checked a few minutes ago, and it was just the dogs in here."

"Bathroom break." I leaned back in my chair. "What can I do for you?"

Adrienne let herself all the way inside. Without trying to be too obvious about it, I looked her up and down. There wasn't any indication of pregnancy on her trim, athletic frame. Her leggings and snugly fitting light jacket didn't hide anything. But I knew that some women didn't show right away. Maeve had been one of those. She didn't look pregnant until her last trimester for both Julianne and Liam.

"Bryan's widow is here picking up his things," she said, closing the door and sitting down in one of the vacant desk chairs. "I just wanted to make sure we didn't have any uncomfortable encounters, you know?"

Too late.

"I was just working on some plans for the additional classes Clarice and I have been talking about," I said. "I want to do some drop-in classes that are focused on a particular problem area. Recall, loose leash walking, barking, stuff like that."

"Oh, cool! That sounds like it'll be super helpful. I know a lot of people call wanting to work on a specific behavior but are a little leery of committing to a six- or eight-week round of classes right of the bat."

I noticed that she was resting the palm of one hand on her seemingly flat stomach as we spoke. Just a habit, or was she doing that caressing the baby thing that came naturally to mothers? I leaned forward in my chair, squinting slightly, trying to get a better view.

"Nell?"

"Yes?" I straightened.

"You okay?"

"Sure."

"It's been a pretty wild first week, huh?"

"That's one word for it."

Rush lifted his head and whined softly. I beckoned him over and buried my hands in the thick fur around his neck. He leaned into the caress, closing his eyes.

"I know that it got a little intense in that meeting, but no one believes you could have done that to Bryan. Not really."

"I'll feel better when this is all over, for sure. In fact, I'm actually going to head over to the police station this evening."

"Really?" It was Adrienne's turn to lean forward this time, her hand still resting lightly on her stomach.

"Yeah. I figure, no one is as invested as I am in proving I'm innocent, right? I might have found some information that could help." Rush, always one to spread the love, pranced over to Adrienne, bobtail wiggling and his lips lifted slightly in a canine grin. Adrienne patted him absently, without even looking down at him. Her eyes remained fixed on mine.

"What did you find?" she asked.

I hesitated a few seconds. I hadn't meant to bring up the photo, even indirectly. But now that I had, maybe I could use it to my advantage. See what Adrienne's reaction to some careful phrasing might be.

"I probably shouldn't have mentioned it," I said, dropping my gaze, "and I kind of want to keep it between myself and the police for now. No offense, but especially after hearing what some people had to say at that meeting, I'm not really sure I can trust anyone around here at the moment."

"I'm so sorry you had to hear that." Adrienne truly seemed

distressed. "It's just because you're new. No one wants to suspect their friends. We're like family, you know?"

"I get it. I'm sure it's so much easier to think it was the new person instead of trying to wrap your head around the idea that someone you've known for years is capable of murder. Or hiding something from the rest of the group."

My eyes met Adrienne's and I arched one brow meaningfully. Adrienne's hand fell from her stomach, and her gaze sliding sideways, to where Simon was curled in an impossibly small ball on the dog bed.

"Right," she murmured. "Well, I supposed I'd better get going. Clarice is expecting me up at the house. When's your next class?"

"Day after tomorrow."

"Well." Adrienne stood and moved toward the door. "I'll probably see you then. Don't work too hard."

She sure made a quick exit after I mentioned people keeping secrets. Curious.

I retrieved the photo once again. Something like that would very likely be of interest to police. And I definitely didn't want to have to explain myself if someone found it on me.

I laid the photo out on the desk and snapped a picture with my phone. Just in case.

"Okay, guys," I said to the dogs. "Ready to take a trip downtown?"

Chapter 19

I watched the progression of the sun setting over the mountains as I drove west into town. By the time I reached the police station it disappeared for good. I drove around the block a few times, scoping out parking spots. Parking with the intention of leaving dogs in the vehicle always required a little extra thought. During the daytime adequate shade was a must. At night, I wanted more light. I finally found a spot beneath a streetlight, albeit a little farther from the station than I would have chosen if I was alone.

"I won't be long," I promised as I went through my routine of making sure their water pail was full, the blankets in order, and that each had a chew toy. I slid the van door shut and pressed the lock button on my key fob. The horn gave several sharp honks and I heard the locks click into place. I gave the handles on the driver's door and the sliding side door a try for good measure. Finally satisfied, I walked away.

"Detective Rodriguez, please," I said to the uniformed officer at the front desk. "I may have found a piece of evidence pertaining to his murder investigation."

Another officer in uniform led me to the same room I'd

been interrogated in. I sat with my back to the two-way glass, wondering if Detective Rodriguez was behind it, watching me and looking for signs of guilt. I pulled out my phone and busied myself checking the weather for the next few days, texting Maeve that I'd be home soon and asking if she wanted me to pick up anything for dinner, and reading Patricia McConnell's latest blog post and the methodology discussion that had begun in the comments. I just finished adding my own comment about reinforcement timing when a soft knock sounded at the door. Detective Rodriguez slipped through.

"Ms. McLinton," he greeted with a polite nod and. As with our previous interaction, he got right to the point. "How may I help you today?"

His quiet, yet purposeful way of moving around the room and the calm way he spoke reminded me of Maeve. He sat opposite me and set a thick file folder on the table, folding his hands on top of it.

"How's the investigation going?" I asked.

"It's coming along."

Of course, I wasn't really expecting any details. Secretly, I was hoping he would tell me I was off the hook because they found a new suspect. I shifted in my seat and fished the photo from the pocket of my jeans. It was a bit of a process. Those jeans really were a little on the tight side. Diet tomorrow, I decided as I finally freed the photo. For real this time.

"Maybe this will help," I said, sliding the photo across the table in his direction. It was slightly wrinkled, and one of the corners had a small rip, but it had mostly survived its time stuffed in my pocket.

The detective's eyebrows lifted slightly, but he didn't otherwise react. Probably a good trait for a detective, but I was hoping for something a little more satisfying.

"I found it in Bryan's desk, at the dog Club," I said, as he studied the black and white image before him. "It was taken just a week ago."

"You took this from Mr. Reed's desk? When?"

I hesitated, wondering if I'd committed a crime by taking the photo. I couldn't have, I decided. Not if I was turning it in to the police.

"Today."

"That desk was thoroughly searched the day of Mr. Reed's death."

I shrugged.

"It must have been missed. I think it was in that locked drawer on the bottom and somehow slid into one of the cracks. It fell out when the drawer moved a little."

"When the drawer moved a little," Detective Rodriguez repeated drily. "And am I right to assume that the drawer was *moving* due to an attempt to force it open?"

Uh oh. This wasn't exactly the direction I hoped the conversation would take. I suddenly didn't know what to do with my hands, and fiddled with my dog club keychain, running my fingers over the raised lettering and logo, lightly tracing the contours of the dog's paw.

"Ms. McLinton?" Detective Rodriguez prompted.

"You can call me Nell," I said.

The look Detective Rodriguez shot me made it evident that he knew I was stalling. I cleared my throat.

"I wasn't trying to force it open," I said. "I was just jiggling it a little to see if it was stuck as opposed to locked. I wasn't trying to *steal* anything. The door to the office wasn't locked. Once it became clear that the drawer was, I stopped trying to open it."

Detective Rodriguez remained silent. He folded his hands on top of the file once more and regarded me with interest. In fact, he looked a little *too* interested. Like we might be drifting back into suspect territory.

I sighed.

"Look. You just accused me of murder. I'm trying to prove my innocence. I thought I'd take a look around. When I found something, I brought it directly to you. We're on the same side, here, I promise. I want to find out who murdered Bryan as much as you do. Maybe even more."

He nodded.

"I see. Well then, thank you for coming to us. We'll look into the photo. You can stop by the front desk and confirm your contact information on your way out."

We both slid our chairs back and stood. Detective Rodriguez held the door open and motioned for me to go ahead. I thanked him as I passed.

"Oh, and Ms. McLinton?"

I turned back toward him.

"You won't be leaving town any time soon, will you?"

Shih tzu's.

———

I dutifully repeated my address, phone number, and place of employment to the officer at the desk before making my escape. Outside, I took a long, deep breath, savoring the crisp, juniper-scented air. What was it about police stations that seemed so claustrophobic, like I'd never breathe fresh air again? Maybe it wasn't the actual police station, I mused as I rounded the corner onto the sidewalk. Maybe it was that every time I was there, I was accused of murder.

A familiar scream-bark jolted me back to reality, and I whirled around to see Rush several feet away. Behind him, looking out of breath and a bit disheveled, one hand clamped tightly around Rush's collar, was Dan Friedman. Rush screeched again and lunged toward me, yanking Dan forward a few steps. I looked in the direction of the Green Machine, and saw it was just where I'd left it, under the streetlight, but the side door was wide open. Simon was nowhere in sight. My chest felt tight. No. No way this was happening.

"What are you doing?" I demanded, closing the distance between us with three giant steps. "Where's Simon?"

"Who's Simon?" Dan gasped, struggling to remain upright as Rush twisted and contorted himself every which way in his attempts to get to me.

"Let him go!" I commanded.

Dan complied, and Rush zoomed straight at me, leaping from side to side anxiously, and uttering short, shrill whines.

"Lie down," I said quietly, and he hit the pavement, his entire body vibrating as he struggled to hold his position.

"Is Simon the other dog?" Dan asked. "The skinny one?"

"Yes."

"He wouldn't let me catch him. I tried to chase him—"

I groaned. Rule number one of catching a loose dog. Don't chase.

"But he kept trotting just far enough ahead that I couldn't grab him. And then the fluffy one saw you and started pulling me in the other direction."

I asked Rush to heel and headed off the way Dan indicated. I told myself if it really was that recent, Simon couldn't have gone too far. Nonetheless, my heart rate accelerated and my eyes filled with tears. I knew that Simon, speedy little sighthound that he was, could be long gone. Lost dogs could become almost feral in their fear and confusion, avoiding all people, even those they knew and loved. And Simon, with those whippet genes of his, might not stop to rest until he was miles and miles away. Who knew what he might encounter. Cars on a dark, busy roadway. Wild animals. Unfriendly humans.

I'd spent enough time working at veterinary clinics and humane societies that I knew the worst that could happen. My breath caught in my throat as I recalled those sad, sad cases. I hastily swiped at my eyes. Crying wasn't going to help anything. I forced myself to stop imagining what might happen, and to focus on where Simon would most likely be.

There was a large park nearby, in the direction Dan indicated Simon had gone. I stood just inside the entrance, called Simon's name, and waited. Silence. I called again, taking care to keep my voice happy and upbeat, as if this was just a game. Still silence. I counted the seconds, and was just about to call again when I heard it; the jingle of tags in the distance.

"Yes!" I called into the darkness, "Good boy, Simon! Over here!"

A few more seconds and the sound of clinking tags became louder. I could hear paws beating against the ground, galloping toward me. Simon sprinted into view, leaping over a large clump of sagebrush in a single bound, not even stopping when he reached me. Instead, he launched his entire sinewy frame into my arms.

I caught him, staggering back a few steps. Simon only weighed about thirty pounds soaking wet, but even thirty pounds packs quite a punch when projectile blasted right into one's solar plexus. Even with the wind knocked out of me, my chest felt lighter than it had for the past five minutes.

Tears that threatened ever since the horrible moment when I saw the van door ajar and realized Simon was missing finally spilled over. Simon frantically licked them from my cheeks as I told him over and over again what a good boy he was. Rush, naturally, wanted to get in on the action, and their combined weight finally made me lose my balance. The three of us went down in a heap on a (luckily) soft patch of grass. Which was just fine with me. After all, my boys were back and in my arms.

That's what I thought, anyway, right up until the sprinklers turned on.

Dan, who had been hovering, seeming unsure of what to do with himself, reflexively jumped back.

I gasped as the shockingly cold water quickly soaked through my clothes. I scrambled to my feet, narrowly avoiding knocking heads with Rush. Simon's wet tail wacked me across the face. Somehow, we managed to move ourselves out of the park, but it must have been quite the spectacle. Once I finally had the dogs situated and was able to look up, I saw the corners of Dan's lips twitching as though he wanted to smile.

"Are you okay?" he asked.

"I'm fine," I said, still focused on the dogs, moving Simon directly beneath one of the streetlights so I could examine him, checking for injuries. I didn't see anything obvious. My relief gave way to anger as I realized why we were even in this situation in the first place. I rounded on Dan.

"What in the world were you thinking?" I demanded.

"Me?"

"Yes, you!" I jabbed a finger in his direction. "Why did you let the dogs loose? Did you break into my van hoping to find more ammunition for another story? Plant some phony evidence, maybe?" I knew I sounded like one of those crazy conspiracy theorists who believe the earth is flat or that the moon landing was faked, but I was beyond caring.

Dan clearly felt the same.

"What are you talking about? I didn't break into your van. The door was wide open —"

"The hell it was!"

"— and the dogs were running loose when I got here. I was trying to help you! Maybe if your dogs were better trained —"

"Excuse me? You're saying that because my dogs didn't immediately run over to a bumbling idiot and obey his every thought, they're not trained?"

"Oh yeah, I'm a real idiot for trying to round up those wild beasts of yours so that they wouldn't get hit by car or disappear! Don't worry, next time I won't bother."

"That is literally the best news I've heard all day."

I turned on my heel and headed back in the direction of the Green Machine, Simon on my left, Rush on my right, one hand curled around each of their collars. They were, of course, perfectly capable of heeling next to me, especially for such a short distance, but I needed that contact. I needed to be touching them to reassure myself that, yes, they were both right there.

Dan fell into step behind us. I turned and glared at him. He stopped short and held up his hands.

"My car is parked in the spot next to yours. I can't help that we're headed in the same direction."

I resumed my march forward without responding. At the van, I reached in and snapped leashes on the dogs. The adrenaline surge that had sustained me through the initial panic had dissipated. I started feeling a little shaky. I turned to Dan, who was in the process of unlocking his Subaru a few feet away.

"You really didn't let the dogs loose?"

He shot an exasperated look in my direction.

"Why would I?"

"Well, you did publish an article accusing me of murder for the whole world to see."

"I think you have an overly optimistic estimation of the *Central Oregon Chronicle's* readership."

I narrowed my eyes.

"But for what it's worth, I'm sorry."

That was unexpected.

"Like I said, my editor was breathing down my neck, and I needed to publish something. The whole rival dog trainers angle was easy pickings."

"Easy pickings," I muttered. "Kind of a cavalier attitude to take about ruining people's lives and reputations, don't you think? I might get fired, not to mention arrested."

I pulled out my phone and dialed the non-emergency number for the police station.

"Hello," I said. "My name is Nell McLinton and I was just in a meeting with Detective Rodriguez? Could you send someone out front, please? My vehicle was broken into while I was inside."

"How do you know it was broken into?" Dan asked once I'd ended the call. "It looks fine to me. Maybe you just didn't latch it all the way. It could happen to anyone."

"I wouldn't be so careless with my dogs. The van was locked. I checked both doors."

"Man plans and God laughs," Dan quoted. "Accidents happen."

"Not to me. Not tonight."

A gust of wind rustled the branches of a nearby Manzanita bush. I shivered. The temperature was dropping fast, and the breeze went right through my soaked clothes. Wet clothes were never an issue before. I always had my entire wardrobe at my disposal in the Green Machine. Now, all of my clothing was in Maeve's guest house.

Dan opened the door to his Subaru and started to get inside. He glanced in my direction, straightened, and let the car door fall closed.

"I could wait with you," he offered.

I waved him away.

"No need," I managed, through chattering teeth.

He shrugged out of his puffy down jacket.

"Take this, at least."

Now he wanted to be a gentleman? Please.

"No thank you," I said primly.

He held the jacket out for a few moments, and sighed when I made no move to take it.

"Okay," he said. "Let's start over. I'm sorry about the article. And I'm sorry for apparently making things worse when I tried to detain your dogs."

If I hadn't just called the police to come outside, I would have loaded up the dogs and driven away. Holding a grudge was definitely not one of my better qualities. I didn't want to apologize for being hostile. I just wanted to leave.

To make matters worse, as the last of my adrenalin ebbed away, my knees buckled. I hastily sat down on the curb, not particularly gracefully, but mostly controlled. The dogs swarmed around me. Since we were all still soaked, it wasn't particularly comforting.

"Go lie down," I said, which was the cue to find a spot and get comfortable for a while. Simon and Rush obliged. Dan hurried over, sinking to a crouch at my side.

"I'm fine," I said, before he could speak. "I just need a minute."

Wordlessly, he draped the jacket over my shoulders and jogged back to his car. I automatically snuggled into the warmth of the soft fabric. Dan then surprised me further by shoving a to-go cup of coffee into my hand as he sat down on the curb next to me. It was still hot. I wrapped both hands around it, the heat slowly bringing feeling back to my numb fingers.

"Thank you," I said, grudgingly. "What are you even doing here, anyway?"

"I could ask you the same."

"But you wouldn't, considering what happened the last time I answered your questions."

I thought I saw a hint of a smile.

"Fair enough," he said. "I usually come down here around this time. My source is generally midway through their shift. I find if I'm generous with my Spoken Moto coffee, I'll get an interesting tidbit or two. Reporter life, and all that."

Well, that explained the coffee. I raised the cup to my lips and took a sip. The strong, hot brew warmed me from the inside out, and tasted slightly of hazelnut. My favorite.

"Best coffee in Bend," Dan said upon seeing my obvious enjoyment.

"Thanks," I said again. Why was it so much easier to thank him for the coffee than it was to thank him for trying to help with the dogs? I took a deep breath. "And thanks for trying to catch the dogs," I said in a rush.

He smiled for real this time, his eyes crinkling at the corners. My instinct was still to flee. It's how I'd handled these types of situations for the last ten years, and it was hard to ignore that kind of conditioning. But I kept my butt on the curb and even managed a tiny smile in response to Dan's. I still didn't trust him. And I certainly didn't forgive him. But I appreciated the coffee and the jacket. So that was progress, right?

Chapter 20

"The police really don't think it's odd that your van door just happened to fall open while you were inside the police station handing over potentially important evidence?" Maeve asked the next morning, as the Green Machine bumped over the ruts in the gravel road leading away from the house.

"No. They think I just didn't latch the door all the way in my haste to get to my meeting with Detective Rodriguez."

Maeve shook her head in annoyance, staring down at the calendar app on her phone.

"Everything all right?" I asked.

"Just a lot going on. I could have done without this event today, what with the divorce not even final, a custody battle, three deadlines next month, and two children that I'm trying to not let become completely feral."

"I'm helping with the feral part," I said.

"I think you're encouraging the feral part," Maeve countered. "Have you seen my bathroom lately?"

"The tub's not permanently stained. It'll wear off eventually. Same with their hair. A few weeks of washes and they'll be so blond you'd never know anything happened."

"I'm not sure if I believe you. That neon pink of Liam's is … vivid."

"You gave permission," I reminded her. "And besides, he loves it. He's a celebrity at school."

"That he is. I've had calls from four parents this week who are saying their kids want the same thing. Three of them asked about the product you used, and one of them just wanted to complain that we're setting a bad example."

"What is pink hair an example of, exactly?"

Maeve shrugged.

"I'm not sure. Anarchism, probably."

"Ah, yes. Today the kids with bright pink hair are taking over the school. Tomorrow, the world!" I gave my best attempt at a maniacal laugh.

Maeve gave an amused snort. Gentle Ben poked his head between the two front seats, snuffling Maeve's arm. She ran a hand over his head and dropped a kiss on his muzzle.

"Watch the road up ahead," she cautioned, pointing. "There's a few potholes."

"I've discovered that for myself, thanks," I said, carefully maneuvering the van. "This road is like an obstacle course."

"Welcome to Central Oregon. Road maintenance here is an afterthought."

We finally hit pavement after one last large crater. I patted the Green Machine's steering wheel comfortingly.

"Okay, buddy. Smooth sailing now. You got this." I glanced at Maeve. "How far is this bookstore, exactly?"

I volunteered to drive Maeve to a local book signing. It was the first event of hers I'd ever attended. I was looking forward to hearing Maeve speak and read aloud from her latest release.

"About a half hour. You're going to love it. Marnie, the owner, has done a fabulous job with the place. Plus, she's super supportive of local indie authors, which is a bonus."

The bookstore was part of a small plaza that seemed to

appear out of nowhere in the middle of the woods. The businesses around it consisted of a Mexican restaurant, an optometrist, a few specialty boutiques, and a small pet supply store.

I found a parking spot in front of two enormous Ponderosa Pine trees. I jumped out of the driver's seat and drew in a long, deep breath of the pine scented air. Just a half hour of driving and it felt like we were in another world. From the desert Tumalo to the endless forest that was Sunriver.

Maeve slowly climbed down from the passenger seat and got herself situated, with Gentle Ben waiting patiently at her side. I slid the side door of the van open and surveyed the dozens of signed books packed neatly into three containers.

"You go on inside," I said. "I'll take care of these boxes."

"Are you sure?" Maeve asked. "They're heavy."

I flexed my bicep. Which was admittedly not super impressive, considering the layers I was wearing. The forecast warned the temperature likely wouldn't get above forty-five degrees that day. Mornings in Central Oregon were always a little chilly, even in the spring.

"Need some help?" A deep voice sounded from behind me.

I turned around to find Calvin Overby a few feet away. He wore a casual gray jacket that perfectly matched his eyes. A laptop bag was slung over his shoulder. He looked amazing.

"Hi," I said. Smooth, Nell. Real smooth.

Calvin gestured to the boxes.

"Looks like a decent sized haul, there," he said.

"Maeve always draws a crowd."

He hefted one box on top of another and removed them from the van. He opened the one of the cardboard flaps of the top box.

"*Lost in Time, Not Space*," he read the book's title aloud. "By Maeve McLinton. Any relation?"

"She's my sister."

I grabbed the last box.

"To the bookstore, I presume?" Calvin asked.

"If it's not too much trouble," I said.

"No trouble at all. I was heading there anyway. Sometimes I get sick of working at the office, you know? I didn't realize there was an event today, though. That always makes things a little tricky."

"You're working on a Sunday?"

He shrugged.

"The curse of the self-employed."

We'd reached the entrance to the store. I smiled at the store's name, *Dog-Eared Books,* ornately carved into the wooden trim above the door. Calvin had his hands full with the two heavy boxes, so I shifted my load to balance on one hip and opened the door.

"Go ahead," I said. He smiled and nodded his thanks as he passed. I nearly swooned. Good greyhounds. I had to pull myself together.

"Calvin!" a voice sounded from somewhere amidst the stacks of books. "I see you're making yourself useful this morning!"

"Anything for you, Marnie! Where do you want these?"

I rounded the corner of one of the bookshelves just in time to see an outdoorsy looking woman, her white hair cropped short, gesturing toward a long table in the rear of the store. I deposited my box of books next to Calvin's. Maeve and Ben were just a few feet away, where a space was set up for her to sit while she did her presentation. Marnie even provided a dog bed for Ben.

"You must be Nell," Marnie said as she approached.

"I am. And you're Marnie?"

"The one and only."

She held out her hand. Her handshake was firm and businesslike, but the smile she gave me was wide and friendly.

"The area that you set up for Maeve is perfect," I said. "The dog bed is a nice touch."

"We want to make sure our authors are comfortable. And Bobbie doesn't mind giving up her bed for an hour or two."

The sound of the name was accompanied by the jingling of metal tags. A most peculiar looking dog ambled up to Marnie's side, shooting her a sideways glance.

"I'm not sure Bobbie agrees with you," I said.

Bobbie was built like a less extreme version of a boxer, with a short muzzle and adorable underbite. She was brindle in color, slightly darker over her muzzle. Unlike a boxer, her coat was wild and wiry. I'd never seen anything like her before.

"Bobbie's a little miffed right now because she can't go say hi to Ben," Marnie said. "They're good friends. After the event, Maeve will take Ben's harness off and we'll let them play for a while."

"Aw, that sounds like fun."

The next half hour was spent arranging Maeve's books on her table, making sure she had plenty of pens and markers, and organizing chairs for the audience. During that time, I also found a few moments here and there to browse the contents of the bookshelves. Marnie kept the place well stocked, including what looked to be the majority of Maeve's backlist on its own shelf.

"I don't usually keep that many books by one author," Marnie said, seeing where my attention was focused. She was holding two steaming mugs of coffee. "But people at Maeve's events seem to like to get caught up on her other series, so I always make sure to stock extra."

She offered me both mugs of coffee.

"One for you," she said. "And would you mind taking the other one over to Calvin? He's sitting at that table by the window. Tell him it's on the house for helping to bring the books inside."

Would I mind? Not in a million years. I carefully made my way over to the table Marnie had indicated. Calvin looked up as I approached.

"Is one of those for me?" he asked hopefully.

"No charge," I said, setting the mug down. It was emblazoned with the phrase *Booklovers Never Go to Bed Alone.* Mine read, *I love that sound you make when you shut up and let me read.* "Marnie wanted to thank you for helping with the books earlier."

"It was my pleasure," Calvin said. He indicated the other seat at the table. "Join me? I'm looking forward to your sister's presentation. Marnie says her events are always really popular."

"Thanks," I said, settling into the seat. "Marnie told me that as well. She said that even people who don't normally read science fiction will try her books."

"I might be one of those," Calvin said. "I'm not usually one for genre fiction, but the summary on the back of the book she's talking about today sounded interesting."

"What do you like to read?"

He took a sip of his coffee, nodded approvingly, and set the mug aside.

"Non-fiction, mostly. Biographies and history books. Dog training books."

"Finally, one we have in common."

"Behavior is pretty fascinating, no matter what species."

I sampled my own coffee, nodding in agreement.

"I also like the psychology behind it. I love knowing why dogs, and people, do the things they do."

"Like why someone might be driven to violence in a particular situation?"

I stared down at my brightly colored mug, suddenly feeling

a little sick. I couldn't help but think back to that day. Of Bryan, crumpled at the bottom of the stairs. Calvin leaned forward and rested a palm on my forearm.

"Hey," he said. "For what it's worth, I don't think you had anything to do with Bryan's death."

"So, what, you're a profiler, now?"

Calvin's hand slid from my arm. I could still feel the warmth of his palm through my sleeve.

"Kind of," he said. "I'm in marketing, and lot of advertising is actually profiling. Identifying which people would be likely to buy a product and then figuring out the best way to get their attention."

He took another sip of coffee.

"You are not a violent person," he said, after a moment. "I can see it in the way you work with dogs, and the way you interact with people. You practically dissolved into a puddle on the floor when you threw that remote. I don't think you're capable of whacking someone over the head and pushing them down a flight of stairs. Correct me if I'm wrong, of course."

I pushed my coffee away. He wasn't wrong. I thought I'd be happy to hear that someone was so firmly convinced of my innocence, but instead, I was a little unnerved at the fact he was paying such close attention to me.

"So, who do you think did do it?" I asked after a moment or two. After all, if Calvin had such great insight into me, someone he'd only known for a few days, he must have just as good of an idea of the inclinations and proclivities of the rest of the club members.

"Doing a little investigating of your own?"

"Something like that. I can't just let the whole world go on thinking I'm a murderer."

"Good morning, everyone!" Marnie's voice filled the store, even though there wasn't a microphone system set up. She stood next to Maeve's chair, on the opposite side of Gentle Ben. Calvin, who had opened his mouth to respond, abruptly closed it and sat back in his chair, focusing his attention on the front of the store.

Though I was pleased he intended to devote his full concentration to Maeve's presentation, I was curious to hear what he had to say.

"We have a special treat for you today," Marnie continued. "It's always my pleasure to welcome back local science fiction author Maeve McLinton!"

The audience applauded. Most of the chairs were full, I noted with satisfaction. I resolved to quit speculating about Calvin's amateur profiling hobby and tried to focus on Maeve. After a few minutes, it stopped requiring much effort. Maeve was a talented speaker, and the way she talked about her books made even me, who'd read all of them multiple times before and after publication, want to start all over from the beginning.

"Is it MS?" Calvin murmured to me when Maeve paused to find her place in the book she'd brought to read from.

"I'm sorry?" I said, not sure I'd heard him correctly. Calvin gestured to Maeve's cane leaning against her chair, and to Gentle Ben, who was snoozing at her side, his Service Dog vest clearly visible.

"Multiple Sclerosis," he said. "Is that her diagnosis?"

I hesitated. Calvin was little more than a stranger, after all.

"My aunt was just diagnosed last year," Calvin said. "It's been a journey."

I nodded in understanding, relaxing.

"Yes, it's MS. She was only twenty-three when they diagnosed it."

"How old were you?"

"Fifteen. Old enough to understand what was happening, but too young to be of any help at all."

Maeve started reading. I turned back to the audience, eager to see their reactions. Every single person seemed riveted. A few were even following along in copies they either brought from home or purchased that day. I skimmed over the various faces, not expecting to recognize anyone. When my eyes finally did find someone familiar, I nearly knocked my coffee over in surprise. Calvin noticed, and leaned toward me, his eyebrows raised questioningly.

"Isn't that Kyle from the Club?" I asked quietly.

Calvin followed my gaze to the young man sitting on one end of the middle row. He had a new copy of Maeve's book in his lap, but he wasn't reading along like some of the others. His attention was focused up front on Maeve. He seemed interested in what she was saying, smiling and nodding when she came to a funny passage.

"Yeah, that's Kyle. Not surprised he's a Sci Fi fan."

"Now, is that profiling or stereotyping?"

"Hey, the guy's here at a science fiction book reading, isn't he? You tell me."

I chuckled softly. Maeve finished reading and invited the audience to come up to the table and get their books signed or even just to have a chat. Everyone seemed to jump up at once and mob the table. Maeve and Ben soon disappeared from view.

"Well," I said. "Seems like we may be here a while."

"They certainly seem enthusiastic." Calvin stretched his long legs beneath the table. I got the impression that he was studying Maeve and the crowd almost like a science experiment.

"Haven't you ever been a fan of anyone?" I asked. "Not necessarily a writer or actor. A trainer, maybe. Michael Ellis is the Schutzhund guy, isn't he? Wouldn't you like to meet him?"

"Michael Ellis," Calvin repeated thoughtfully. "Now who's stereotyping?"

"Am I?" Michael Ellis was pretty popular in protection sport circles. He utilized electronic collars quite a bit, and though I might not have agreed with him on some of his ideas, I respected him as a trainer.

Calvin drained the last of his coffee.

"I think my fanboy moment came from meeting Denise Fenzi herself," he said, setting his empty mug to the side.

Denise Fenzi. Huh. That was interesting. Denise Fenzi did her fair share of competing in protection sports as well, but her training philosophy was more in line with mine.

"Rendered you speechless, I see," Calvin said after a few moments, grinning.

"Just processing," I said.

"So, you *are* surprised."

"A little."

"You should come out to the club sometime," Calvin said. "See how we operate."

"I've been to a Schutzhund club before," I informed him. "Half a dozen at least."

"You haven't been to mine."

I'd been about to accept the invitation when Kyle approached, still holding his book. From the way he was carrying it, with the front cover slightly open, I surmised it had just been signed.

"Hey Calvin," he said. "Nell."

"How're you doing, Kyle?" Calvin greeted.

"Fine," Kyle said. "The reading was good. Do you like Ms. McLinton's books too?"

"I haven't read any, actually," Calvin said. "But I'm pretty sure Nell has."

"Kind of hard to avoid it, considering she's my sister," I said, smiling. "I'm glad you enjoyed her presentation."

"Oh, you're sisters? That's cool."

Kyle shifted awkwardly from one foot to the other.

"Well," he said. "I guess I better get going. I promised Felicia I'd take a look at the chain on the A-frame. She's worried it might have some rust starting."

"Rust? On Felicia's chains!" Calvin exclaimed in mock horror.

Kyle laughed and said his goodbyes. We watched as he wove through the crowd and headed for the door.

"He comes out to the IGP club sometimes," Calvin said. "He can't afford membership, but I work with him when I have time."

"He has a lab, doesn't he?"

"Lab mix. I don't think he's done a DNA test on her. But she's a great little dog. Amazing retriever. Not really suited for IGP, but Kyle can practice the basics with her so he'll be better prepared with his next dog."

The crowd was starting to thin, and I saw Marnie beginning the process of clearing chairs. I got up to help.

"You and your sister are out in Tumalo, right?" Calvin said, and I turned back.

"That's right."

"Have you had the dogs out hiking around there at all?"

"Just around Maeve's property and one other trail so far," I said. "There hasn't been a lot of time for exploring just yet."

"Do you want to come out with Axel and me on Tuesday? There's a spot just west of Redmond that I bet you'd love."

Did he just ask me out? Could a hike with the dogs be considered a date? Did I want it to be? Maybe. It would certainly be a departure from my usual routine of rolling into town, swiping right on a likely looking photo, and rolling out the next morning. The routine had been as close to the opposite of my fundamentalist upbringing as I'd been able to manage, and this, in addition to the whole settling down thing, felt like I was taking a step backward.

Calvin set his mug aside, waiting for me to answer to what I'm sure he considered a simple question. And it was, I tried to convince myself. The simplest of questions. Did I want to go hiking with Calvin? All the rest could be figured out later.

"A hike sounds great," I said.

Chapter 21

"He asked you out?" Maeve set her coffee cup down on the table. "Tell me everything."

The event was officially over. Maeve signed a mountain of books. From the way she moved and how she held her coffee cup, I could tell she was exhausted and sore. Still, her eyes sparkled as she leaned forward in anticipation. We never discussed boys and dating as kids. Age difference aside, dating was forbidden. It was a miracle Frank was able to break through our father's defenses to win the opportunity to spend (supervised) time with Maeve.

"Well, it's nothing special," I said. "We're just going hiking with the dogs on Tuesday."

"Where?"

"He didn't actually say. Somewhere west of Redmond."

Maeve frowned.

"That doesn't exactly narrow things down. There's all kinds of beautiful trails out that way."

"Out which way?" Marnie asked, emerging from the storeroom with a cup of coffee of her own and joining us at our table. She smiled down at the dogs. Maeve had removed Ben's vest, giving him freedom to do as he liked for a while. He and Bobbie settled down next to us and were engaged in a pretty serious game of bitey face.

"Out past Redmond," Maeve said. "Calvin and Nell are going hiking."

"Oh, that sounds like fun!" Marnie said. "And there's definitely plenty of trails out that way. I'm pretty sure Calvin would have scoped them all out. That dog of his isn't the couch potato type."

"Neither are Nell's," Maeve replied. "Seems like it'll be a good match."

A customer stopped by our table and, after admiring the dogs' antics for a while, asked for help finding a particular book. Marnie directed her to the romance section and told her she'd be with her shortly.

"Thanks again for hosting such a great event," Maeve said.

Marnie drained the rest of her coffee and got to her feet. "Oh, it's always my pleasure, Maeve, you know that." Marnie stacked our coffee mugs and cradled them in one hand. "It was lovely to meet you, Nell. I hope we'll be seeing more of you in the future."

My stomach did the tiniest of flip flops at the indirect implication of me being there long enough to become a regular anywhere, even at a place as inviting as Dog Eared Books. I plastered on a smile.

"You most definitely will be seeing more of me," I said. "This place is fantastic. Coffee shop and bookstore all rolled into one. I might just follow Calvin's example and come here some days to try and get some work done."

"I have a few regulars who like to do that," Marnie said. "I think it's the books. Helps get people in that working mindset."

"You'd think it would be a little distracting," Maeve mused.

"It would be for me. I can't have any books in my office at all. Too tempting."

Bobbie and Ben's silent wrestling match migrated next to my chair. Bobbie in particular seemed to think my foot made a good backrest.

"You know, I would have thought so too," Marnie answered. "I mean, people don't come to a bookstore unless they like to read, right? But one young man who comes here to work says the books are inspiring. He says when he looks at all of those completed works, whether they're novels or non-fiction, he feels like if so many people were able to finish their projects, he can certainly manage to eke out enough words to make his deadline."

"That's an interesting perspective," Maeve allowed.

"He's a local reporter," Marnie said. "You may know of him. There was an article …"

I groaned.

"Daniel Friedman?"

"That's him!" Marnie said.

"Did you read that article?" Maeve asked, cheeks flushed. "Not the best bit of reporting. A little fast and loose with the actual truth."

"I did read it. And I must say, until you mentioned what really happened, he had me convinced. The boy can write, you have to give him credit for that."

I wasn't inclined to give Dan credit for anything.

"Well, I better get a move on," Marnie said. "Before Judy thinks I've abandoned her in the romance section. Nell, I'll be looking forward to seeing you back here. And I hope you'll bring your dogs next time. Bobbie always likes to meet new friends."

"Rush and Simon will be delighted to come," I said.

Marnie beckoned to Bobbie.

"All right, Bobbie, let's go on a Patricia Scanlan hunt. I know we've got a few of hers stashed around here somewhere." Bobbie rose and shook herself thoroughly before following Marnie deeper into the store. Ben rolled onto one side, tongue lolling from his mouth, eyes on Maeve to see what was next.

"I suppose, we'd better get going," Maeve said, checking the time. "I want to get some words in on the draft I'm working on before the kids get back from Frank's."

"And I should get Simon and Rush out for a walk," I said, making a face at the mention of Frank. "They've been cooped up all day."

I grabbed the single remaining box, which only had a half dozen or so signed books shifting around inside. It was all that remained from the haul we brought inside that morning.

"I'll get these into the van and pull right up to the front," I said. It was a measure of exactly how exhausting the event had been for Maeve that she didn't argue, just nodded and began the task of replacing Ben's service dog vest.

The sunlight was blinding as I emerged from the store. The temperature warmed, and I briefly closed my eyes and turned my face toward the sun, basking in the glow. My eyes had adjusted by the time I made it to the van. I fumbled with my key fob, but it must have been dying because the Green Machine remained locked.

Grumbling, I set the box down and went to fit the key into the lock the old-fashioned way. I stopped just before the key made contact and leaned forward, squinting for a better look. There were tiny, nearly unnoticeable scratches on the lock. I hadn't been able to see them in the dark last night, or in the early morning gloom as we left the house this morning, but in the bright sunlight they were starkly visible. I was sure they hadn't been there before. The Green Machine had his share of dents and scratches, to be sure, but I was aware of every single one. I took meticulous care of my boy. It had been imperative, when he'd been both our home and means of travel.

I gently touched the lock, running my finger over the scratches. Was it worth going to the police? They'd seemed pretty disinterested, even last night. I took a few pictures before carrying on with unlocking the door. I wanted to have some documentation, just in case.

Chapter 22

I stood, just a touch apprehensive, on the balcony at the Club, looking down at the training arena. It was my second obedience class, and my first class after Bryan's death. Despite the Club's official decision to let things proceed as usual, and the positive feedback from clients, I still had my worries about how things would go.

The six dog and human teams who made up my class were milling around the individual stations Stacey and I set up for them. I looked from team to team, matching names with faces.

There was Joe, a fit looking man in his fifties and his Great Pyrenees and Golden Retriever mix, Barley, Stephanie and her corgi, Chet, and Dottie with an adorable pittie mix named Tonks. That dog got points both for cuteness as well as her magical name. And then there was Tianna and her fluff ball combination of shepherd and husky with the hilariously apt name of Jill, Rhonda with her little terrier, Maxx, who looked almost exactly like the Grinch's dog in *How the Grinch Stole Christmas*. Lastly was Cara with her Glen of Imaal terrier, Abbey.

Ages ranged from eight-month-old pure puppy Tonks to

stately eleven-year-old Abbey, who, Cara had told me, was just there for the mental stimulation of being in a new place around different people and dogs. Such things tended to be very beneficial to senior dogs. I just hoped the two of them wouldn't be too bored. Abbey seemed to have a handle on the basics.

Stacey stepped onto the landing and stood next to me.

"Everyone's here and ready," she said.

"It looks great down there," I told her. "Thanks for your help getting everything set up."

Stacey flashed a dazzling smile.

"No problem."

"Hey," I said, just as she started to turn away to rejoin the class. "Is everything okay?"

"Everything's fine," she said.

"It just seemed a little intense with Jeff the last time I saw you two. If there's a problem —"

"There isn't," she said quickly, cutting me off. "Jeff's great. He was just having a bad day yesterday. He couldn't ... he was having a rough time at work."

"Oh, I've been there," I said. I had to fight to keep from adding that I certainly wouldn't treat my significant other, or anyone for that matter, so rudely even in that situation. Well, maybe Dan Friedman. But it's not like he wouldn't deserve it.

"What does Jeff do?" I asked, instead.

"He's a locksmith."

I'm pretty sure my eyebrows shot straight up at that, but Stacey was looking down at the assembled class, and didn't seem to notice. Would Jeff have had a reason to break into my van, I wondered? I'd come right out and told him I'd be at the police station. Maybe what I'd said about presenting evidence to the detective had made him nervous. Hmm. I wanted to ask Stacey for more details, but she spoke first.

"That little white dog," she said, pointing. "She's some kind of fancy terrier, right?"

I was pretty sure she read the class roster, and knew what breeds the class was comprised of, same as I did. Was she trying to steer the conversation to a safer topic? Curious.

"She's a Glen of Imaal terrier," I said, deciding to go along. After all, if Stacey wasn't willing to talk, nothing I had to say was going to change her mind. Not in the limited amount of time we had before class began, anyway.

"She looks like a doodle," Stacey said, using the dog world euphemism for anything mixed with poodle.

"Glen of Imaal terriers are pretty rare," I allowed. "I've only ever seen a few. And Abbey's coat is softer and a little curlier that you'd typically see. But that just comes from grooming by clipping verses hand stripping."

I pushed away from the railing. Clearly, this was going nowhere. Maybe Stacey would be more inclined to talk after class.

"I suppose we'd better get this show on the road."

———

The class went great. It was remarkable how easy it was to focus without someone heckling from the sidelines. As soon as the thought formed in my mind, I forced it out. Even to me, it sounded like I was glad Bryan was dead. Which was definitely not the case. Someone out there was, though. Was that person Jeff? I tried to recall if I'd ever seen or heard him interact with Bryan at all.

"Make sure you reward her when she's in the position you want her to be in," I advised Dottie during the loose leash walking portion of the class. Tonks, full of adolescent energy and enthusiasm, liked to bound ahead to the end of her leash. Dottie had been doing an excellent job of not moving forward when there was tension on the leash, but tended to click and offer a treat as Tonks trotted back to her, which was resulting in Tonks running ahead, turning back for her treat, and then sprinting ahead again.

"May I?" I asked, holding out my hand for the leash.

"Please," Dottie said. "I don't even know what I'm doing anymore."

"That is perfectly normal at this stage," I assured her. "Puppies are a lot."

I took Tonks' leash and stepped a few feet away from Dottie. Tonks, who was a little on the timid side, stayed planted, reluctant to leave her owner's side. I approached from the side, angling my body so that I wasn't facing her head on, and tossed one of my homemade tuna treats her way. Homemade, of course, meaning made in Maeve's oven. Maeve had been less than impressed, threatening me with eviction when she'd emerged from her office and smelled them baking. It was worth the threat, though. Those treats were like crack. I'd encountered very few dogs able to resist them.

Sure enough, Tonks dipped her head to investigate the treat on the ground. She sniffed it for a second or two before lapping it up. I tossed another one, which she pounced on immediately. I dropped a few more on the floor, forming a trail that led her closer and closer to me. As she snarfed up the last on, she eyed the treat pouch at my hip, clearly eager for more. I quietly asked her to sit, typically the cue most familiar to the majority of dogs. Tonks complied, and I clicked the clicker the second her rear end hit the ground and fed her a tuna treat from my hand.

She accepted the treat and then looked up at me, her eyes twinkling with excitement and anticipation, no longer wary. Perfect. Now we were ready to work. I used a treat to guide Tonks into heel position on my right side. Dogs traditionally used to be trained to heel on the left, but unless you're competing in obedience trials, it really doesn't matter in the slightest which side they are on. I preferred to teach dogs to work on both sides. Dottie mentioned earlier that it was easier for her to have Tonks on the right, so that's where I started her. Holding one treat just in front of Tonks' nose, I took a step forward. Just one. Tonks stood up and did the same. I immediately clicked and gave her the treat as she stood next to me, facing forward. We took another three steps in the same fashion, treat in front of nose, reward for taking a single step. Then, I asked her to sit again. Now familiar with what was expected of her, she quickly complied.

We did another round of one step forward with a reward at a time, and then I moved to taking two steps before rewarding, and then three. Tonks was now glued to my side, happy to stay in place next to me. As we did some circles, I noticed a woman with a Shiba Inu on leash standing off to the side, far enough away from the dog and handler teams so as not to be a distraction or bother. She seemed content to observe, so I didn't give her presence too much thought, figuring she'd either finished up with or was waiting for one of Felicia's agility classes and was killing time. We heeled back to Dottie, with Tonks only needing a few treats to keep her focused and in position.

"I didn't know she could do that," Dottie said in amazement.

"In the beginning it's a lot of work," I said. "Especially once they've learned that pulling on the leash gets them where they want to go. But if you're consistent with it, she'll get it."

Out of the corner of my eye, I saw Jeff enter the building from the front door. Stacey, who was in the process of refilling the water bowls at each station, didn't immediately acknowledge him, but began looking around the room. Not wanting to be caught staring, I moved over to Abbey and began working with Cara on encouraging Abbey to improve her sit posture by shifting her weight forward. When I looked up again, both Jeff and Stacey were gone.

I checked the time. Class was due to end in a minute anyway. I decided now was as good a time as any. I moved to a central position, where everyone could easily see me from their stations.

"Okay, everyone!" I said. "You all did great work today! This week, continue to work on sitting with attention and good posture, and continue practicing getting into and walking in heel position. Remember, in the beginning you are going to be using a lot of rewards to help them learn what is expected of them. Later on, we'll start to fade them out, but we want to make sure the behavior is well established first. Does anyone have any questions?"

Very few people came up to me for questions after class. The large arena gave everyone ample space to work with their dogs, and allowed me to move from pair to pair to answer questions multiple times during class. I was really liking this set up. Clarice knew what she was doing when she built the place.

Joe and Barley were the last to leave, with Barley charging toward the door, and Joe just hanging on for the ride. As much as I wanted to go see what Stacey and Jeff were up to, I instead intercepted the pair, and we worked on heeling toward a goal.

"He was doing great in class," Joe said, giving the leash a tug in his frustration.

"Barley was doing awesome in class," I said. "But it's a different situation now. Everyone was making a beeline for the door, and there's a lot of excitement. So we have to take a few steps back."

I gave Joe a handful of the crack tuna treats and coached him in working with Barley as they approached the door. Barley's personality lent itself more to the singlemindedness of a Great Pyrenees at times like this, verses the more biddable Golden

Retriever, so it was slow going at first. But in the end, Joe and
Barley walked out the door together, the leash drooping between
them. I cheered them on the rest of the way to Joe's car.

Deanna had a private lesson scheduled with a student from
one of her competition obedience classes, and after that there
was going to be an educational seminar presented by the
veterinary rehab facility where Felicia worked. I needed to get
all of the equipment from my class cleared away so the space
was ready. Stacey was supposed to help with that. But where
was she? I surmised she went somewhere with Jeff. Was she
okay? Did she need help?

I decided to take quick look around the rest of the building,
starting with the fenced yard where I first met the two of them.
The sun was shining, and the yard was warm and inviting.
Unfortunately, it was also empty. I took another spin around
the arena, ending my circle as Deanna entered through the
back door, seeming a little out of breath.

"Hey," I greeted her. "Don't worry, I'm going to take care
of my mess. I've just lost my assistant, and I want to make sure
she's okay. You haven't seen Stacey around here anywhere,
have you?"

"No, but I just got here," Deanna pitched her voice low,
and I leaned forward to hear what she had to say next, "Don't
tell Clarice."

"I won't," I said with a laugh, straightening. Clarice's rule
was that instructors were supposed to arrive at least a half an
hour before their classes or lessons were scheduled, in order to
prepare and be there in case clients decided to show up early.
Not a bad policy, but life happens sometimes.

"I hope Stacey's not with that fiancé of hers," Deanna said
as I headed toward the stairs. "That boy is trouble."

I figured that much out for myself, but I wanted details.
Unfortunately, I still had Stacey to find and a mess in the arena

to deal with. Besides, Deanna had a lesson to prepare for, so I let it go.

I took the stairs two at a time and started from the beginning of the hallway, poking my head into each office that I came to. I heard the murmur of voices coming from the direction of Bryan's office, then, and quickened my pace. I rounded the corner and found Stacey and Jeff in the middle of what seemed to be a pretty heated, if whispered, argument. They both fell silent as I approached, and I only managed to catch Jeff's final two words,

"— was blackmail!"

"Hey, guys," I said. "How're things going?"

"We're fine," Jeff said. "Not that it's any of your business."

Stacey, who'd been leaning with her back against the wall while Jeff loomed over her, ducked beneath his arm. Her eyes were suspiciously bright.

"I need to borrow Stacey for a few minutes," I said. "We just need to get some equipment put away before the next class."

"Oh!" Stacey exclaimed. "I forgot! I'm sorry."

Jeff pushed away from the wall, muttering to himself as he passed us and stalked down the hallway.

"He's just having a bad day," Stacey said.

"Seems like he's been having a lot of those lately."

Stacey wouldn't meet my eyes.

"I'll get started on those chairs," she said, and began speed walking in the direction of the stairs.

I didn't follow right away, turning instead toward Bryan's office. There wasn't much else along this section of the hallway. Had they been blackmailing Bryan? Was the evidence somewhere in his office? I checked the time and decided I could take a minute or two to investigate.

Once again, the door was unlocked, and I slipped quietly inside. Everything looked about the same. I made the rounds, checking the closet, the filing cabinet, and the desk, moving quickly, looking for anything that seemed different from the last time. I was coming up empty until I got to the desk, where I began opening drawers. I tried the locked drawer automatically and gasped in shock when it slipped open easily.

My enthusiasm was short lived. I dropped down to my knees to look inside the drawer, only to discover it was completely empty.

"Shih tzus," I muttered.

I felt around inside, making sure I wasn't missing anything jammed into a corner, and then slowly slid the drawer closed. I was about to stand up when a glint on metal caught my eye. I leaned closer, focused on the lock itself. Was that … I flicked my phone's flashlight on and took a closer look. There, on the lock, were scratches similar to what I'd found the previous day on the Green Machine.

"Jumping Jack Russells," I breathed, and snapped a photo.

"Nell?" a voiced sounded from the doorway. "What are you doing in here?"

Chapter 23

For an instant I froze, crouched behind the desk, phone in hand. My eyes darted around the room, looking for something, anything, that might save me.

"Nell?" Adrienne's voice sounded again, and I heard her take a step into the room. I opened the first unlocked drawer in reach, scanning the jumbled contents. Aha! I grabbed a pad of yellow Post Its and straightened.

"Found some!" I said, hoping I'd injected the right amount of triumph in my tone. Adrienne stopped in her tracks.

"You were looking for Post Its in here?"

I slipped the pack into my pocket and pretended to check my phone, as though everything was normal and my heart wasn't about to leap right out of my chest.

"Someone told me there might be some," I said.

"Who?"

Oops. Hadn't thought that far ahead. There were plenty of people around to help with the seminar, I knew. I wasn't willing to throw anyone under the bus as the person who'd told me to search for Post Its in a dead man's desk, though. I mentally tried and rejected a few options and decided to go with the abrupt subject change.

"Hey, how did Aurora's agility debut go on Sunday?" I hoped that would be a sufficient enough distraction. First performances are important for a lot of reasons and can be the topic of endless conversation.

Adrienne rolled her eyes and groaned.

"We were the talk of the trial," she said, and her tone indicated that it likely wasn't in a superstar kind of way. "Aurora decided that the course set by the judge wasn't to her liking, so she made up her own."

"Uh oh," I said, but couldn't help smiling. "Tell me there's video."

"It will never see the light of day," Adrienne declared, shaking her head, but returning my smile. "It was probably too soon to start trialing. We've done a few fun runs, of course, but she *is* only two and a half. Huskies are pretty slow to mentally mature. I think the earliest I'd ever started trialing any other dog was three."

"I can see why you wanted to start," I said. "I watched a few of her runs at class. She looked good. And she's fast."

"Which definitely contributed to our issues. She's still not great with distance work and needs a lot of support from me on the course. Normally it's not an issue and I can keep up, but I wasn't on top of my game on Sunday, and once she got ahead of me it was all over."

We'd left the office by then, and Adrienne turned around and locked the door securely behind her. I wondered what she meant by not at the top of her game, and once again found myself studying her midsection like a creeper.

"I should have just stayed in town for the book signing," she said, tucking her keys into her pocket. The keychain got stuck on her belt loop, and we paused in the middle of the hallway as she worked to get it free.

"Maeve's book signing?" I asked.

Adrienne, still concentrating on her keychain situation, wasn't looking at me.

"Yeah," she said, her voice slightly muffled from the way she'd tucked her head to see what she was doing. "Maeve McLinton is… oh!" she exclaimed and looked up. "Are you two—"

"Sisters," I said, grinning. "And I've got some extra signed books in the van, if you'd like one."

"Oh, I'd love that!" she said, finally yanking the keychain free. "These things are so ridiculous sometimes."

I pulled out my own set of keys.

"I think they're kind of nice," I said, studying the logo. "And so sweet of Clarice to hand them out to employees."

"Not just employees," Adrienne said. "People who hold higher positions in the club and some longer-term members have them as well. Excluding the actual keys to the premises, of course. Clarice means them to be a symbol of how we're all family, I think."

"Still, I like it."

"I like the idea of it. I just wish they were a little smaller," Adrienne said, this time succeeding in jamming the keys into her pocket. And then it was her turn to change the topic. "So, you and Maeve McLinton are sisters?"

"We are," I said. "It's why I decided to move out to Central Oregon."

"That I knew. I don't think you'd mentioned her name before."

"Have you read her books?"

"Have I!" Adrienne's thumb swiped across her phone, and she tapped the screen a few times. "Look," she said, turning it in my direction. "I'm a member of her Facebook group, see? And I subscribe to her newsletter. And I try to leave a review on every book. I know how important that is."

"Well, I know for a fact she really appreciates that."

"Every time she has a book signing in town, I have something else planned," Adrienne moaned.

"You don't have to wait for a signing to meet her," I said. "We could all get coffee sometime."

Adrienne's eyes lit up.

"That would be wonderful!"

"And I'll get you one of the signed copies of the new book," I promised.

————

By the time I'd managed to disengage myself from Adrienne and get back downstairs, all remnants of my class had been cleared away, and Stacey was gone. Shih tzus. I didn't mean for her to do it all. I hoped she wasn't upset. I joined several other club members in setting up chairs and projection equipment in preparation for the presentation from Leaps and Bounds.

I'd wondered how many people would come out for something like that on a weekday, but by the time the veterinarian and technician delivering the presentation arrived, every seat was full.

"Big crowd," I murmured to Felicia. We and several other club members had staked out places on the sidelines.

"There's always a huge turnout for these presentations," Felicia responded.

"Excuse me."

Felicia and I both turned to see the woman with the Shiba Inu I'd noticed during my class earlier approaching.

"Hey, Alexis," Felicia greeted her. "Everything okay with Taiko?"

"Hello, Felicia," Alexis answered. She looked to be in her fifties and was pale, with very fine, light brown hair that was expertly highlighted. "Taiko is doing wonderfully, as usual. I'd actually like to speak with Ms. McLinton, if that's okay."

"Of course," Felicia said, moving aside so that I could squeeze past her.

"Let's go outside so we can sit in the sun," Alexis said. "Taiko loves sunbathing."

"Does he?" I said with a chuckle. "Most Shibas I've known have been confirmed snow dogs."

"Taiko is the exception," Alexis assured me, and sure enough, once we'd sat ourselves on a bench near the old grooming building, Taiko settled himself at our feet, his rear legs stretched out behind him like a frog's. His little black nose pointed skyward.

"What a character!" I said in delight. For a moment I forgot that I didn't know this woman and had no idea why she brought me out here when the event was about to begin.

Alexis smiled at my reaction.

"I can tell you appreciate dogs for who they are," she said.

"I — of course I do," I said.

Alexis must have seen the bewilderment in my expression.

"Let me start over," she said. "My name is Alexis James. And this, of course, is Taiko."

The way she said her dog's name made it seem like I should know who he was, but I was sure no one at the club had ever mentioned him before. I tried to recall if I'd seen his photo up on the wall, but there were so many dog and handler teams I couldn't remember if he and Alexis were amongst them.

"I just wanted to tell you that I was observing your class today."

"Yes," I said. "I think I saw you there."

"I didn't want to distract you while you were teaching, but I just wanted to tell you how impressed I was. It brought tears to my eyes, actually."

And sure enough, her eyes were a little wet. But nothing spectacular had happened at that class. It was a typical beginner manners class. We worked on the basics, I answered questions, and sent everyone home with instructions on what to work on for the next week. Pretty straightforward.

"Oh, I can see you're confused," she continued. "But, you see, I've been waiting to see who they'd get to replace Bryan so they could finally kick him out of this place for good."

I blinked. She did realize the man was dead, didn't she?

"That man nearly killed my precious Taiko."

"He did? How?"

"Well, I'm sure you know that Shiba Inu are special dogs. You can't treat them like you would any other dog."

I nodded, pretty sure I knew where this was headed. Shibas were unique, no lie there. I loved working with them in a training environment. They were independent, whip smart, funny little dogs who didn't always respond well to traditional training. I liked them a little less in a veterinary setting, where even the simplest act, like trying to auscultate the heart and lungs, could set off an ear-splitting chorus of screams. But none of that meant they couldn't be treated like dogs. They were, after all, dogs.

"Well, Taiko was given to me as a puppy by my late husband four years ago. He was the sweetest, most adorable little baby. He looked like a fox, with that dark fawn coloring of his and those dear little ears. I fell in love. But I'd never even heard of a Shiba Inu before, and had no idea how different they were from so-called normal dogs."

That was, of course, why professionals in the industry caution against giving pets as gifts, but that was neither here nor there, and I certainly wasn't going to mention it.

"But as much as I loved him, little Taiko was turning my life upside down. He would dig these monstrous holes in the yard and tear apart anything he could reach -- big things, like my furniture and Ted's most valuable antiques. And this was as a ten-week-old puppy! I was terrified of what he'd be capable of as an adult. And the screaming. If you did something he didn't like, oh my. I was worried the neighbors would call animal control on me just for trying to give my puppy a bath!"

Taiko closed his eyes and rolled onto his back, wriggling around in the soft grass for a bit before finding a position that satisfied him. He then fell asleep right there in the open, lying on his back with his rear legs outstretched and his front legs curled against his chest. He *was* pretty adorable.

"He sounds like a handful," I said. "I've had those moments before. Where it feels like it's never going to end and you're going to be trapped at the mercy of this little whirling dervish for the rest of your life." I glanced down at the pawprint inked onto my left wrist as I spoke. Sebastian had been a handful, but I still missed him more than I could put into words.

"Exactly!" Alexis exclaimed. "Oh, you do understand! So, when I contacted the Club about taking some puppy classes, I thought I was doing the responsible thing to make sure that this dog didn't wind up running my life. From the first class, I felt like I made a mistake. There was all this talk of dominance this and pack leader that. Even I could see that Taiko wasn't trying to dominate me. He was just a baby, and just needed some training. But I figured the trainer knew best, right? And the Cascade Canine Club was supposed to be the best place to go around here."

My stomach churned a little, the same as when I was at the beginning of a horror novel and things were going perfectly and everyone was happy. You just knew it wasn't going to last.

"What happened?" I asked.

"Bryan told me that Taiko would never respect me until I established myself as his alpha. He told me to roll him over on his back and hold him there until he submitted. I tried it at home, once. He'd just gotten into my knitting basket. Total carnage. Yarn everywhere. Including the beautiful qiviut I'd just had ordered. All destroyed. I was just so angry! So I grabbed him and told him he was bad, and tried to get him on his side. He wasn't having any of it. He only weighed about ten pounds at the time, but he was strong! And when I continued to try and force him, he attacked me! I can still see those little white teeth of his lunging for my face!"

I scuffed one foot through the grass. I hated stories like that. They were nothing new in the dog training world, of course. I'd heard some variation of what Alexis was telling me more times than I could count, and about any breed or mix you could think of. Communicating with another species can be difficult. And we humans are more prideful than we'd like to admit sometimes. We tend to expect every other creature on the planet to bow to our obvious superiority and do what we say without question.

Alexis cleared her throat and continued.

"I told Bryan what had happened in class the next day. He said he'd show me how it was done. Except, he got pretty much the same results I did. So, he declared Taiko was the most aggressive puppy he'd ever seen, and I should either have him put down, or I'd have to get serious about my training in order to prevent him from becoming a danger to the public."

"And I'm guessing getting serious meant using an electric collar?"

Alexis nodded. I felt a new surge of anger at Bryan. Even trainers who regularly used electric collars would never put one on a three-month-old puppy. How had he managed to keep his position at the club so long? Four years wasn't that far in the past. There had been plenty of information out there about more humane methods of training. There was no excuse for that kind of gross incompetence.

"I can imagine how that went," I said.

Alexis' eyes were full of tears, but when she spoke her voice was steady.

"Good," she said. "Then I won't have to go into detail. But by the end of class, Taiko was a shivering ball, huddled on the floor in his own puddle. His eyes … I'll never forget the fear in them. And Bryan had the nerve to declare the session a success."

"I'm so sorry that happened to you both," I said.

"I wanted Bryan arrested for animal cruelty. I wanted this place shut down. Clarice managed to convince me otherwise, though. She said she'd talk to Bryan and make some changes in how puppies were trained. She introduced me to Felicia, who's been a godsend. Felicia helped me to see that Taiko wasn't a bad dog, and that I wasn't a bad owner. She even came to my house to work with us for nearly a year, because Taiko was so traumatized that he refused to get out of the car when we were on the property."

"Felicia is an amazing trainer," I said. "I've had the chance to see her work a few times since I started."

Alexis nodded vigorously.

"Yes, when I first started training, my only goal was to get Taiko to a point where we could live together peacefully. But Felicia convinced me to try agility with him. We never looked back after that! Taiko just got the second leg of his Advanced title this past weekend."

"Congratulations to both of you!" I said. An Advanced title can only be achieved through years of training and trialing. And with a Shiba it was even more of an accomplishment. Especially for a novice handler.

"Oh, I know it's nothing special like Felicia's endless string of Masters," Alexis said. "But I'm pretty thrilled with it. And when I think what I almost allowed to happen to Taiko …" she trailed off and paused for a moment to collect herself before continuing. "Clarice made some good changes. She made a rule that shock collars couldn't be used on puppies younger than eight months of age, and Bryan was eventually phased out of teaching puppy classes altogether. But it was never enough for me. I didn't think Bryan had any business trying to teach *anyone* how to train their dog."

Taiko woke from his nap and bounced to his feet. He sank forward, his neck extended, the nails of his front paws digging into the grass, his rump in the air as he stretched. He straightened, had a good shake, and jumped up onto the bench next to Alexis, eyes sparkling in anticipation of the fun she had planned for him next.

"Well," Alexis said, standing up too. "I guess that's my cue. I'm glad I got to meet you. I knew from the moment I saw your bio added to the club website that you'd be an asset. And that it would finally be time for Bryan to move on."

Was it just me, or did that sound kind of ominous? Had she meant move on to other endeavors or move on to another plane of existence? It was impossible to tell from her tone. And the raw pain still lurking beneath the surface of her eyes.

"Thank you," I said, as she clearly expected some kind of response. The conversation had left me cold, though, despite the happy (for Alexis and Taiko) ending. Something didn't feel right.

———

Still a little shellshocked, I took a few minutes to let Simon and Rush run around one of the larger paddocks before heading back inside with a signed copy of Maeve's book tucked under one arm. The people from Leaps and Bounds seemed to be nearing the end of their presentation.

"And, finally," one of them said. I was too far away to see her nametag, but her polo shirt had the letters *DVM* embroidered just below the left shoulder, "the fitness of senior dogs is something that is very often neglected. As our older dogs slow down, it's all too easy to just chalk it up to age, and let things progress. But fitness work has many benefits for senior dogs, and those benefits are not only physical. Learning new things and practicing on new equipment in a new environment also helps them to stay mentally sharp. We'll just do one quick demo, here. Come on up here, Abbey, and show 'em how it's done!"

I smiled as little Abbey, the Glen of Imaal terrier from my obedience class, trotted to the front of the room. The veterinarian began putting her through her paces, using a variety of equipment while her owner watched with a proud smile.

"I should look into this for Denali," Adrienne said from right next to me, and I jumped. I hadn't heard her approach. "He still has tons of energy, but he just can't do the jumping, running, or pulling that he'd like to do. This kind of thing, though, I bet he'd be great at it."

Her eyes were focused up front, where Abbey was balancing her front paws on a lime green foam square as she scooted her rear feet forward into a sit.

"This may look simple," the veterinarian cautioned, "But this exercise puts extra weight on the front, aiding in developing strength, works the core, and promotes good balance."

"From what I've heard of Denali," I said, "I'd imagine he'd dive right in."

"He most certainly would."

I offered her the book, then, and she hopped up and down a few times like a little kid as she read the signature on the inside cover.

"Wow," she whispered, so as not to disrupt Abbey's demonstration, "This is so cool! I can't believe I'm standing here with Maeve McLinton's sister."

"You'd better believe it, Adrienne," Calvin said, coming up to stand next to us with Axel. "I saw it with my own two eyes."

Up front, Abbey was now walking back and forth over a narrow foam plank a few inches above the ground. At various points the veterinarian asked her to pause, holding either a sit or stand for a few seconds before continuing on. A crowd of other club members and trainers had gathered near Adrienne, Calvin, and me, ready to prepare for the evening round of classes that would start after the presentation.

"What's that you're looking at with those beautiful eyes of yours?" Jared's voice sounded from a short distance away. He emerged from the crush of people, with the same black tri aussie from the flyball class at his side. This time his shirt was decorated in dancing yellow pineapples.

"Just a local celebrity," Calvin said.

"Local celebrity? Honey, if you want to see a local celebrity all you have to do is ask. I'm available twenty-four/seven," Jared drawled, adding a wink for good measure.

Calvin rolled his eyes.

Abbey finished off her demonstration by walking backward up a small incline. She paused when hear rear feet neared the top, her front feet braced on the floor. Her fuzzy white plume of a tail wagged slowly back and forth. She looked enormously pleased with herself.

Calvin and Axel moved a little closer to where I was standing.

"So, how does eight o'clock tomorrow morning sound for the hike?" he asked.

"Sounds great," I said. "Where are we going?"

I noticed more than one person lean forward with interest as Calvin gave directions to an unofficial trail just outside of Redmond. I didn't think much of it. People, especially dog people, in Central Oregon always seemed to be on the lookout for a good hiking trail. Nothing strange about that.

Chapter 24

"I don't think I've ever even heard of this trail you're going to," Maeve fretted as I set a plate of blueberry pancakes in front of her. I'd become the unofficial breakfast maker of the household. Maeve never mentioned it and I certainly wasn't going to, lest she get some nonsense in her head about me doing too much. Besides, I enjoyed making breakfast. One drawback to life in the Green Machine...traditional breakfasts were hard to pull off. Rush and Simon danced around my feet, still not quite used to this whole cooking in a real kitchen thing. Ben, perfect boy that he was, lay on his dog bed, eyes on Maeve.

"Well, that doesn't necessarily mean anything," I said. "Central Oregon is full of unofficial trails, and miles upon miles of Bureau of Land Management space that anyone can access. You've said so yourself dozens of times, at least."

"Right, but I didn't mean you should go somewhere so remote with some random guy. When you told me he invited you out, I thought maybe you'd go to one of the more popular trails. You don't even really know him."

"Sure I do. We're at the club together all the time. And we

talked for a while at your signing. You should eat that, by the way. Cold pancakes are gross."

Maeve picked up her knife and fork and began cutting her pancakes into bite sized pieces. Rush stationed himself at her side, not begging, but ever hopeful that a piece would fall in his direction. Julianne had already cut hers into little triangles and was drizzling syrup over them. Liam was in the process of constructing some sort of pancake roll-up with bacon and strawberries. It looked revolting, but he seemed to be enjoying himself.

"That's not enough to go out into the middle of nowhere with him," Maeve set her knife down and sampled a bit of pancake. "Mmmm, just like Mom's. So good."

"Don't let her hear you say that," I said. "She'd be horrified that I would dare use her recipes after my betrayal." (Betrayal being her preferred term for me striking out on my own). Maeve took another bite of pancake, but didn't dispute what I'd said. She knew our mother as well as I did.

"He could be a serial killer!" Julianne piped up, setting down her glass of orange juice.

Maeve frowned at her.

"How do you even know what a serial killer is?" she asked.

"Mom, please. I'm twelve." Julianne said, a hint of superiority in her tone. And I was suddenly struck by the fact that she really wasn't a little kid anymore. The teen years were closing in fast.

"He's not a serial killer," I said. "Serial killers are not that gorgeous."

"Oh no?" Maeve said. "The name Ted Bundy ring a bell?"

I ate the last bite of my pancake and got up to take my plate to the sink. Simon and Rush leapt up to accompany me. Just in case I needed help.

"People exaggerate Bundy's looks," I said. "I was never that impressed."

"Well, there's no accounting for taste, Nell. Plenty of women would have disagreed with you. And you know what happened to them."

———

I would have liked to say serial killers weren't the first thing that popped into my mind when I saw Calvin and Axel at the trailhead but, thanks to Maeve and Julianne, that is, of course, exactly what happened.

"Good morning," Calvin greeted as I locked up the Green Machine, checking and re-checking the doors. There was no doubt in my mind that I'd locked the van the night the dogs had been turned loose, but I was still being extra careful. I kept Simon and Rush on short leashes. The parking area was right off the highway. The cars whizzing by were a little disconcerting.

Calvin motioned for us to move away from the road, climbing over a few rocks and retreating behind a clump of junipers. I hesitated for just an instant, snippets of the true crime podcasts I listened to swirling around my mind. Maeve was right, I didn't really know Calvin. Probably would have been wisest to maybe get together a few more times in public places before heading off to the wilderness. But then I remembered Calvin had announced to pretty much the entire Club where we'd be going and when. That seemed like a poor strategy if he did, in fact, have nefarious intent.

I followed him behind the junipers. We let the dogs off leash, watching closely as they sniffed and circled. Simon, ever the prickly pear, raised his hackles and growled softly as Axel got a little too enthusiastic in his investigation. Axel wisely backed off.

"Let's get them moving," Calvin said. "I'm sure everyone will settle down."

He slipped the remote to Axel's collar into his pocket.

"Just a precaution," he said, though I hadn't commented. "Axel's gone after deer before. His prey drive is pretty intense."

"So is Simon's," I said. "It took a lot of work before I trusted him off leash."

We headed down a steep canyon wall, the dogs racing ahead with Simon in the lead. His high-pitched squeak-barks and Rush's excited screams made for a unique combination.

"Nice," Calvin said. "That'll scare the mountain lions away for sure. I've seen evidence of them from time to time in this canyon."

Well, that was good to know. I knew mountain lions lived in Oregon, but had always heard that actually running into one was pretty unlikely. Calvin grinned and donned his sunglasses. I was left to wonder exactly how much of what he'd just said was truth verses just messing with the newbie.

We walked the bottom of the canyon for a while, admiring the steep, jagged rock face that rose to either side. The dogs scaled huge boulders, pausing every now and again to take in the view or follow a scent trail. The sun warmed our backs, and was bright enough that I retrieved my own pair of sunglasses from my pack.

Calvin uttered a low whistle of appreciation as Simon climbed right up the side of a seemingly smooth looking boulder. It was at least six feet tall. Rush, a little less confident when it came to such things, placed his front paws up on the rock and whined. Simon looked down at him from his perch, the tip of his tail waving gently. He reminded me of the kid on the playground who was able to climb the highest on the jungle gym, and then spent the rest of his time mocking the other kids from his perch.

"You ever done any protection sports with him?" Calvin asked, nodding in Simon's direction.

"No," I puffed. We'd started climbing the other side of the

canyon wall, and I was already feeling it. Calvin wasn't even out of breath.

"You should come out to the IGP club sometime," he said, pausing and waiting for me to catch up. He took a drink from his camelback and flipped the mouthpiece over his shoulder. I stopped once I caught up to them on the pretense of offering the dogs some water. Really, though, I was the one who needed a breather. Calling the canyon steep was an understatement; I felt like I was climbing at a ninety-degree angle.

"I didn't think border/whippets were all that common in IGP circles," I said, once I could speak again.

Calvin shrugged.

"You don't need a traditional breed just to come hang out and train," he said. "And Simon may be border collie and whippet, but he looks and acts like a mini-Malinois. I bet he'd be a lot of fun to work with."

I packed away my collapsible dog bowl and water bottle and slung my pack over my shoulders, eyeing the distance left to the top.

"The view is worth it, I promise," Calvin said. "We're almost there."

We were halfway. If that.

"Definitely, one hundred percent starting my diet tomorrow," I muttered to myself as I huffed and puffed my way up the wall. Axel scouted our way, ranging about fifteen feet ahead of Calvin. Rush and Simon sprinted ahead and then back to me to make sure I hadn't died, then raced ahead again. Calvin continued talking about the IGP Club as he climbed.

"We have plenty of people who are there with other breeds, just for the experience," he said. "Like I said at the book signing, Kyle comes with that little lab mutt of his. She's an outstanding tracker, that dog."

"I ... heard she's ... a good little ... retriever, too," I said, between gasps.

"Yeah, she's one of those do it all types. Good first dog. Kyle will be able to try all sorts of things with her, and then decide what will be best for his next dog. He's already in contact with some of the shepherd breeders at the club. Talking about trading work for a puppy a few years down the line."

I tried to respond but settled for flashing a thumbs up. Really, though, except for being out of breath, I was having a phenomenal time. The sky was the clear, endless blue I learned to associate with Central Oregon. The gnarled junipers, round sagebrush, and gigantic rocks and boulders every few feet ensured that there was always something exciting to look at. And, of course, if I ever got bored of the landscape, I could always admire Calvin.

Calvin took another rest break (for my benefit, I was sure) about three quarters of the way to the top.

"That was one good thing about Bryan," he said. "He was always so welcoming of new people. He convinced Clarice to offer Kyle the handyman job in exchange for classes and club membership, and suggested I do that same. Really, there's nothing that kid can't build or fix. He's a hard worker, too."

"I think," I said, after I'd caught my breath, "That that's one of the first nice things I've heard anyone say about Bryan."

Calvin shrugged and took another pull from his camelback. Was I a teensy bit distracted by the way his Adam's apple bobbed up and down as he swallowed? Perhaps. And serial killers were the farthest thing from my mind at that moment, most definitely.

"He wasn't the best trainer. And his ethics left a lot to be desired. But he wasn't all bad. He was one of my instructors when I was just getting into Schutzhund back in the day."

"Oh?"

Calvin nodded.

"For a while there, I thought the guy walked on water. I

probably owe my involvement in Sport to him. But he couldn't evolve with the times, and I know that caused a lot of discord." He looked toward the canyon rim. "Ready to get going again?"

"I was born ready!" I declared, bouncing on the balls of my feet. I hoped he'd ignore my red face and heavy breathing once we resumed climbing. Maybe if he had a distraction ... a distraction that would also prove helpful to my agenda.

"Have you noticed more discord with anyone in particular?" I asked as I restarted my trek.

"Felicia," he said immediately. "The two of them would butt heads all the time. They were both strong personalities -- and they weren't shy about speaking their minds."

From what I saw, that was putting it mildly.

Calvin continued, "Deanna. There was something going on with Clarice, too, but I'm not sure what. Lots of history there."

"So I hear," I said.

Calvin paused near the remnants of an old barbed-wire fence, making sure the dogs steered clear of it. Once they'd passed, he vaulted onto a large rock that jutted out into the middle of the trail and offered me his hand, helping me to scramble up as well. How, I wondered, were we going to get back down?

"And, of course," Calvin added, as we finally crested the top of the rim. "There's Adrienne. Those two ..." He blew out a breath and shook his head.

I was too winded to respond, but I knew what he was talking about. I witnessed an argument or two. Not to mention the ultrasound photo with the partial name, beginning with 'A.' Did that have anything to do with the murder? Or was it completely unrelated?

Calvin wordlessly waved an arm, indicating I should take in the view from all sides. I straightened, finally registering that I started deep in the bottom of a canyon and was now at the top, having survived a climb that made Pilot Butte seem like a mere anthill in comparison.

Calvin was right about the view being worth it. I turned in a full circle, taking in the canyon floor below me, the snow-capped Cascade Mountains to the west, the desert to the east, and the looming shadow of Smith Rock in the distance to the north. Simon and Rush stood on the edge of one of flat rocks that comprised the rim and looked out at the endless hills. They too, seemed in awe. Calvin lifted his phone and snapped a photo.

"That's a great shot," he said, one hand dropping down to stroke Axel between his large ears.

We walked along the rim for a while, taking in the mountain views from a few different angles and admiring the tenacity of the junipers, some of which seemed to grow straight out of the very rocks we stood on.

"Have you heard anything from the police about likely culprits?" Calvin asked.

"You mean other than me?" I deadpanned, shaking my head. "The police aren't exactly forthcoming with information on an active investigation; especially with their prime suspect."

We found a shady spot beneath a large juniper tree that had to be hundreds of years old and sat down. The dogs stuck close, having formed a small pack, and sniffed around the area together. Axel had managed to rein in his interest in Simon, and Simon, in turn, was content to ignore him.

"Have you ever met Alexis James?" I asked.

Calvin's brow furrowed for a moment as he thought about it.

"Shiba Inu lady?" he said, finally.

"That's her."

"She was most definitely not Bryan's biggest fan."

"You do have a talent for understatement," I said. He laughed. "There's a lot of hostility there."

"Are you saying the police should be looking in her direction?"

I hesitated. I'd never accused someone of murder before, and felt it wasn't something that should be taken lightly.

"We had a strange conversation yesterday, and I can't stop thinking about it. It sounds like Bryan caused her and her dog a lot of trauma. I get being upset, but it seemed like she was on a mission to destroy the guy professionally. And she said something else … something about how since I was hired, she felt it was time for Bryan to move on. Just her tone of voice and her choice of words made me wonder what she's capable of."

"I don't think I've ever had a conversation with her," Calvin said. "She does agility, mostly. But I'll keep an ear out, and let you know if I find out anything useful."

Chapter 25

The return hike was easier than the hike in, but not without its own challenges. Climbing straight down a canyon wall wasn't quite as cardio vascularly taxing as the climb up, but it was more treacherous. It was a gorgeous outing, though, and I enjoyed the experience. And the company.

I loaded the dogs into the van immediately after unlocking it, filling their water pail before closing the door. I really was not a fan of the traffic zooming past so close to the parking area. I then turned to Calvin, who was parked just in front of me in the turnaround.

"That was really fun," I said. "Thanks for inviting us."

"We should do it again sometime," Calvin said. "It's not often I come across dogs that can actually keep up with Axel."

"For sure," I said.

I waited a beat, hoping he'd suggest another day or trail, but he simply unlocked his Toyota and loaded Axel into the travel crate in back. Disappointed, I headed for the driver's door of the Green Machine.

Something glinting in the sun, half covered by the sandy dirt, caught my eye. I bent over and retrieved a Cascade

Canine Club keychain. I first checked my own keyring, and everything, including my keychain, was there.

"Calvin!" I called.

Luckily, his windows were open. His brake lights flashed as he rolled to a stop.

"You dropped your keychain," I said, jogging over to his car.

Calvin pointed to his keys, dangling from the ignition. A Canine Club keychain was clearly visible.

"It's not yours?" he asked.

"No, I have mine."

"Huh. That's odd."

It certainly was. I was pretty confident the keychain wasn't in the parking area when we arrived. I waved Calvin off and returned to the Green Machine. I carefully looked him over, top to bottom, inside and out. Nothing seemed to be missing or damaged.

Was I overreacting? It seemed like an unbelievable coincidence that someone from the Club would have stopped at this tiny, unmarked parking area while Calvin and I were hiking, and just leave.

I considered calling the police, but after taking a second to imagine how that conversation might go, I decided against it. They didn't take the first break-in seriously. It was unlikely they would rush right over if I told them I was concerned about finding a keychain in the dirt.

I made one last check of the van. When I still didn't see anything out of the ordinary, I cautiously started him up. He seemed to be running just fine. I sat there for a few minutes, analyzing every sound and vibration, trying to discern if there was anything that seemed odd.

I nearly jumped out of my seat when my phone buzzed in my pocket.

"Hello, this is Daniel Friedman, from the *Central Oregon Chronicle?*"

"I know who you are, Dan," I said, relaxing against the backrest.

"Right, right," he said, speaking fast. "Hey, are you busy today?"

"Not at the moment."

"Good, good. Can you meet me? Say, at Dog Eared Books in Sunriver? Do you know it?"

"Yeah, I know it, but it's a bit of a drive, considering I'm in Redmond right now."

"I'll be here for a while," Dan said. "Gotta get caffeinated and all that."

"I don't know," I said. "You sound plenty caffeinated all ready."

"I got some information about Bryan Reed that you should hear about. But I don't want to say anything over the phone. Just in case."

"In case what?" I said, lowering my voice theatrically. "You think we're bugged?"

"Is it the drive?" Dan asked, ignoring my question. "We could meet somewhere closer. There's some nice places in Bend that would be a good midway point."

I checked the time. It wasn't even noon. Maeve was deep into her next rough draft and the kids were at school. I didn't have to teach any classes that day. Though the drive was long, it was beautiful. I did promise Marnie I'd come back with the dogs. And then there was the matter of Dan's jacket, which was folded neatly on the passenger seat. I could kill a bunch of birds with one stone if I just made the drive to Sunriver.

"No, no," I said. "You stay put. I'm leaving now."

"Excellent," Dan said.

———

Considering the length of the drive, the Green Machine made it in record time. I found a shady parking spot and began my routine of making sure the vehicle was secure and the dogs were comfortable. I decided to leave the dogs in the van for now, just in case Marnie was busy.

I hurried inside with Dan's jacket draped over one arm, scanning the tables along one end of the building, where Marnie served coffee. Since Dan mentioned caffeinating, I figured that would be a good area to start.

"Nell! Over here!"

I winced. Dan was a little loud, and a few of the patrons browsing the bookshelves turned to glare at him. I avoided making eye contact with any of them as I scurried across the room to where Dan was frantically waving one arm over his head at a secluded little table.

"Do I really need to remind you to use your inside voice in my bookstore, Mr. Friedman?" Marnie asked. She arrived at the table just as I did and deposited two mugs of coffee before speeding away. The place was packed.

"Your blood must be ninety percent caffeine at this point," I said, handing Dan his jacket and sitting down in the chair opposite him.

"Hyperbole," Dan scoffed, draping his jacket over his chair. "Eighty-five percent is my max. Otherwise I get the shakes. But, now that you mention it ..."

Dan paused for a moment, fishing around in his messenger bag before withdrawing a small plastic box, almost like an old-school pager or beeper, complete with digital display. A glucometer, I realized, familiar with the devices that measured blood sugar levels from my time working at veterinary clinics. He then produced another small bit of plastic, about the size of a pen cap, and pressed it quickly to his finger. A drop of blood appeared. Carefully keeping the finger elevated, Dan used his other hand to insert a small, coded strip into the glucometer. He studied the digital display, and in a second it beeped and flashed a number.

"Okay," Dan said, packing away the glucometer and lancet. "We are good to go."

"You're a diabetic?" I asked.

Dan nodded.

"Since I was nine." He took a long gulp from one of the mugs while gesturing to the other. "That one's yours," he said, once he swallowed. "I noticed you liked the hazelnut Spoken Moto stuff, so I ordered you Marnie's version." He lowered his voice, "It's not quite as good, but it'll do."

"Thank you, I love hazelnut." I raised my voice slightly as Marnie passed on her way to another table. "And I think Marnie's coffee is fantastic."

"Flatter all you want," Dan said with a grin. "But I'm still Marnie's favorite. Right, Marnie?"

"In your dreams, Friedman," Marie called over her shoulder.

I hid my smirk by taking a sip of my coffee. I thought it was tasty. At least as good as what Dan got from Spoken Whatever.

"So," I said, as Dan continued mainlining his gigantic mug of Marnie's house blend. "What was so important that I had to immediately drive all the way out here?"

Dan motioned for me to lean in closer. I complied.

"Okay, Double O Seven," I whispered. "Spill."

"Turns out, Bryan Reed played things a little fast and loose with his marriage vows," Dan said, and sat back, a look of triumph on his face.

"What? Like he was having an affair?"

"Exactly."

"With who?"

"Whom," Dan corrected, and I glared at him. He shrank back in his chair. "Sorry, force of habit."

Writers. Maeve was exactly the same.

"Well unforce it," I said. "It's annoying."

"Noted."

"With *whom*," I emphasized, "Was Bryan having an affair?"

"Not sure."

I threw up my hands.

"So really you don't know anything. Who is this source of yours anyway?"

"A good reporter never reveals his source," Dan said. "But this affair business opens up all sorts of possibilities. The wife, for example. You know what they say about a woman scorned."

"That it's an incredibly sexist and offensive saying?"

"Still," Dan said. "It's usually the wife."

"The spouse," I said. "Plenty of murdering husbands out there."

Dan sighed.

"Fine," he said. "The spouse. Katherine Reed. What do you know about her?"

"Next to nothing. How do you know it wasn't the girl-friend? And who *was* the girlfriend? Were they still together at the time of Bryan's death?"

"My source didn't give a name. But I was told to also look into the president of the Cascade Canine Club. Clarice Abernathy?"

"What about Clarice?"

"You tell me."

I sat back in my chair and folded my arms over my chest.

"I'm not telling you anything about anyone until you give *me* some answers for once. Like, who is this source of yours?"

"I told you, I can't say."

"Okay, then." I tossed some cash on the table for my coffee and slid my chair back.

"Hold on," Dan said. I continued to gather my things.

"Wait just a second," he said. "Please. I can't give you the name of my source. I promised to keep them anonymous."

"Sure," I said. "Just like you promised to keep what I told you the night of the murder off the record?"

Dan didn't have a response. Good. I didn't really want to hear any more of his excuses anyway. Coming here was a mistake. I strode out the door, not looking back or even slowing down at Dan's repeated attempts to get my attention. I tossed my purse on the Green Machine's passenger seat and slammed the driver's side door closed. Dan stood under Dog Eared Books' awning, looking defeated. He deserved as much, I decided as I released the parking brake, fired up the Green Machine's engine, and shifted him into reverse.

A squirrel darted into my path as I started to back out of my parking space. I hit the brake pedal probably harder than I needed to. The van lurched to a stop, but something felt off as I cautiously released the brake after the squirrel was safely out of the way. We started rolling backward, and I lightly pressed the brake again. Except nothing happened. The Green Machine gained speed, and I punched the brake all the way to the floor. Still nothing. The brakes were out.

We were rolling downhill uncontrolled.

Chapter 26

Instinctively, I kept my foot on the brake pedal. For ten years the van always slowed down or stopped when I pushed the brake. My body kept insisting, *This time it'll work! This always works!*

It most definitely was *not* working. I used my mirrors to see what was behind us. Luckily, there weren't any humans or animals in our path. Unfortunately, there wasn't anything else, either. If I kept going, I'd roll right into the busy cross street.

Simon and Rush knew something wasn't right. They stood stiff legged, at attention.

"We're okay, guys," I murmured, trying my best to remain calm.

And then I saw them. Behind us and to the left were the two enormous Ponderosas I parked under the day of Maeve's book signing. I frantically yanked at the wheel, hand over hand, hoping I had enough time to get us lined up. It was a strange sensation, actually trying to hit something.

"Lie down!" I ordered the dogs, bracing myself for impact.

The sound of crunching metal and cracking glass was spectacular. I was thrown back into my seat, and heard the dogs slide backwards behind me. The Green Machine was surely a little worse for wear, but we were stopped, at least.

"Sorry, buddy," I whispered, patting the steering wheel.

I turned to check on Simon and Rush. They stared at me with wide, frightened eyes, but both still held their downs.

"Okay," I released them.

They both bounced to their feet, swarming into the front seat. I moved them to where I could better check them over. A cursory exam didn't reveal anything obvious. We really weren't going that fast, even though it felt that way.

"Nell!" Dan called. He started pounding on the side of the Green Machine. "Is everyone okay in there?"

"Take it easy," I said, sliding the door open. "He's had a tough enough day without you beating on him."

Dan visibly sagged with relief.

"Oh good," he said. "When I didn't see you in the driver's seat I thought someone was hurt."

"I think we're all fine."

"Nell!"

I turned toward the bookstore to see Marnie sprinting over to us, her floral pattered apron flapping in the breeze.

"Nell!" she gasped, once she reached us. "What in the world?"

"I think the van's been tampered with," I said, and told them about the keychain I found at the trailhead, and the similar scratch marks I discovered on the locks of the Green Machine and Bryan's drawer.

Marnie immediately called the police and told us not to touch anything. I did my best, only re-entering the van to grab my purse and the dogs' leashes.

While we waited for the police, I kept a close eye on the dogs, watching for any change in their breathing, movement, or demeanor. Instances like this, of course, are why it's safest to always have dogs restrained in vehicles, preferably in crates.

Our previous life in the Green Machine made constantly having crates set up impractical. And I hadn't even begun to investigate the possibilities since settling in at Maeve's. I hoped that Rush and Simon wouldn't have to pay too dearly for my shoddy preparations.

————

The police, including Detective Rodriguez, arrived faster than I expected. I repeated the whole story about noticing the similar scratches (Detective Rodriguez called them "tool marks") on both the Green Machine and the desk drawer, and finding the keychain. Detective Rodriguez frowned at the latter, especially after I told him about the tiny, unmarked parking area.

"Did any of your co-workers know where you were going this morning?" he asked.

"A bunch of them were around when Calvin was giving me directions," I said.

"Full name?"

"Calvin Overby," I said. "He's a member of the Cascade Canine Club, and is the training director at the Central Oregon IGP club."

"Do you have reason to believe he had anything to do with this?"

"I don't see how he could have," I said. "He arrived before I did, and we spent the entire time with each other. Plus, he had his keychain on him when he left. He showed it to me."

Detective Rodriguez nodded, scribbling in the small note-book he carried. Dan was off to the side, typing furiously on his phone. One of the other officers approached. His name was Olsen, according to his nametag.

"The brake line's definitely been tampered with, Detective," Officer Olsen said, nodding at me in acknowledgement but directing his comments to Detective Rodriguez. "I won't know the full extent of the damage until I can take a closer look at the yard, but whatever happened, it was deliberate. Looks like someone only partially cut the line, and then it snapped the rest of the way when you were avoiding the squirrel."

"You're taking the van?" I blurted, then blushed. Of course, they'd have to take the Green Machine. It's not like I'd even be able to drive him in his current condition. At least it meant they were taking me seriously, for once. Though, the idea of someone cutting my brake line was terrifying. Didn't this kind of stuff only happen in movies?

"Yes, I'm afraid we'll have to," Detective Rodriguez said gently. "But we'll release it back to you as soon as possible."

"I understand," I said. "I just didn't think it through, I guess."

It was more than that. The Green Machine was my home for the past ten years. I was having a hard enough time reconciling with the whole living at Maeve's thing. It was nice to know that I always had the option to just pack my stuff and leave if things got too bad. Or if my parents announced a visit.

"I'll also need the keychain you found," Detective Rodriguez continued.

"Of course," I said, fishing it out of my purse. "Um ... sorry, but I did touch it a few times. Will that affect anything?"

"We have your prints on file," Detective Rodriguez said. "We know you've been handling it. People seldom glove up just to pick something shiny off the ground." He smiled at his own joke, surprising me. He'd always seemed so serious and straightlaced.

"We'll be in touch," he said, tucking the notebook into his pocket and motioning for the rest of the team to finish up.

————

"Need a ride?" Dan asked, after the police and the tow truck carting the Green Machine left. My chest felt tight as I watched the Green Machine being hauled away. I told myself I was being maudlin, and turned away before my home for the last ten years disappeared altogether

Rush pushed his nose into my hand, sensing my distress. I ran a hand over his head and smiled down at him. He wiggled his whole rear end in response, his lips lifting in a toothy grin.

"The dogs are welcome, too, of course," Dan continued. "And obviously I won't charge you."

For a moment I was confused. Then I remembered he drove for Lyft, and the last time I'd accepted a ride from him I paid him for it. I also remembered the consequences of that ride.

"Working on another article?" I sneered.

"No," Dan said. "I mean, yes, always, but that isn't what this is about."

"What's it about, then?"

"It's about you and the dogs nearly dying today, and you being stranded forty minutes from home. I just want to help. You don't have to say one word during the drive if you don't want to."

I didn't believe him. But my other options were paying a fortune for Lyft or dragging Maeve away from her writing.

"This doesn't mean I forgive you," I said, motioning for the dogs to head toward the white Subaru at the other end of the parking lot.

"Perish the thought," Dan muttered, falling into step behind me.

We did spend the first twenty minutes or so of the drive without speaking. Dan seemed determined to keep his word about not pressuring me to talk. I played on my phone, texting Maeve to let her know what happened, and reading up on the various methods of damaging a brake line.

"The police don't seem to be making much headway," Dan said, as we approached Bend.

"Are you serious, right now?"

"It's boring, driving in complete silence."

"So, turn on some music, or a podcast, or something."

"Or we could just have a normal conversation. Like adults do."

I sighed.

"I saw you writing down everything Detective Rodriguez was saying back there," I said. "I don't want to see any of this in a *Chronicle* article."

"You won't."

I shook my head, wincing as the stiffness from backing into the tree started setting in. Ugh. Tomorrow was going to be brutal.

"I wish I could believe you," I said, already partially checked out. I was reading the reviews of various local veterinary clinics. I wanted to get Rush and Simon checked out to make sure the crash hadn't resulted in any injuries I'd missed.

"What do I have to do to convince you that I'm not a bad guy?"

What would he have to do indeed? Leave me alone for the rest of our lives? That sounded good, though not particularly helpful. Still … there was that anonymous source. Maybe that could be useful. I lowered my phone.

"Help me solve Bryan's murder," I said turning to face him. "Since, as you say, the police aren't making much headway. Solve it, and don't write about it."

"Don't write about it?" he repeated. "That's a little unfair, don't you think?"

"You want to talk about unfair?"

"No thanks. You've already made your point on that."

I shrugged.

"Actions have consequences. Some of them affect careers.

You're just going to have to do what Hannah says, and *try harder, be better.*"

I didn't expect him to get the reference to the British true crime podcast, but he briefly took his eyes off the road to glance in my direction.

"Hannah Maguire from *RedHanded?*" he asked.

"You're a listener?"

"Am I a listener?" Dan checked his mirrors and made a quick turn into a gas station. There, he put the car into park and unzipped his hoodie.

"I'm a bonafide Spooky Bitch," he proclaimed, revealing a black and white T-shirt with the same moniker. It was what the RedHanded hosts referred to themselves and their listeners as. It seemed apt, given the subject matter they covered.

"Well, you're half right," I said.

Dan shifted back into drive.

"Meaning?"

"I don't think you're all that spooky."

Chapter 27

"Still, it was nice of him to give you a ride," Maeve said, pouring a little oil into the popcorn popper and adding some kernels from the economy sized bag stashed in the pantry. Popcorn was Maeve's one vice. At least it was the only one I knew of.

"Especially since it was all the way from Sunriver," she added, when it became clear I wasn't going to respond. She fixed the lid onto the popper and gave me nod.

I plugged it in.

"Popcorn, popcorn!" Liam chanted, dancing around the kitchen, wearing his favorite red and orange patterned ceramic bowl as a hat. It clashed horribly with his hot pink hair.

Maeve plucked the bowl from his head as he twirled past.

"Have you finished your homework?" she asked, poking the bowl in the direction of the kitchen table, where his iPad lay.

"Can we have Dan, Dan, the newspaper man over for dinner sometime?" Liam asked, ignoring her question and performing a less than graceful arabesque in the middle of the kitchen.

"Why?" I asked, busying myself setting all of Maeve's

popcorn goodies in a row on the kitchen counter. Anything you could think of to put on popcorn, Maeve had at least two containers. There was butter and salt, of course. Plus, seasoned salt, coconut flakes, ranch seasoning, barbeque seasoning, chocolate sauce, caramel sauce, and marshmallows.

Julianne looked up from her perch at the end of the counter, where she was peeling the foil off Hershey's kisses and placing the unwrapped chocolate into a bowl. All three dogs were stationed around her, each ready to snatch up any stray kisses that might fall from the counter.

"Yeah, why?" she asked, popping a kiss into her mouth. "All he's ever done is give Nell a ride home and write a mean article about her. The two kind of cancel each other out."

"And her math teacher says she doesn't have a firm grasp of algebra," Maeve said, raising her hand for a high five.

Julianne gave her hand a gentle slap, careful not to hurt her mother or make her lose her balance.

"He gave you his coffee that night, too," Liam said, clicking his heels together. "It would be so fun. We never have company."

"Homework," Maeve said.

Liam danced a jig back to his seat at the table. I pulled out his chair for him, and he doffed an imaginary hat.

"Thank you, milady," he said.

"You are full of beans tonight," I told him.

"I'm about to be full of popcorn!" he said, wriggling in his seat and swiping the iPad's home screen.

"What do you mean he's full of beans *tonight*?" Maeve said. "He's been full of beans since he was in the womb."

"Since I was a womb-baby!" Liam exclaimed, fingers now flying over the screen as he organized his assignments.

"It's called a fetus, stupid," Julianne said, adding her bowl of kisses to the row of fixings on the counter.

"You're a fetus," Liam retorted.

"Okay, guys, settle down. It's been nearly a decade since anyone in this room has been a fetus," Maeve said.

That reminded me.

"Hey," I said, pulling out my phone. "I want to get your opinion on something."

The popcorn started popping as I searched through my photos for the ultrasound picture. It smelled delicious. Maeve leaned toward me to get a better look.

"Really, Nell?" she said. "I write science fiction, you know, not science fact. And surely not ultrasound reports."

"But you've had ultrasounds before. And I bet you got a few of these printouts, right?"

"Sure."

"So? Is there any way to get information about the parents from this?"

"Like whether it resembles the mom or the dad?"

Julianne and Liam cracked up, which set the dogs off in a chorus of barking. Good greyhounds. Everyone was bonkers tonight.

"Maeve," I said. "I'm serious. I found this in Bryan's desk, and look. The date is just a week before the ... you know."

"Brutal murder?" Julianne offered.

"Thanks," I said. "Are you sure *your* homework is done?"

Julianne grinned and settled into the chair next to Liam.

"All done. Even algebra."

"Well here, then. Make yourself useful and melt some butter." Maeve handed her a small glass bowl and spatula before taking the phone from me and studying the photo from all angles and sizes.

"What, exactly, do you want to know?" she asked, as Julianne beep-beeped the microwave timer, "All of the identifying information has been removed."

"There's a rumor that Bryan was having an affair," I said. "If the photo belongs to her ..." I trailed off. "I don't know. I thought maybe there would be a serial number on the paper and we could use that to trace it back to the particular doctor's office."

Maeve handed me my phone back.

"You've been listening to too many true crime podcasts."

"Like *RedHanded*," Liam sing-songed. "Spooky, spooky, spooky bi —"

"You finish that word and there will be no popcorn for you tonight," Maeve threatened.

Liam hastily returned his attention to his homework. Wise choice.

"Any guesses as to who he was having an affair with?" Maeve asked, indicating with her cane which cabinet to find other ceramic bowls from the set Liam's belonged to.

"Well," I said, stretching to reach the top shelf, "you can see what looks like the letter 'A' at the part where the paper was ripped. So one could make the assumption that the mother's name begins with 'A'."

"Right," Maeve said, moving closer to the popcorn maker as it neared the end of its cycle.

"Initially, the only person I could think of with an 'A' name was Adrienne, the Club vice-president."

"The one with the huskies?" Maeve asked, transferring the popcorn into a giant bowl.

"Yes," I said. "But a few days ago I met a woman named Alexis James."

"So that's two." Maeve accepted the melted butter from Julianne and began drizzling little bits over the popcorn, shaking the bowl thoroughly after each little bit that she added.

"The problem is, both of them really seemed to dislike Bryan. And that was putting it mildly. Plus, Alexis has to be in her fifties."

"Certainly not too old for an affair."

"But it's getting kind of up there for making babies," I pointed out.

"Not impossible, though," Julianne piped up, choosing a green and blue bowl and filling it with popcorn. "My social studies teacher just went on maternity leave, and she's *old*."

"Ms. Connolly is only thirty-five, my dear," Maeve said. "If she's old, then I may as well be geriatric. But Julianne is right. It's not impossible. Especially in this day and age."

"Well, you sure do *sound* geriatric after that last part," I said, maneuvering between Rush and Gentle Ben to fill Maeve's bowl and my own.

Maeve studied the array of toppings before her. Julianne made a beeline for the barbeque seasoning. Liam watched them longingly. I made typing motions with my free hand, and he returned to his work.

"You know," Maeve mused as she sprinkled some salt into her bowl, "Just because they didn't seem to like each other in public doesn't mean they weren't a little more ... friendly ... in private."

"It's possible."

"But you don't think it's likely." Maeve dropped a few kisses into her bowl.

Yum. If you've never tried salted popcorn with chocolate kisses before, you've never lived. I was tempted to go that route with my own popcorn, but then remembered the difficult canyon wall climb earlier. I settled for a small sprinkle of the ranch seasoning.

"I mean, if you're going by that theory, Bryan could be having affairs with the entire training staff," I said, shaking my bowl to make sure the popcorn was evenly coated.

"Busy boy," Maeve said, settling herself into a chair at the kitchen table.

I sat down next to her, directly across from Julianne.

"I think," I said, "as much as I hate to admit it, I'm going to have to figure out a way to talk to Clarice. By all accounts she knew Bryan the best, and she also knows everyone else at the club, tool."

"Why do you hate to admit it?" Julianne asked.

"Who brought Clarice up in the first place, that's why."

"Newspaper man?" Liam asked, looking up from his laptop.

"Give the boy a gold star," I said.

"I'd rather have some popcorn," Liam grumbled.

"Would you like a kiss?" Maeve asked, giving her bowl a nudge.

Liam nodded vigorously.

"Yes, please!"

Maeve leaned over and dropped a quick kiss in the middle of his forehead.

"Mom!" he complained, as Julianne and I chuckled. "That's not what I meant!"

Maeve pushed the protective flap over the iPad.

"Go on and get yourself some popcorn," she said. "And we'll all help you finish your homework later."

Chapter 28

Driving Maeve's compact sedan was an adjustment after the roominess of the Green Machine. Simon and Rush each staked out a corner of the backseat and were looking out their respective windows. Their vet exam was clear and neither seemed any the worse for wear after yesterday's crash.

I resolved to find a moment to talk to Clarice before I left the club for the day. It should be easy enough; all I had planned was drawing up an agenda for the drop-in classes I presented to Clarice a few days ago.

I parked Maeve's car and made a futile attempt at locking it. The lock on the driver's door had been broken for some time. Maeve warned me not to leave anything valuable inside. She had an appointment to get it fixed but canceled it when the police impounded the Green Machine.

I brought the dogs to one of the fenced paddocks to run around before we went inside. My phone buzzed. It was Dan.

I swiped my thumb across the screen. "What's up, Dan?"

"Just checking in," he said. "Wanted to make sure you and the dogs are okay."

"We're fine. Thanks again for the ride." Ugh. That

sounded so formal, but I wasn't sure what else to say to him. I was grateful for his help, but I was still wary that anything I said to him might wind up in the paper, no matter his claims to the contrary. There was a strained silence on both our ends, and I wondered if, perhaps, it wouldn't be best to just feign a random disconnect.

Dan spoke up before I could put my plan into action. "So, uh, could you get me a list of the people at the kennel club the day of the murder? I have a free day today and thought I might as well do some digging."

"You don't have to," I said quickly. "Just forget about what I said about solving the —"

"No," he interrupted. "I want to help."

"All right, I'll get you the list," I said, and ended the call.

I motioned to the dogs and hurried inside. Once everyone was settled in the office, I booted up my laptop and sent Dan the list I made. As the email processed, I stared idly out the window. It was a warm, sunny day, and several club members were making use of the grounds. Dottie and Tonks practiced loose leash walking along the paths. Several people commandeered one of the large paddocks, using it as a dog park of sorts, flinging tennis balls with a Chuckit! for four dogs of various breeds.

Some movement in the distance caught my eye. I looked past the others to see Clarice, accompanied by her salukis, trekking up the hill to her house. Sensing the opportunity was at hand, I told the dogs to stay where they were and shut them inside the office.

I sprinted across the yard, slowing down only a little as I started climbing the hill. I actually managed to outpace Clarice, who had no idea that we were racing. She was just out for a leisurely walk with her dogs.

"Hi!" I said, breathlessly, rounding the curve of Clarice's

driveway just as she was about to enter the security code to her gate.

Clarice turned around, clearly startled.

"Nell!" she said. Her tone wasn't exactly welcoming.

The salukis eyed me with disinterest. They were even more stunning in the daylight, Inanna in particular. The sunlight glinted off the black of her coat, providing even more of a contrast with her silver points. She had just enough feathering to provide an added touch of elegance to her already lean, willowy frame.

I tore my eyes from the dogs, trying not to let myself become distracted. It was tough, though. I'd much rather discuss salukis than the secret pregnancy, affairs, and murder.

"Do you have a minute?" I asked. "I think we need to talk."

"Oh, Nell, I'd love to, but I have so many things I need to get done around here."

She opened the gate slightly and squeezed through. Her dogs, even slimmer than she was, followed suit.

"Clarice," I said, as she closed and locked the gate. "Since I've been hired, I've been harassed and berated by a fellow trainer, accused of murder, and have had my life and the lives of my dogs threatened. I think you can spare ten minutes."

She hesitated, and for a second, I thought she was going to refuse. But she sighed and pushed the gate open.

"Thank you," I said, following her up the long gravel drive to the ornately carved front door. She hung her jacket and leashes in the grand entrance hall and led me to a tastefully designed sitting room decorated in neutral tones. My hair was probably the brightest thing in the entire house.

"Can I get you something to drink?" Clarice asked, as the dogs settled themselves onto the various thick, cushy dog beds strategically placed around the room.

I decided it was best to get right down to it.

"Were you having an affair with Bryan?" I asked.

Clarice paled, and quickly sat down on one of the opulent sofas in the room.

"No," she said, so softly that I had to strain to hear her. "No, we never had an affair."

I sensed there was a little more to it and didn't respond.

Clarice's hands twisted in her lap. "We never had an affair," she repeated. "But I was ... and maybe still am ... in love with him."

I'm not sure why I was so shocked by her declaration since I already suspected a relationship. Maybe it was the idea of refined, stately Clarice pining after someone as odious as Bryan. Still, as Maeve pointed out during the Ted Bundy discussion, there was no accounting for taste.

Clarice looked up and, upon seeing my expression, gave a small smile.

"You might as well sit down," she said. "And I'll tell you everything. I've been needing to get it off my chest."

She motioned to the other end of the sofa. Now it was my turn to hesitate -- not because I didn't have the time -- but because that sofa was a beautiful cream color. I was pretty sure I was covered in dog hair and a decent amount of that wonderful Central Oregon dust that coated every surface. Every surface except those in Clarice's house.

"I don't want to get it dirty," I said.

"Sit."

I sat.

Clarice stood up and crossed the room to a large bookcase built into the wall. For one wild moment I thought she was going to pull a book out and reveal a secret passageway. Instead, she removed several books and withdrew a battered wooden box. It would have been somewhat of an anti-climax; except I was pretty sure I knew what the box was. And to whom it had belonged.

"I was never romantically involved with Bryan," Clarice

said. "Partly due to my own morals. A married man is always off limits. But also because I wanted to protect both Bryan and Katherine. Katherine has always been a dear friend, and I never wanted to hurt her. As for Bryan, well, unrequited love is a funny thing. I would've done almost anything to protect him and his reputation. Even now."

"Why?" I couldn't help asking. From what I'd known of Bryan, he wasn't exactly deserving of that kind of devotion.

Clarice set the box down on the coffee table in front of us and withdrew a small key from her pocket before reclaiming her seat next to me.

"I know that you and Bryan didn't get off to the best start," she said. "But he could be the sweetest man. He did a lot for the Club over the years, starting from the very beginning. He helped so many young people get involved in their chosen sports, and would move heaven and earth to match clients to dogs suited to their needs. He had such a passion for training."

"I've heard from people who had a different perspective," I said.

"Let me guess. Alexis James?"

"She's one example."

"I'm not defending Bryan's training techniques," Clarice said. "Goodness knows, I don't have enough knowledge on the subject to even know where to begin. And there's no question he took things too far with the Shiba Inu puppy. But you have to understand that for every Alexis James out there, there's another person singing Bryan's praises."

Ra got up from his dog bed and place his head in Clarice's lap. She absently played with the feathering on his ears with two fingers.

"Back when the Club was newly formed, when it could hardly even be called a club, I was lost. I had my vision, but I wasn't clear how to go about implementing it. Bryan, on the other hand, was at the top of his game. His methods were more widely accepted back then, and he was the most popular trainer in town by far."

I thought back to the articles I'd found in Bryan's office, and Maeve's mention of hearing about him when she first moved to Bend. I nodded, encouraging Clarice to go on.

"He jumped into this project with both feet. He helped me design the training arenas, and he put the word out to all of his contacts when we were about to open. This Club would not be what it is now without Bryan's generosity and work ethic. I owe him for the life I lead now, this business, and my reputation in the community."

"That makes sense," I said. "I get why you're so loyal to him."

Clarice fitted the key into the box's lock.

"A few days before Bryan's death, he asked me to keep an eye out for anyone hanging around his office. He implied that it had something to do with this box. So, after I found out what had happened, I snuck into the training building through the back. No one noticed me. None of the officers seemed concerned about that entrance, most likely because Diesel was there. But I've known that dog since he was seven weeks old, so he didn't make a sound when I approached. Once I had the box, I took it back up to the house and hid it. To keep up appearances, I came back to the club and demanded to be allowed inside."

I thought back to that day, and how it had been quite a long time before Clarice appeared at the barricades. I hadn't noticed her in the building, but I was distracted by the police and evidence technicians.

Clarice stared off into space, one hand still resting on Ra's head. "I needed to protect him," she said again, almost to herself.

"I know about the pregnancy," I said, figuring that was what Clarice was tiptoeing around.

Clarice raised her eyebrows slightly, and refocused on the key. A few seconds later, the box was open. It took all my self-control to keep from grabbing the thing and examining its contents for myself.

"It's been killing me, this past week, keeping this from Katherine," Clarice continued. "I know there are important documents in here, things that she'll need to settle the estate, plus a hefty amount of cash. I know Bryan always intended for her to have those things."

"You can still give it to her."

"It's just … this photo," Clarice said.

"Oh," I said. "I already found the ultrasound photo. It wasn't even in the box. It was stuck between —"

Before I could finish, Clarice reached into the box and pulled out a four by six Kodak color print of a smiling blond toddler holding a bouquet of daisies out to the person taking the photo.

I gasped, and all three of the salukis lifted their heads and stared at me.

"The ultrasound picture I found was dated just two weeks ago!"

"I don't know what you're talking about," Clarice said. "Bryan had an affair nearly twenty years ago, but he broke things off with the woman when she became pregnant. As far as I knew, they were never in contact afterward. But then I found this."

She passed the photo to me. I studied the child, for all the good it did. She looked like any generic little girl. She could have been Julianne nine years earlier. Or even me, for that matter, but that certainly would have required more than a nine-year time jump. Just how much more, I wasn't in the mood to contemplate. I flipped the photo over. Scrawled on the back were the words, *Baby A. She has your eyes.*

"'A?'" I asked, looking up. "Who's the mother?"

"I don't know," Clarice said. "She wasn't dog person. None of us here ever met her. And after the pregnancy, Bryan never mentioned her again. Not that he ever really talked about her before." She held out a hand for the photo, and I gave it back to her.

"I can see why you'd be concerned about showing this to Katherine," I said.

"I thought about removing the photo and giving her the rest, but that doesn't feel right either."

"I'd want to know, if it were me," I said.

Clarice stared at the photo for a few seconds before replacing it in the box. The salukis, sensing her distress, gathered around her on the floor, obviously trained to avoid the pristine white sofa. Clarice stroked them all, murmuring endearments. Their long tails waved gently back and forth. I thought I saw her swipe at her eyes a few times.

"Would you mind," she said, after a few moments, her voice slightly unsteady, "taking this to Katherine for me? I can get you the address."

"Me? Clarice, no. She thinks I murdered her husband!"

"She doesn't," Clarice assured me. "She's been in contact with the detectives and, according to her, while they haven't ruled you out completely, they've been focusing the investigation on other areas."

Well, that would have been nice to know. I had some choice words for Detective Rodriguez next time I saw him.

"What other areas?" I asked.

"I'm not sure," Clarice said, and pushed the box toward me. "Would you please?"

I hesitated.

"I don't know," I said, staring at the box. "It would still be awkward. Isn't there anyone else you could ask? Someone who has at least met Katherine before?"

"Please, Nell," Clarice said again. "I can't stand having this secret any longer. You're the only one who knows. I just ... I can't tell anyone else. Please."

I'd never seen Clarice, elegant, dignified Clarice, so close to losing control. My heart went out to her. After all, she was only trying to protect Katherine.

But still. Showing up on the doorstep of a woman I've never met, the widow of the man I'd been accused of killing, was a lot to ask.

Chapter 29

Pushover, I thought, as I left Clarice's house with the box tucked under one arm. I couldn't see a way that this would end well. I trudged back to my office.

"Just a second, guys," I said to Rush and Simon as they swarmed around me, excited to see me after my brief absence. I shoved the box deep inside my backpack. I didn't want to be seen carrying it around.

I'd just finished stowing the box and was finally greeting the dogs properly when Felicia poked her head in the room.

"Nell!" she exclaimed. "I'm so glad to see you!"

"Um," I said, pushing back my chair. "Glad to see you, too, Felicia."

"I have this humungous agility class due to start in a few minutes," Felicia said, without missing a beat as she ran a hand through her faux hawk. "Adrienne was going to help me out, but she wasn't feeling well today and went home. Are you free?"

"Sure," I said, standing. Anything to delay the trip to Katherine's. "Is Adrienne okay?"

Felicia waved a hand dismissively.

"It was some sort of stomach bug, she said. I'm sure she'll be fine. So, you'll help?"

"Of course," I said, but my mind was racing. Adrienne had mentioned feeling a little under the weather the previous weekend as well. Did that mean what I suspected it meant? I hurried to catch up to Felicia, who was already halfway across the yard to the Agility building.

"This is just a run-through class, for people who are already competing," Felicia said. "We're running Advanced and Masters level courses. I'll need your help with setting up and taking down, and general managing of everyone. We're doing Masters courses on the north end of the building, and Advanced on the south end. Do you have a preference?"

I shook my head.

"Okay. I'll take Masters, you take Advanced." Felicia did some tapping on her phone, and a second later I received text with the diagrams for a handful of courses.

"Just go from the top down," Felicia said. "Let everyone have two runs per course. The people in the class should be pretty familiar with the routine. Any questions or issues you don't want to deal with, just let me know."

"Gotcha," I said, as we entered the building.

We split up and started setting up our respective courses. Felicia, no surprise, was a genius course maker. Everything flowed well and made sense, but each course had its own particular set of challenges. I just placed my last jump when dog and handler teams started arriving.

"Advanced over there with Nell, Masters over here," Felicia directed people as soon as they'd stepped through the door.

"Nell!" exclaimed Jared as he and his aussie bounced our way. It was the dog he'd had with him at Deanna's class the day of the murder, a larger boned red merle male.

"Hey," I said. "Who's this handsome guy?"

Jared placed a hand over his heart and batted his eyelashes.

His shirt that day was full on tie dye. I felt like I was staring into a kaleidoscope.

"Why Nell, I'm flattered," he said.

"Not to damage your fragile little ego, but I was talking about your dog."

"Ouch." Jared mimed pulling a knife from his heart. "You do wound me, Nell."

"You'll survive, I'm sure," I said, kneeling to greet the red and white speckled dog as he approached.

"That's Gusto," Jared said. "He lives up to his name. He throws his whole heart and soul into anything I ask him to do. Conformation, obedience, agility, or sheepherding. He's got the versatility part of the standard nailed."

Gusto buried his face in the crook of my elbow, as though Jared's effusive praise was embarrassing him.

"Say," Jared said, suddenly, interrupting my cuddle session with his dog. "Is Stacey helping out today?"

I straightened, my hands falling to my sides. Gusto was too polite to continue to force the issue, but he did place himself in a beautiful free stack, as if to drive home exactly what I was missing by not fawning all over him. He and Jared seemed to have a lot in common.

"I don't think so," I said, mentally running through my day thus far. "I haven't seen her."

"I did, just now," Jared said. "And she and that fiancé of hers were having one humdinger of a shouting match."

The rest of the class had gathered by then. While I was curious to continue questioning Jared about Stacey and Jeff's argument, I focused on the clients who migrated over to the Advanced course. The class seemed pretty evenly divided between Felicia and me. Alexis and Taiko joined us, as well as three other teams that I didn't recognize. I had an interesting mix of breeds in my group, as opposed to the contingent of border collies gathered on the Masters course.

In addition to Gusto and Taiko there was a blue and tan pittie mix called Raina, a fuzzy, black and white Pomeranian named Nova, and, most surprisingly of all, a little Pug called Harley, who seemed to enjoy spending the majority of his time standing up on his rear legs, taking in the sights.

"He's so cute!" I said to his owner, a formidable looking middle-aged woman. Her blonde hair fell just below her shoulders and was streaked with gray, and the treat pouch belted around her waist was fashioned in the shape of a wide, smiling pug face. "Well done on getting him to this level. You don't see many pugs running Advanced."

"Maybe _you_ don't," she snapped. "But I've put titles on all of my pugs."

I stepped back for a moment, stunned at her vehemence. Pugs, in general, had been irresponsibly bred to the point of living their lives in varying amounts of discomfort and with limited function. It was rare to see one like Harley, who was fit and athletic. I didn't think my comment was out of line. I was complimenting her breeding program and training skill.

Jared and Gusto sidled up next to me.

"Don't mind Heather," he said, after she and Harley drifted away. "She's always so defensive about those dogs. And those titles she's talking about? CGC's, mostly. Harley's the only one who's ever gone beyond that."

"A Canine Good Citizen Certificate is nothing to sneeze at," I whispered back.

"No, but it's also not comparable to any other high-level performance or breed title. And it's not fair to play up what is essentially a certificate stating your dog has basic leash manners and pretending it's the equivalent of an OTCH or MACH," he said, referring, respectively, to the highest-level titles in both obedience and agility. "So don't worry. You didn't say anything wrong."

"What's going on over there?" called Heather. "Are we supposed to be walking this course or not?"

I snapped to attention.

"Yes, go ahead and walk it as many times as you need, and then we'll start run throughs in order of size. Anyone here jumping twenty-four inches?"

No one responded.

"Twenty?"

Jared, and Raina's owner, Holly, raised their hands.

"Okay," I said. "We'll start with a jump height of twenty inches and work our way down."

Jared told Holly she could go first, and she and Raina had a nice run, though Raina tended to knock bars when her excitement got the better of her.

"Excuse me," a voice said, just as Holly and Raina had started their second run. Jared and I both turned to see one of the border collie and human teams from Felicia's side of the room approaching.

"Hi, Dana," Jared said. "What're you doing over here slumming it with us Advanced runners?"

Dana barely spared him a glance.

"I was actually looking for you," she said to me. "You're Nell, right? Or is there someone else with purple, pink, orange, and yellow hair I should be looking for?"

"No, I'm pretty sure I'm the only one who fits that description," I said. "What can I do for you?"

"Well, I was just over at the other building, using the restroom. That girl who helps out with classes sometimes? What's her name, Tracey?"

"Stacey," I said.

"Right, that's it. I'm horrible with names. Anyway, she was in the stall next to me, and sounded very upset. She wouldn't respond when I asked her if she needed anything. When I got back here, one of the other people in class said that you know her?"

"She's assisted in my classes a few times," I said, "But we aren't exactly close."

"Well, someone should probably go find her," Dana said. "My turn is coming up soon but let me know if there's anything else I can do to help."

She crossed back over to the other side of the room. I chewed on my lower lip. Holly and Raina finished their second attempt at the course and waited patiently for my feedback.

"Whoo Hoo, girl! Welcome to the Clean Run club!" Jared called out, thankfully saving me from having to pull something out of thin air to say to her. "Not a single dropped bar!"

I checked the time. Still forty-five minutes left of class. I looked over at Felicia. She seemed to have her hands full on the Masters course as she tried to mediate a dispute over run order between two of the border collie handlers. Yuck. Competition classes were exciting, certainly, but I missed the simplicity of my puppy classes and pet manners classes. Much less drama between owners over there.

"Why don't you go ahead and see what's going on?" Jared said. "I don't mind doing my runs solo, and I'll cover for you until you get back."

"Thanks," I said. "I just want to make sure she's okay."

"Go on," Jared made a shooing motion.

I didn't need to hear him say it again and beat a hasty retreat. The main training building was dark and quiet.

"Hello?" I called. "Stacey?"

Silence. I checked the restrooms first, but there was no evidence that anyone had been in there. I pulled out my phone and tapped out a text. *Are you okay?* I figured simpler was better, and headed upstairs, taking them two at a time, to start a more thorough search of the building.

By the time I'd checked every office and the equipment storage room downstairs, Stacey still hadn't responded. I had to get back to class, but I didn't just want to leave if Stacey was in trouble. It was pretty clear that, whatever was going on, she was no longer in the building. I turned in a slow circle at the top of the landing. From that position I could see most of the training building, except for a few of the offices. I didn't see anything out of the ordinary until I'd nearly completed my circle.

Directly in front of me, on the closet door, was a reddish-brown smear.

"Shih tzus."

Things didn't get more ominous than that. I neglected to check inside the closet the first time around. It was just a tiny storage closet. I didn't think there'd be room inside for a fully grown person.

"Maybe it's nothing," I said aloud, trying to calm my racing heart as I reached for the knob. "It could be paint. Or maybe someone's dog had an upset stomach and they missed a spot cleaning."

I turned the knob, half-hoping it would be locked. No such luck. The knob turned easily. I took a deep breath and yanked the door open. Stacey's fiancé, Jeff, tumbled out of the small space, landing at my feet. The hair on one side of his head was matted, wet, and stained the same reddish brown that was on the wall. His eyes were empty, wide-open, and staring.

He was dead.

Chapter 30

"All right, Ms. McLinton," Detective Rodriguez said, pen poised above his notebook. "From the top."

I'd already gone over this with him, and with the officer who first arrived on scene. And with the 911 dispatcher as well.

I didn't want to make light of Jeff's death, but it was getting late. The dogs were still locked in my office. I could hear Simon whining faintly even from where I'd been parked, in a metal folding chair at the foot of the stairs. And I still had to go to Katherine's to drop off that confounded box.

"I told you," I said. "I came here looking for his girlfriend. Someone from the class I was teaching said Stacey and her fiancé were arguing and that she was upset. I wanted to make sure she way okay."

I glanced over to where Stacey sat in a metal folding chair, far enough away from me that we couldn't do any conspiring. She'd been devastated when she'd first joined the crowd gathering outside the building. Tears streamed down her face as she pleaded to be allowed to go to be with Jeff. When the police were occupied elsewhere, she even tried to scale the barricades. Kyle managed to grab her at the last second.

The police eventually allowed her to come inside after the coroner had removed Jeff's body. Stacey sat silently, shoulders hunched, wrapped in a gray blanket. She stared at the floor, giving only single word, monotone responses when asked a question. She seemed to be in shock.

"Ms. McLinton."

I shifted my gaze from Stacey.

"Sorry, Detective," I said. "Um … by the time I got over here, the building seemed empty. I checked everywhere just in case. That's when I found Jeff." I took a deep breath. "It looked like he was hit over the head. Just like Bryan, right?"

"You know I can't answer that. Now, do you commonly check cramped and tiny storage closets when you're looking for someone?"

"Only when there's blood smeared on the door," I snapped, heartily sick of being accused of something I had nothing to do with.

———

By the time the police told me I could go, it was quite late. Relieved that I wasn't dragged down to the station this time, I hurried upstairs to collect my bag and the dogs.

Once outside, I hesitated. Maeve's car wasn't exactly set up for dogs to spend extended amounts of time. Since it was getting to be later in the day, I didn't think I'd have time to drive to Tumalo and back to drop them off, and still make it to Katherine's place at a reasonable hour. I definitely did not want that box in my possession overnight.

There was still a huge crowd gathered at the barricades, even though there really wasn't anything to see.

"They cut you loose, I see!" Jared said, as he and Gusto trotted in my direction.

Did the man ever walk? He seemed to be capable only of

running, jumping, or bouncing. Much like his chosen breed, come to think of it. Aussies are always on the lookout for ways to jazz things up, even something as simple as walking across a parking lot.

Sure enough, Gusto pranced alongside Jared on his tippy toes, and sat down when Jared halted in front of me. Gusto threw his head back, as though demanding the world notice how beautiful he was.

"Once word got out that Jeff was found dead," Jared said, "I and a few of the others from class told every cop we saw that you were only gone for a few minutes. Clearly, not enough time to pull something like that off."

"Thanks," I said.

Rush whimpered softly, wanting very much to go over and say hello to either Gusto or Jared. I wasn't sure which. Who was I kidding? He likely wanted to greet them both simultaneously. Simon remained quietly at my side, throwing out disdainful looks at the aussies' antics.

The crowd fell silent as Detective Rodriguez led Stacey from the building and over to his vehicle. She wasn't in handcuffs, and he allowed her to ride next to him in the front seat.

"Do you think she did it?" Felicia asked as she and Holly veered off one of the paths to come stand with us.

"She's always been so nice to me," Holly said.

Raina sat calmly at her side, surveying the scene with a somewhat grumpy countenance. Holly warned me at the beginning of class that Raina's default expression was a classic RBF; she wasn't wrong.

"She's always had good things to say about Raina," Holly continued.

"Loving dogs doesn't automatically exclude someone from being a murderer," Felicia said.

Holly shrugged.

"Just an observation," she said. "I've always had good inter-actions with her."

"Far be it from me to speak ill of the dead," Jared said, "but that Jeff was trouble with a capital 'T'. Everyone has a breaking point. Maybe she hit hers."

I'd witnessed some heated interactions between them, for sure. But Stacey always seemed to be the one who wanted to avoid conflict. Try as I might, I couldn't imagine her taking the heavy, steel bolt cutter found in the closet with Jeff, to his skull.

"I suppose, we'll be hearing from the police soon enough," Felicia said, clearly done with the topic. "Nell, if I could have a quick word?"

"Sure," I said, following her a short distance from the others. "I actually wanted to speak to you too. Would it be okay if I leave the dogs in the agility building while I run a quick errand? In one of the spare ex-pens, maybe?"

"That's fine," Felicia said. "Classes have obviously been canceled for the rest of the day. It's getting to be our standard murder protocol."

The corners of my lips twitched, though it wasn't really a laughing matter.

"I wanted to talk to you about class today," Felicia contin-ued. "I heard that you left in the middle of the session. Now, I assume that you didn't set out to discover a dead body and intended to be back in just a few minutes. But I just wanted to let you know that's not something I condone. Classes are usually only forty-five minutes to an hour. There's really no reason to leave in the middle. I've received complaints."

"Complaints?" I repeated, shocked. "From whom?"

"I'm not going to name names," Felicia said, but I noticed her gaze drifting over my left shoulder. On the pretense of adjusting Rush's collar, I turned in that direction. Heather stood just a few feet away, seeming very interested in our conversation, her lips twisted in a triumphant sneer. The woman took an instant dislike to me. Was it really all because of the single comment I made at the beginning of class?

I considered arguing my case but decided it was more trouble than it was worth.

"Of course," I said. "It won't happen again."

Chapter 31

It was very nearly sunset when I reached Katherine's house. I broke several traffic laws on my way over; I was nervous enough about dropping in on her like this without the added worry of doing it after dark. She and Bryan had lived in a cozy little house in a quiet neighborhood near Pilot Butte. It was right around the corner from where Maeve and Frank lived when they first moved to Bend.

I parked in front of the well-maintained home. The Rottweilers painted on the planter out front confirmed I was at the right place.

I pulled the box from my bag, took a deep breath, and rang the doorbell. The volume of the Diesel's deep barks increased as he rushed to the door. The frame shuddered with the impact. I took a step back.

Katherine opened the door, flushed and flustered, struggling to keep hold of the collar of a dog who outweighed her.

"Sorry!" she called, raising her voice to be heard over the barking.

I had no desire to stand on the porch shouting at her, so I mimed putting Diesel in another room and closing the door.

She disappeared from view for a few moments, and then the barking became, blessedly, muffled.

"Please, come in," she said, as she came back into view, patting her hair into place. "Nell McLinton, right? Clarice called to say you'd be stopping by."

Well, that was something.

"Did she say why I was coming?"

Katherine led me to a living room furnished with comfortable, yet attractive couches and chairs. Unlike Clarice's lavish decorating style, each piece looked to have been chosen with care and acquired over time.

"She said Bryan's box was found, and you were going to drop it off as a favor," Katherine said, directing me to one end of the couch. "But that was all Clarice said in her message. She didn't answer when I called her back."

It seemed she was about to say more, when she was interrupted by Diesel throwing himself against whatever door was separating us.

"Sorry about that. I can't seem to find the remote to his collar. Bryan usually took care of these things."

I cringed at the memory of the remote in pieces on the floor of the training arena, and very nearly blurted out exactly what happened. I stopped myself just in time, reasoning that it made sense to get through this particular issue first. I'd find some way to made amends afterward. Either to replace the collar and remote, or offer some private training sessions as an alternative.

Katherine sat down beside me.

"Diesel is just beside himself. He's lost without Bryan. So am I, to be honest. We've been married for nearly forty years. Most of my life."

"I'm so sorry," I said, trying to imagine having a partner for that amount of time and then suddenly losing them.

"Thank you," Katherine said. "I'm beginning to get over

the shock of it, at least. Now, I'm focusing on finding out who did this and making sure they answer for their actions."

Awkward. I shifted uneasily on the couch. Perhaps that was my cue to shove the box at her and make a hasty departure.

"Oh, no, my dear! I wasn't talking about you!" Katherine said, noticing my discomfort.

Katherine glanced down the hall, at the closed door Diesel was presumably behind.

"He's quiet, now," she said. "Do you think I should let him out?"

I couldn't think of anything I wanted less than to throw a nervous, insecure dog into the mix. I was having a hard enough time trying to process the idea that I might not be the sole official suspect in Bryan's murder. And then there was the matter of the photo tucked away in the box.

"Maybe it's best just to leave him for now," I said. "From what I've seen of Diesel, he seems to be a little anxious around new people. He could probably do without the pressure of that kind of interaction, considering everything else that's going on."

Thankfully, Katherine nodded in agreement.

"You're right, I'm sure. I keep forgetting how hard this must be for him. He and Bryan were never apart. Sometimes it seems like he's searching the house for him. He's been waking up in the middle of the night and whining until I walk him around the house and show him Bryan's not here. A few nights ago, he was completely beside himself, barking and howling."

"Maybe he needed to go out?"

"No. He's always been impeccably housebroken and never asks to go out at night. Once we got down the stairs, he didn't run to the back door like he normally does when he needs to get outside. He went to the front door and was just hurling himself at it. He did that for nearly ten minutes. I thought he was going to break the door down. I was afraid the neighbors were going to call the police."

"But he eventually settled down?"

"Well, he stopped trying to get through the door. But the rest of the night he was on edge. He couldn't settle. He just paced the room, growling at every little noise. And then, the next morning, I went out to get the paper, and found this."

She pulled her cell phone out of her pocket, tapped the screen a few times, and then turned it to face me. I raised my eyebrows. The photo showed a clump of yellow daffodils on the porch, next to a white envelope. Katherine motioned for me to swipe to the next photo.

The next picture was of a plain white card, with the words *I'M SORRY* printed in block letters. I gasped and dropped the phone.

"The police are testing it for DNA," Katherine said, retrieving her phone. "They didn't find any fingerprints, but analyzed the writing. I think that's when they started moving away from you as a suspect. I honestly never thought they were on the right track about you to begin with."

"You ... you didn't?"

"I know Bryan wasn't popular with this current team of trainers. You aren't the only person he's had conflicts with. Bryan could be ... set in his ways."

Understatement.

"If they were only basing their suspicions on you because the two of you didn't get along, they'd have to place the entire training staff on the suspect list, wouldn't they?"

She wasn't wrong.

"I don't mean to seem as though I'm speaking badly of him," Katherine continued. "He was a wonderful husband. Always so generous and attentive."

I was in the process of handing her the box, but her words caused me to reflexively hold it tighter. I couldn't get the image of that beaming toddler and her flowers out of my mind. Maybe Clarice was right. Maybe it was better if Katherine didn't know.

"Nell?" Katherine asked, one hand still outstretched for the box.

I sighed. Probably no way to avoid it at this point.

"The box wasn't missing," I said.

"I'm sorry?"

Shih tzus. How did I let Clarice convince me to do this?

"Clarice had it this whole time. She wasn't trying to steal it or keep if from you. She was trying to protect you."

I expected Katherine to ask why she needed to be protected, but instead she became very still; her hands fell to her lap.

"I see," she said, quietly. "Was she ... did she and Bryan —"

"No," I interrupted. "No, she would never have done anything like that to you. But there were others."

Katherine nodded, lifting her gaze to the framed portrait above the mantle. She and Bryan on their wedding day. A lifetime ago. He'd been attractive back then, in his Marine Corps uniform with his hair buzzed short. The camera caught them mid-laugh, and they seemed blissfully happy together. I realized I'd never before seen warmth in Bryan's ice blue eyes.

"Bryan wasn't perfect," she said, after a few moments. She looked away from the portrait. "But I knew he'd never leave me. He was never serious about any of them."

"You ... You knew about the pregnancies?"

Katherine paled, and I worried she might faint. I hastily set the box on the end table nearest to me and scooted closer to her, hands outstretched to steady her if required.

"No," she said, dropping her gaze to her clenched hands. "No, I didn't know about ..." She trailed off, still looking down at her hands. She seemed a little stronger, so I moved back to my original spot on the couch and retrieved the box.

"Are there children?"

Katherine asked the question so softly I nearly missed it. I offered her the box once more. She slowly opened the lid and began silently sifting through the contents. When she found the photo of the little girl, she went completely still, her eyes full of longing.

"Do you know who she is?" Katherine asked.

I shook my head.

"No," I said. "Clarice doesn't either."

"You said pregnancies. As in, plural?"

"There was an ultrasound photo in Bryan's desk," I said. "It was dated only a week before the murder. I thought it might be yours."

I felt my face flush as I said the words. Clearly Katherine knew nothing about the photo. She closed the box and set it aside but kept the photo of the toddler in her hand.

"It's not mine. I was never able to ..." she trailed off, brushing a tear from her cheek. "No matter how I wished otherwise."

"I'm so sorry," I said. "I had no idea."

Katherine sniffed and swiped at another tear. Catching sight of a box of tissues on one of the lower bookshelves, I got up and brought it to her.

"Thank you," she said, accepting a tissue and dabbing at her eyes with it. "I thought I long since made my peace with never being able to have children. But this little girl ... I can see Bryan in her every feature. Her smile, her dimples. And the eyes. Especially the eyes."

Chapter 32

Back at the Club, I parked Maeve's car directly beneath the streetlight closest to the Agility building. I hated coming here at night, especially after running into Clarice in the dark the night after Bryan's death. I shivered at the memory, recalling Clarice's words from earlier in the day. *I would've done almost anything to protect him and his reputation. Even now.* Nope. Definitely didn't want to be alone out here any longer than necessary.

I realized I needed to get my laptop from the main building so that I could work on some informational handouts for my next class. Grumbling under my breath, I turned and jogged toward the training building.

The police tape was taken down, and there weren't any signs warning people not to enter. I pulled out my keys and let myself in, flicking on the lights before even stepping one foot inside. The pristine arena looked just as it always did. The equipment was stacked neatly against the walls. The familiar smell of the rubber floor mats was comforting.

Still, two people lost their lives in this very building in as many weeks, and I didn't dawdle. I took the stairs two at a time, flipping light switches as they came, bathing the entire building in a florescent glow.

As I approached my office, the door opened. I froze. Adrienne emerged, pulling the door closed and fitting her key into the lock. She jumped a little when she saw me.

"Nell!" she gasped, placing a hand over her heart theatrically. "You scared me!"

I licked my dry lips, struggling to regain my powers of speech.

"I scared *you*? You're the one creeping around in the dark!" It came out a little more accusingly than intended, but jumping Jack Russells. My heart was racing. What was she doing in the office Deanna, Felicia, and I shared? She had her own office.

"I was looking to see if Felicia had a master list of all of her classes and attendees," Adrienne said, answering my unspoken question. "We're going to be suspending classes for a while until things calm down."

"Probably for the best," I acknowledged. "Did you get everything you needed?"

"Mostly."

Adrienne's keys clanked against each other as she wiggled the one in the lock free. I noticed that her Dog Club keychain was missing. Goosebumps erupted over my forearms. I rubbed both arms vigorously through my sweatshirt sleeves.

"What happened to your keychain?" I asked, trying to sound nonchalant.

Adrienne looked down at the keys in her hand.

"I don't know," she said with a shrug. "I must have lost it somewhere."

The dusty parking lot of a canyon trailhead, perhaps?

"Seems like the thing was always giving you trouble," I said. "Funny you didn't even notice it was gone."

Adrienne slipped the keys into her pocket.

"I guess I've had a lot on my mind recently," she said, and

inclined her head toward my office door. "Was there something you needed, Nell?"

"My laptop."

"You should grab it, then. It's getting late."

———

Holy shih tzus. I clutched my laptop to my chest, trying not to be too obvious about checking to see if anyone (okay, Adrienne) was following me as I hightailed it out of the main training building. That was nerve-wracking.

I let myself into the Agility building. I could hear Rush whining, and I hurriedly turned the lights on. He and Simon were still exactly where I'd placed them, in an ex-pen set up in an out of the way corner. I set my laptop down on the blue painted pause table.

"Hey guys," I greeted, letting them out to run around the building while I folded up the ex-pen and emptied their water bowl. I was just starting to relax slightly when Simon suddenly let out a warning bark. Rush squealed with joy. I whirled around, the metal bowl falling to the turf-covered floor with a hollow sounding thud.

"Sorry," Stacey said. "I didn't mean to scare you. I didn't think anyone else was here, and then the lights came on."

"You were just ... hanging out here in the dark?" I asked, retrieving the bowl.

Rush wiggled his way up to Stacey. His back was toward me, so I couldn't see exactly what he was doing. I surmised that he must have greeted Stacey with a pretty phenomenal grin, because she took a step back, turning slightly away and curving her body awkwardly.

"He's just smiling," I assured her, crossing the room.

Sure enough, Rush's lips were peeled so far back from his teeth that he looked like a canine version of a Jack-O'-Lantern.

"He looks kind of scary when he does that," Stacey said, hesitantly reaching out a hand. Rush leaned into the caress.

"It can be a little disconcerting if you're not used to it. But he only does it when he's happy and wants to interact."

Stacey knelt next to Rush and ruffled her hands through the impressive mane of hair on his chest. Rush leaned his whole body against her, slowly pushing her back until she was sitting on the turf, and he was sprawled across her lap. She gave a soft laugh that ended in a sob and buried her face in his white ruff.

I sat down next to her. Simon curled up beside me and rested his head in my lap.

"I'm so sorry about Jeff," I said.

It was a few moments before Stacey was able to respond. She slowly raised her head, sniffling. Rush licked the tears from her cheeks.

"Thank you," she said.

"Have you been sitting here in the dark this whole time?" I asked

She shook her head.

"No, I just got back from the police department maybe forty-five minutes ago. They called me a cab. That was nice of them, especially after they accused me of murdering my fiancé."

It was more than they did for me, that's for sure.

"I think it's just some sort of protocol they have to follow," I told her. "Rule out the people closest to the victim first. Like family and close friends."

"I guess," Stacey said, and heaved a long, shuddering sigh. "It was horrible, though."

"I understand."

Stacey looked up, as if seeing me for the first time.

"Yeah," she said. "I suppose you would."

Rush rolled over onto his back, white paws playfully slapping at Stacey's hands. She leaned forward and hugged him, something most dogs tend not to appreciate. Rush was willing to put up with all kinds of human shenanigans for attention, and sure enough, he pressed himself even closer to Stacey, snuffling the blond curl that drifted over his nose.

"My car wouldn't start," Stacey said, her voice slightly muffled by Rush's fur. "And, of course, by the time I came to terms with that, the cab left. I have a friend coming to pick me up, and I'm going to stay with her tonight. I thought I'd wait here. I kept the lights off because I was afraid Clarice might come down to investigate. I wouldn't want to meet her here alone at night."

"Why would you worry about Clarice?" I asked, even though I had the same worry earlier. I wanted Stacey's perspective.

Stacey gave a helpless shrug.

"I know it seems crazy," she said. "But I feel like Clarice is following me sometimes. She always seems to turn up wherever I am. And she never liked Jeff. I could tell."

Well, not liking Jeff certainly wasn't unique to Clarice. But following Stacey around did seem strange. I was about to ask her to tell me more when Stacey wriggled herself out from under Rush. She started to stand up. The color drained from her face, and she put a hand to her forehead, quickly sitting back down.

"Are you okay?" I asked.

"I'm fine," Stacey said. "It'll pass. It always does."

"Try to put your head between your knees," I advised. "And take some deep breaths."

"I'm fine, really," Stacey insisted. "Mints help sometimes. They should be in my purse."

I looked around the arena, and spotted Stacey's purse draped over the puppy A-frame. I grabbed it and attempted to hand it to her.

"Would you mind?" she asked, weakly, not looking up.

I unzipped it and rummaged around inside. In my haste, I dislodged her pocketbook, which fell to the green turf at my feet. My hand closed around the tin of mints just then, and I popped it open and held it out to her.

"Thanks," she said gratefully, taking two.

I slipped the tin back into her purse and bent to retrieve the pocketbook. It opened when it hit the floor. Stacey's driver's license faced up, with her smiling photo next to her name. Anastasia Marie Callahan.

"Hey," Stacey said, already sounding a little more with it. "What're you doing with that?"

"Sorry, it fell," I said, my eyes meeting hers.

Anastasia. And those eyes. A light, icy blue. Just like …

"Baby 'A'?" I gasped. She was the right age.

"Huh?" Stacey said.

I shoved the pocketbook back into Stacey's purse and dug out my phone, pulling up the picture of the smiling toddler.

"Is this you?" I asked.

"Where did you get that? That's private!"

"Was Bryan your father?"

Stacey rose to her feet, wobbling slightly. She slapped my hand away when I reached out to help.

"That's none of your business!"

"I'm sorry," I said. "I was just —"

Stacey snatched her purse and stormed out of the building.

I stood in the empty arena; stunned. Rush and Simon crowded around me, gazing up in confusion. I stared down at the photo on my phone. It was obviously Stacey. Once I made the connection I couldn't unsee it.

I wondered if I should go after her. She was upset, had nearly passed out, and just ran into a dark and empty parking lot.

I just reached the exit when I heard a car door slam and

the roar of an engine. By the time the dogs and I made it outside, the parking lot was empty. The only indication someone else had been there was a cloud of dust.

The drive back to Maeve's seemed to take forever as my mind worked overtime trying to make sense of everything. Stacey was Bryan's daughter? Could that be true? If it was, it meant two people close to Stacey died in quick succession.

I parked in Maeve's garage, trying to decide whether to call Dan. I absently gathered my laptop, purse, and leashes from the passenger seat. I brushed aside some of my other gear and discovered one of Maeve's books, laying facedown. Had she left it there as a joke?

Smiling, I picked it up and turned it over to see which book it was. I gave a small cry and dropped the book into the footwell. The cover was shredded, the binding frayed, and a bunch of pages were ripped out or crumpled. Only a small portion of Maeve's signature remained on the title page. Printed in block letters, just like the card on Katherine's porch, was a single word. **STOP**.

Chapter 33

Detective Rodriguez turned the mutilated book over in his gloved hands, examining it from every angle. He stood in the entryway, just outside of Maeve's kitchen. Maeve and I were finishing preparations for a salad bar we hoped would be something fun for the kids' dinner.

"This was just lying on the front seat of the vehicle?" Detective Rodriguez asked. He lightly ran a finger over the printed block letters next to what remained of Maeve's signature. Simon and Rush watched him attentively from their down-stays on Gentle Ben's bed.

I nodded, keeping an eye on the chicken and couscous I had on the stove as I crumbled several strips of turkey bacon.

"And you only just noticed it now?"

"There was a lot of stuff on that seat," I said, trying not to sound defensive. Maeve's car isn't set up for hauling around dogs and equipment, and you people still have my van. So yeah. There was a bunch of gear on top of the book. I didn't notice it until I got here and started taking things out of the car."

Maeve looked up from where she sat at the kitchen table,

chopping a colorful variety of bell peppers. Gentle Ben, ever eager to be of assistance, was instantly at her side.

"Why does it matter how long it took her to find it?" Maeve asked. "Shouldn't figuring out who put it there take priority?" The question, far from accusing, was delivered in Maeve's typical calm, quiet tone with just the merest hint of reproach.

Detective Rodriguez looked up from placing the battered remnant of the book into an evidence baggie, the nuance clearly not lost on him. He studied Maeve as though really seeing her for the first time, though he'd been introduced upon his arrival. Maeve tended to have the effect.

She seemed just tiny and blond at first glance. But the longer you looked at her, the more you started to see the natural highlights in her hair that were more prominent when she'd been out in the sun, the hint of rosiness to her cheeks that wasn't a result of any make-up, and the way her hazel eyes seemed to lighten or darken according to her mood.

"I'm just trying to figure out when the book may have been placed in the car," he said, returning his attention to the evidence bag. "It's important to establish an accurate timeline."

"I see," Maeve said. "Because it kind of sounded like you were trying to find a way to turn this into Nell's fault, somehow."

"I was out and about all day," I said, steering the conversation back on course. "It could have happened any time. The car was empty when I loaded up in the morning."

"And it wasn't locked?"

"The lock is broken," I said.

"It was supposed to be fixed today, but since Nell's van is out of commission … you know, since the last time someone tried to kill her … I had to cancel." Maeve sounded a little less composed. A bell pepper chunk went flying off the cutting board. Rush and Simon both aborted moves forward before remembering that they'd been asked to stay. They each got a morsel of bacon crumble for their trouble. Gentle Ben lapped up the bell pepper chunk from the floor.

"The investigation into whomever broke into Nell's vehicle is definitely a high priority," Detective Rodriguez assured her.

I could tell Maeve wasn't convinced. Neither was I. Maybe a little information sharing would help move things along.

"Today at the club, I noticed Adrienne Santi was missing her keychain," I said, gathering supplies and ingredients for mixing a few different salad dressings. "I know for a fact she had it the day before my van was broken into."

Detective Rodriguez produced his notebook and pen. After confirming the correct spelling of Adrienne's name, he asked, "Is she a trainer at the Club?"

"No," I said. "The vice-president. She has huskies."

Detective Rodriguez's pen stopped moving.

"Huskies," he repeated. "Okay."

Oh, right. Non-dog people tend to consider those types of details irrelevant. They weren't, though. You could tell a lot about a person by their dogs.

"Adrienne and Bryan didn't get along," I added hastily. "And she's been acting strange ever since his death."

I decided not to mention the connotation between her name and the fragment of a name on the ultrasound photo. The man likely wouldn't have earned the title of Detective if he hadn't been able to put two and two together.

"I also couldn't help but notice the similarity between the printing of the word 'stop' on Maeve's book and the 'I'm sorry' on the card Katherine Reed found at her house," I continued. "Don't you think?"

"How —"

"It's a free country," I said. "No law against me having a conversation with Katherine, is there?"

"Of course not," Detective Rodriguez said. "I just wouldn't have expected the two of you to be in contact."

I sampled a bit of the raspberry vinaigrette I was concocting and added a little more salt.

"Katherine is very focused on bringing her husband's killer to justice," I told him, setting the raspberry vinaigrette aside and gathering ingredients for Greek yogurt ranch. "She's not wasting her time and effort on people who should be ruled out."

He didn't take the bait. Not that I expected him to. Still, it would have been nice to hear that maybe I didn't have to be so worried about suddenly being bundled into the back of a police cruiser and thrown in prison.

"Analyzing writing styles isn't typically something that can be done at a glance," Detective Rodriguez said instead. "We'll have to see what the experts have to say."

Of course that would be his response. Okay. I decided to take one more try at this information sharing thing.

"And, of course, you know that Bryan has a child."

Detective Rodriguez blinked.

"Are you referring to the photo you turned in?"

"No, I mean an actual flesh and blood, grown adult daughter. The result of an affair he had twenty years ago."

"Do you know the name of this woman?"

"The mother? No. No one seems to. But the daughter's name is Stacey Callahan."

Detective Rodriguez scribbled in his notebook.

"You've been busy," he commented.

"Somebody ought to be," Maeve grumbled, slicing off the top of her last pepper a little too forcefully. The green stem flew through the air and landed a few feet away on the floor. Gentle Ben leapt toward it.

"Leave it," Maeve said, in a completely neutral, almost sing song tone. Ben halted in mid-leap, dropping to a sit and keeping an eye on the stem until I was able to dispose of it.

Maeve looked as though she were about to say more about

what she thought of Detective Rodriguez's investigative technique, but was interrupted by a clattering of footsteps on the stairs.

"Mom, did you know that camels can actually close their nostrils during a sandstorm?" Julianne's voice floated from the living room. "Just close 'em right up to keep out the sand. I thought it sounded like something from one of your books, but it's true!"

Julianne stopped short when she entered the kitchen and saw Detective Rodriguez, tripping over her own feet. At the last second, I grabbed her arm and hauled her upright.

"They also have two sets of eyelashes," Detective Rodriguez said with a small smile.

Julianne flushed bright red and looked at the floor.

"I didn't realize anyone else was here," she muttered.

"Detective Rodriguez, this is Julianne. Julianne, Detective Rodriguez," I said. "He's just collecting some information for his investigation. If you're done with your homework, you can help me finish up the salad bar."

"Salads!" Liam zoomed into the room at top speed. The kid had a sixth sense when it came to food. And such obvious glee over a salad? More power to him. I was wishing for a cheeseburger.

Simon sat up as Liam sped past, excited by the movement. I reminded him to lie down. He did so with a sigh, casting a longing look in Liam's direction. Liam skidded to a halt in front of Detective Rodriguez.

"Liam, this is Detective Rodriguez," Maeve said, rising from her chair to carry the bowl of peppers to the counter. I offered to help, but she shook her head. Maeve crossed the kitchen steadily and at a good speed without the aid of either her cane or Gentle Ben. She deposited the bowl next to the other vegetables and toppings I'd arranged.

"Detective Rodriguez!" Liam exclaimed, seemingly over-joyed at his presence. "Where's your uniform?"

"You're looking at it," Detective Rodriguez said.

"It's just a suit."

"And a tie," Maeve said, coming to stand behind Liam and placing her hands on his shoulders.

"Well, the department won't let us have pink hair like yours," Detective Rodriguez said. His tone softened, and his smile widened. He seemed to have a genuine fondness for kids. "It would make it too easy for the criminals to spot us."

"Do you have a badge? And a gun?"

Detective Rodriguez reached into the pocket of his suit jacket and handed his badge to Liam.

"Cool!" Liam said, running his fingers over the brass badge in its leather holder and examining the accompanying ID card.

"Fer-Fer-n-," Liam attempted to read the name.

"Fernando," Detective Rodriguez said.

"Fernando Rodriguez," Liam repeated slowly, imitating Detective Rodriguez's accent, even expertly rolling his r's.

"Hey, that's not bad!" Detective Rodriguez sounded impressed.

"But you can call him Detective," Maeve said, and then prompted, "Because ..."

"Because it's respectful," Liam said, handing Detective Rodriguez back his badge.

"That's right," Maeve said, flashing Detective Rodriguez a smile over Liam's head. Liam peered at Detective Rodriguez's suit jacket.

"Where's your gun? Can I hold that next?"

"Liam!" Maeve admonished, giving his shoulders a shake.

A knock sounded at the door. Gentle Ben, the only dog not holding a stay, raced to the door on his own, making his low roo-ing sound to announce the guest. I followed him, peering through the peephole. We weren't expecting anyone else.

Dan Friedman stood on the porch. I opened door.

"What are you doing here?"

"Hey, Nell," Dan responded. "Nice to see you, too."

He peered around me into the entryway and waved.

"Hi, Detective. And Nell's family. Hello."

Detective Rodriguez's expression instantly changed from amused to guarded. Liam, thankfully, seemed to forget about the gun.

"Dan, the newspaper man?" he asked, shrugging out from Maeve's grip and skipping into the hallway.

"My reputation precedes me, I see," Dan said, shaking Liam's hand. "Is that good or bad?"

"Guess," I said.

Chapter 34

Detective Rodriguez left soon after Dan arrived, probably in an attempt to avoid appearing in whatever story Dan happened to be working on. I couldn't fault him for that. I hoped to send Dan on his way as well. But Liam was in fine form and invited Dan to partake in the salad bar. Dan either ignored or didn't notice my attempts to signal to him to decline. I was betting on the former.

"Thanks, I haven't eaten yet," he said. "Is there a bathroom where I can," he made an injecting motion with three fingers, "shoot up?"

Maeve's eyebrows shot up to her hairline.

"He's diabetic," I broke in, glaring at Dan. "He just needs to check his blood sugar and take his insulin."

"There's sugar in your blood?" Liam asked, wide-eyed.

"There's sugar in everyone's blood," I said.

"I just have to be more careful of how much there is in mine," Dan explained.

"How do you check it?" Liam asked.

Dan demonstrated the use of his glucometer. Liam was suitably impressed. Even Julianne came over to watch, though she feigned indifference.

———

"So, someone just straight-up shredded one of Maeve's books?" Dan asked after returning from the bathroom. He zipped the insulated bag containing his insulin supplies into a compartment of his messenger bag, then drizzled some of the ranch dressing onto his salad. "And put it in your car? As like, a warning?"

I nodded, having just taken a bite of my salad.

"Creepy," Dan said, eyeing the rest of the toppings to see if there was anything he missed. "That's like, Hannibal Lector creepy." He added a few croutons to his bowl. "Do you still hear the lambs, Clarice?" he said, referencing the movie.

"Your Hopkins needs work," I said.

Dan rolled his eyes and sat down in the extra chair I dug out of the garage.

"Everyone's a critic," he said. "I'll have you know I did two summers of drama camp in high school." Rush, who'd been lying on the right side of my chair, padded over to settle himself next to Dan. Traitor.

"Who's Clarice?" Liam asked, popping a cherry tomato into his mouth.

"A character from a book," I told him.

"One of Mom's books?"

"Thomas Harris," Julianne said. "They're too scary for you to read."

Maeve raised her eyebrows.

"And for you," she said to Julianne.

Julianne was suddenly very interested in cutting the pieces of chicken on her salad into perfectly sized cubes.

"I think I read my first Dean Koontz at twelve," Dan offered.

"Right," I said. "And look how you turned out."

"Oh, and speaking of childhood deviancy," Dan said, wiping his hands on his napkin and then retrieving his phone from his pocket. "Listen to all the dirt I uncovered on some of your fellow club members. Dog people, man. They're crazy."

I side-eyed him.

"Present company excepted, of course," he amended.

"Don't be too sure about that," Maeve interjected.

"Hey!" I cried. "Whose side are you on?"

Julianne and Liam dissolved into giggles. Gentle Ben added a low, throaty roo as though he were laughing, too. Simon laid his head in my lap.

"At least someone here is in my corner," I said, running a hand over Simon's smooth, soft fur. His tail whipped back and forth as he snuggled in closer.

"Do you want to hear or not?" Dan asked.

"Spill," I said.

"Okay," Dan said. "So, your club president? Clarice? Not to be confused with the *Silence of the Lambs* character."

"It was a good book, though," Julianne said.

"I know it's a good book," Maeve said. "But you're twelve."

"So you'd rather I read *Twilight?*"

"No!" Maeve sounded equally horrified at that prospect.

"At least she's reading," I said. Maeve shot me a glare that made my blood run cold.

"Maeve. When I was twelve you and Frank were helping me smuggle in the *Fear Street* books to hide under the floorboard in my closet. Remember that?"

"That was different," Maeve said.

"How?"

"I wasn't your mother. That's how."

"Oh man," Dan broke in. "R. L. Stein. Loved me some *Goosebumps.*"

"See?" I said. "It's normal. And I'd wager *Silence of the*

Lambs is probably a little more intellectually stimulating than *Who Killed the Homecoming Queen.*"

"Let's finish this discussion another time," Maeve said, which I knew meant we were wearing her down. "Dan, please continue with what you were saying about Clarice Abernathy."

"Right," Dan said. "Apparently she was married before she moved to Central Oregon. Marriage didn't last, split seemed fairly amicable, yada yada."

"So far sounds pretty boring," I said.

"Until her husband decided to remarry. Or, more accurately, until her husband and the new wife decided to separate."

"Okay," I said, motioning for him to go on.

"It was a one-sided split this time. New Wife left for greener pastures. Evidently, Clarice was feeling a little indignant on the husband's behalf. New Wife suddenly found herself the subject of a tax audit, with complaints made to her boss about the way she conducted herself at work. Plus, a virulent rumor that she was infected with and going around spreading an STD."

"Wow," I said, spearing a leaf of kale with my fork, "Remind me never to get on Clarice's bad side."

"Unfortunately for Clarice, New Wife happened to work at a law firm, and her boss went after Clarice. Defamation, harassment, the whole nine. She moved out here to Bend to get a new start."

Rush shifted position and lay his chin on Dan's foot. Dan froze, his fork midway to his mouth.

"What's he doing?"

"Resting," I said. "Does it bother you?"

"No. But what does it mean?"

"Your shoe is comfortable."

"But he's not, like, trying to tell me something? That he's the boss of me?"

"Because his head is on your shoe?"

Julianne started to giggle.

"Hey, I've been reading up on some of this dog behavior stuff. Sometimes the most seemingly innocuous things —"

I stared at the ceiling for a moment, summoning patience. I could only imagine what nonsense he was reading.

"Rush isn't trying to take over the world one shoe at a time," I assured him. "Now, who's next on your list?"

Dan examined his phone.

"Okay, let's see. There's a bunch of juvenile stuff my source was able to dig up. Heather Schultz had an underage drinking citation. Kyle Gilmore had a record of fighting during his sophomore year of high school. Seems like that was in defense of another classmate, though. And Adrienne Santi. Now here's something interesting. At age seventeen, to get even with a cheating boyfriend, she keyed his car and slashed his tires."

"That's intense," I said.

Dan nodded, continuing to scroll.

"And Felicia Yin has been accused of bribing an agility judge to overlook faults on a course."

"I don't believe that," I said.

"Why not?" Maeve asked, drizzling a little more of the raspberry vinaigrette onto her salad. "I'm sure it happens."

"Cheating happens in any sport, I suppose. But I've heard these rumors from time to time about various people who have a lot of success in competition. Usually, it's just from disgruntled rivals. Felicia does enough winning that I'm sure she's made a few enemies."

"Still," Dan said. "Probably worth looking into."

I shrugged and snagged a stray crouton lurking near Julianne's plate.

"Would be hard to prove," I said, after I finished crunching. "Judges are only human. And people watching from the sidelines will never have the same perspective the judge has standing in the middle of the course."

"Fair enough," Dan said. "Okay, who's left? Calvin Overby got into some trouble when he and some partners in college decided to try and launch a software company and he bailed at the last minute."

"It's not Calvin," I said.

"Why not?"

"Because she liiiiikes him!" sang Julianne.

"Hey, now," I said. "Is that any way to pay me back for defending you on the book thing?"

"Calvin and Nell, sitting in a tree!" Liam warbled through a mouthful of cabbage.

"Feel free to chew and swallow before mocking me," I said to him.

"She won't hear anything less than positive about him," Maeve added.

"I can't help but feel a little ganged up on, here," I said. "And, might I remind you, Maeve, that the 'less than positive' I was disputing was you accusing him of being a serial killer!"

"Hey, it's not impossible," Dan said. "It's always the good-looking guys. Like —"

"I have heard the Ted Bundy argument," I said. "We don't need to go there again. Calvin is not a serial killer. And I'm sure he didn't murder Bryan or Jeff."

"Because you have a crush on him?" Dan said.

"Because he has no motive!" I said. "Bailing on his friends about to start a company was a jerky thing to do, yes, but it's hardly evidence of an antisocial personality. Plus, he and Bryan were friendly. And I don't think he ever even had an interaction with Jeff."

"That you know of," Dan pointed out.

"How about we move on?" I said. "I'm sure you have a few more people on your list."

"Fine," Dan said. "But I'm not discounting anyone just yet."

"You do what you need to."

"There's Stacey Callahan," he continued. "Nothing much there ... just a shoplifting charge when she was thirteen."

"It's also likely that she's Bryan's illegitimate daughter."

Dan raised his eyebrows.

"Really?"

I nodded, chasing the last few crumbs of couscous around my bowl with my fork.

"I found out tonight. We ran into each other at the club after the police released her from questioning."

"So they haven't charged her with anything," Dan mused, tapping at his screen. "Interesting." He scrolled through is list once more, seemingly checking to see if he missed anything.

"Oh!" he exclaimed. "I almost forgot this Alexis James lady! Listen to this. Thirty years ago, she was at a club with some friends. It was one of those mosh pit type of places, where everyone's dancing on top of each other? Well, Alexis took offense to someone bumping into her an initiated a knock down drag out fight!"

"Jumping Jack Russells," I said, trying to correlate the well-dressed yuppie I met with the image in my head of an out-of-control party girl. "Was anyone hurt?"

"Yes, as a matter of fact," Dan said. "Alexis was charged with assault after throwing one of her ... what do you call 'em, those really spikey high heels?"

"Stilettos," Maeve said.

"Right, one of those! She threw it at the girl she was fighting with. It hit her in the face, and she had to have stitches and plastic surgery and everything."

"That's why you shouldn't throw shoes," Liam said. "Someone could get hurt."

Words to live by.

Chapter 35

It was my turn to see the kids off to bed. By the time I'd supervised Liam's extensive bedtime ritual and made sure that Julianne was comfortably snuggled up with a book (Anne McGaffrey this time; Maeve would most certainly approve), Maeve had coffee brewing.

"Decaf for him," I said, pointing to Dan, who was typing furiously on his phone.

"Sacrilege!" Dan said, without looking up.

As I entered the kitchen, all three dogs greeted me and escorted me to my chair at the table.

"Hey, Rush," I said, taking his face in my hands and dropping a kiss on his freckled muzzle. "Nice to see you remembered I exist." He sneezed in my face. I couldn't get any respect in this place.

After thanking Maeve profusely, Dan placed his phone onto the table and took a long gulp of the coffee she set next to him. Maeve and I sipped ours rather more sedately.

"I can't find any one suspect who ticks all the boxes as our killer," Dan said.

"Maybe there was more than one," Maeve suggested.

"You know, I was thinking about that," I said. "Especially ever since you mentioned Clarice's history with her ex-husband's second wife. She never went after the husband. It was only the second wife *after* they'd split up."

"Right," Dan said.

"Clarice told me that she'd do anything to protect Bryan. That kind of sounds like what happened with her husband. She was trying to protect him. What if Jeff was the one who murdered Bryan? He'd been sneaking around the Club grounds ever since Bryan's death. I overheard him and Stacey talking about blackmail. What if they were trying to blackmail Bryan and something went wrong?"

"And Jeff killed him!" Dan nodded. "That makes sense. Seems like Bryan had worked pretty hard to make sure no one knew that he fathered a child. Things could have gotten heated."

"And Clarice found out somehow, and decided that Jeff had to pay," I finished. "She was at the training building where Jeff was found earlier that day. She would have had the opportunity – and the motive."

"You're the only one here who's ever met her," Dan said. "Do you think it's her?"

I took another sip of my coffee as I gave the question some thought. I ran a foot along the length of Rush's furry back. Rush's bobtail wagged furiously. He tipped his head back, his lips lifted in another spectacular grin.

"There's something about her that makes me think she'd be capable of anything," I said, finally. "I know Stacey was terrified of running into her tonight, which makes me wonder if she and Jeff had a previous encounter with her that didn't go well."

"But?" Maeve prompted.

"But I just can't see her physically stuffing a body, especially a big guy like Jeff, into a closet without help. Also, this."

I pulled up the photos of the card sent to Katherine and Maeve's destroyed book and passed my phone around the table.

"The writing on both of these looks the same," I said. "And why would Clarice apologize for Bryan's death if she had nothing to do with it?"

"Maybe Jeff wrote both notes," Maeve said, handing the phone to Dan. "And Jeff put the book in the car before he ran into Clarice." She paused, one finger resting on her chin. "But where would he have gotten the book?"

"He's a locksmith," I said. "Technically he could have taken it any one of the times the van was broken into. I never kept count of exactly how many books there were. I guess it's possible," I said.

"It's block letters," Dan pointed out, enlarging the photos and examining them from several different angles. "It's not that hard to make them look uniform. Two different people could have been responsible. You'd have to have a professional analyze it."

"That's what Detective Rodriguez said." I reached out to take my phone back.

"What about Adrienne?" Dan asked, scrolling through his list again. "She has a history of messing with people's cars. Three times now, someone broke into a vehicle you were driving. Maybe she's refined her technique since seventeen."

"The dislike between the two of them was definitely mutual," I said. "But where's the motive?"

"Maybe he was the one blackmailing her about the baby," Maeve said, adding a dollop of creamer to her second cup of coffee. Gentle Ben lay at her feet, watching for any hint that his services might be required.

"Baby?" Dan asked.

"There's a recent ultrasound photo floating around," I said. "I found it in Bryan's desk, but it's a little unclear as to who it actually belongs to. The first letter of the name looks like an 'A'. Adrienne has been acting just strange enough that it could maybe be pregnancy related."

"But why would Bryan use that as a way to blackmail Adrienne?" Maeve asked. "It's not the nineteen fifties anymore. Having a baby is no longer taboo."

"Is there any possibility that it could be Bryan's?" Dan asked. "Maybe Adrienne was doing the blackmailing. Or maybe Bryan had a lovechild limit of one."

"I may have understated Bryan and Adrienne's animosity," I said. "They really, really didn't get along."

"That works for some people, though," Dan said. "You know, you get a real intense fight going, and then you … conciliate."

"Speaking from experience?" I asked.

"Not me," Dan said. "Fighting gives me anxiety."

I guess that explained why he was so eager to make up for the article.

"Adrienne also had access to one of my signed books," Maeve said. "You told me that you gave her one just a few days ago."

"True," I said. "But she genuinely seemed to be a fan. She's a member of all of your groups and everything."

"Annie Wilkes anyone? Being a fan doesn't count in the 'not a killer' column," Dan said.

"And she was missing her keychain when I talked to her tonight. When I saw her before my hike with Calvin, she most definitely had it."

"You said she's a personal trainer," Maeve said, stirring her coffee. "So she's fit."

"Extremely," I said.

"Fit enough to stuff a guy in a closet?" Dan asked.

"Possibly."

Dan nodded, typing a note into his phone. I finished my

coffee and contemplated another cup. The caffeine induced brainpower boost was a benefit for sure, but I also wanted to be able to sleep sometime this century. My phone chimed, signaling a text from Stacey.

Hi, Nell. I just wanted to apologize for the way I acted tonight. You caught me off guard. If it's okay, I'd like a chance to explain. I know there won't be any classes tomorrow, but I figured you'd be at the club anyway. Would you be able to meet me there?

"Whoa," I said.

"What?" Dan asked, leaning over to peer at my screen. I instinctively shielded my phone, but then, realizing that I going to tell him about it anyway, handed it over. He skimmed the text, uttering a low whistle once he'd finished.

"And Stacey is …" he consulted his notes. "The daughter? And Jeff's fiancé?"

I nodded, taking back the phone.

"That's a pretty solid connection to both victims," Maeve remarked, tracing a finger over the design of her empty coffee mug.

"And you said Stacey and Jeff didn't seem to have the best relationship," Dan added.

"Well, no, they didn't," I said. "Jeff seemed pretty controlling."

"Maybe Stacey couldn't take it anymore. Or maybe," Dan's eyes lit up. "Maybe Stacey used Jeff as muscle to get the first murder done, and then got rid of him when he was no longer needed!"

"Ooh," Maeve said approvingly.

"I don't know if she's that devious," I said. "She seems like a very sweet girl. Just tonight she nearly collapsed after Detective Rodriguez interrogated her …" I trailed off, mentally going over the incident.

I'm fine, really, she'd said. *Mints help sometimes. They should be in my purse.* As though it wasn't the first time she had a dizzy spell.

And then I remembered how she seemed to curl into herself at times, like when I bumped into her, or when she was unsure of the meaning behind Rush's excited grin. As though she were protecting something. And then there was the name on her driver's license. Anastasia.

"Holy shih tzus!" I leapt out of my seat.

Simon sprang up also, barking a few times for good measure. Rush spun in a circle, ready for action.

"Settle down, you two," Maeve said. "And Nell, what in the world?"

"The baby is Stacey's," I said, and immediately set about explaining everything I just realized.

"That's what she and Jeff could have been blackmailing Bryan about," I finished, pacing the kitchen, unable to sit back down. Simon and Rush heeled on either side of me, convinced we were practicing some kind of obedience exercise. "Maybe they were trying to get support or something. They're both so young. I can see how they'd be overwhelmed with a baby on the way."

"Things may have escalated, and they killed him!" Dan added, dodging the dogs on his way to the coffee maker, where he poured himself another cup and chugged it without even waiting for it to cool.

"And then, when Jeff got to be too much trouble ..." he made a slashing motion across his throat.

Maeve collected her mug and mine and deposited them in the sink.

"She might have the same in mind for you," Dan said, tipping his cup almost upside down to drain the dregs. He eyed the coffee maker. Maeve took the cup from him.

"I'm cutting you off," she said, plunging the mug into the soapy water. She turned to me, leaning against the counter for balance. "Nell, you cannot meet with this girl. You know that, right? You need to call the police."

I hesitated, crouching down. Rush pressed himself against me, just like he did with Stacey just a few hours ago. She seemed so distraught as she'd sobbed on the floor of the agility building, and had been so gentle with Rush. What if I was wrong? Sending the police after her could cause all kinds of problems.

Dan narrowed his eyes, correctly interpreting my silence.

"Nell, come on," he said. "You can't be serious."

"I don't want to sic the police on an innocent person. Being accused of a murder you didn't commit is not fun. I know that kind of thing doesn't bother you, but it bothers me."

Dan threw up his hands.

"How many times to I have to apologize before you'll forgive me? I'm trying so hard to make it up to you. I'm doing all of this research for a story I'm not even going to write. A story that could, quite possibly, be the biggest of my career."

I looked away, running a hand over Simon's head as he approached from my opposite side. I buried my other into the thick fur on Rush's chest. Maeve turned away and started washing dishes with a singular focus, obviously wanting nothing to do with the turn the conversation had taken.

Dan blew out a breath and ran a hand through his curly mop of hair.

"You know," he said, "When I was a kid, my Rabbi used to say that asking for forgiveness three times was the limit. After that, it stops being my problem and starts being yours."

Ouch. I probably deserved that. Not that I was going to admit it to him any time soon. I stared down at my phone's screen, where Stacey's message was still illuminated.

"I need to be sure," I said, mostly to myself. "Before I say anything to the police. I just couldn't do that to someone."

No one spoke for a few minutes. The only sounds came from Maeve swishing the water around and Gentle Ben's panting.

"How about this?" Dan finally said. "I'll go with you."

"She's not going to talk to me if you're there."

"I'll stay in the car. Call me when you find her and keep the line open. I'll be able to hear your conversation, and the minute she says something incriminating, I'll call the police. And I can always burst in like the lumbering oaf I am if things start to go sideways."

"I don't like it," Maeve said instantly, looking up from watching the water drain from the sink.

I stood, one hand still lightly brushing the top of each dog's head.

"I ... kind of do," I said. "You'd really do that?"

"Yes," Dan nodded to punctuate his point. "But I'm not fooling around. Anything she says that's even slightly suspicious, I'm calling the cops and coming in."

"What makes you think either one of you would stand a chance if this girl actually is a killer?" Maeve demanded.

"Two against one," I said.

"Not the worst odds," Dan added.

Chapter 36

"Ruffwear coupons! Get 'em while they're hot!"

I leaned against the wall of the main training building, enjoying my view of Calvin handing out coupons as Rush and Simon wrestled quietly at my side. Calvin stood in the middle of the room, hawking coupons to anyone who even glanced in his direction. I already two stuffed in my back pocket that Calvin handed over with a friendly smile and nod, but nothing more. I tried not to feel too disappointed. Maybe my huffing and puffing during the canyon walk turned him off.

Several other trainers and Club members were scattered around the arena. Deanna was working with Adrienne and Aurora in one corner. Adrienne looked perfectly normal. She was concentrating hard on fine tuning Aurora's finish behavior. Earlier she greeted me as though the awkward interaction from the previous night never happened.

I ran into Clarice as I'd arrived. She thanked me over and over again for delivering the box to Katherine. She'd also mentioned she saw me at the Club later. Clarice reminded me that trainers were discouraged from using the grounds after hours. I was so shocked, I didn't have the chance to explain I was just picking up the boys. But really, *how* many people were creeping around in the dark last night? There wasn't enough money in the world to entice me to come back here at night again. No way.

I glanced down at my phone. A message from Dan popped up.

Anything?

Not yet, I responded, taking another look around the room.

Jared and Gusto swaggered up to Calvin.

"What, or *who*," he waggled his eyebrows, "do I have to do to get me one of them coupons?" His accent was noticeably thicker and hokier than his norm, and he looked Calvin up and down, grinning at him teasingly. I smiled, waiting for Calvin to roll his eyes and ignore him as usual, but instead he tossed the entire book in Jared's direction.

Jared caught the coupons one handed, looking a little shocked. Calvin leaned toward him, lightly resting a hand on Jared's elbow.

I couldn't quite make out what he was saying, but I got the gist when the two of them locked eyes. *Oh.* Maybe it wasn't my lack of fitness that had turned Calvin off. I looked down at my phone to hide my smile, just in case either of them glanced in my direction.

A hand dropped down on my shoulder and my heart was suddenly in my throat.

"Sorry," Stacey said. "I thought you knew I was there."

"Nope," I said, trying to swallow my heart back down. "Must have been a little distracted."

Rush pranced over to Stacey.

"Hey, buddy," she said, scratching him under the chin.

"No Bruiser today?" I asked.

She shook her head.

"To tell you the truth, I don't think I'll be able to concentrate enough to work him today. I really just wanted to talk to you. Is there somewhere quieter we could go?"

Did she want privacy because she wanted to avoid being overheard, or because she wanted to murder me? I thought about going up to my office, but I knew Deanna was planning on working on some class schedules later and didn't want to be a bother to her. Felicia would be supervising some run-throughs in the agility building. Bryan's office was sure to be empty but was just as surely locked. Plus, under the circum-stances, it didn't seem like the best idea for a location anyway.

"We could try the grooming building," I suggested.

Stacey nodded eagerly.

"Oh, good idea!" she said.

I motioned for her to go on ahead and fell into step behind her. As we walked, I called Dan, just as planned, and slipped my phone into the front pocket of my sweatshirt. It felt weird, knowing the line was open and he could hear everything we said. Could he hear my breathing as we walked across the property? That was even weirder.

Rush and Simon automatically heeled beside me. We'd been on a pretty good walk just prior to arriving at the club, so we didn't need to make any stops on our way to the grooming building. I caught sight of Dan's Subaru parked under a tree in the middle of the lot. He was too far away for me to make out whether he was watching us or his phone. I didn't want to make Stacey suspicious, so I turned my attention forward.

I unlocked the door of the grooming building and stepped aside so Stacey could enter first. She led the way to the main grooming area. The room was neatly organized, with three rubber topped tables each spaced about eight feet apart, and smelling faintly of dog shampoo. A raised steel tub took up the entire back wall, complete with its own ramp and various hoses and spray attachments. A pegboard along another wall held dozens of evenly spaced tools, ranging from slicker brushes, to shedding rakes, to thinning scissors. Right smack in the center was a pair of eight-inch shears made of Japanese steel. Clearly, Cascade Canine Club spared no expense, even when it came to grooming equipment. The Japanese blades were by far the best out there.

The sight of the massive pair of shears gave me pause, and caused me to question my choice of the building. Too late now, I decided, as Stacey strode to the table farthest from the entry and, incidentally, from the mounted tools as well. I thought the wisest course of action would be to station myself at the table in front of the pegboard, but then I would have to shout across the room to Stacey.

Stacey hopped up onto the table and sat, swinging her legs absently as she waited for me to do the same. I hefted myself up onto the table nearer to hers. Rush and Simon lay down under the table, resuming their face biting game. Stacey watched them for a few moments, smiling.

"They are adorable," she said. "Sometimes I wish Bruiser had a friend he could play with. He gets bored sometimes."

"He's welcome to play with my guys," I offered. "Rush, for sure, would be thrilled."

"Thanks," Stacey said.

Did that mean she wasn't planning on killing me? Mindful of the phone in my pocket, I decided it would be best to get right to it.

"So," I said. "About last night."

"Yeah," she responded. "I'm so sorry about the way I acted. I was just so shocked. I wasn't expecting that from you."

"It's true, then? Bryan was your father?"

She nodded.

"My mother was a bartender at his favorite hangout. You know how things go," she said with a shrug.

I mean, I could imagine.

"When my mom found out about me, there was no doubt

in her mind that she wanted to keep me and raise me. Bryan wanted nothing to do with that. He may not have been the most faithful husband, but he said that he didn't want to leave his wife. He made it clear Mom was on her own unless she wanted to terminate. He offered to pay for that."

"What a guy," I said drily.

"Mom respected his decision. She only contacted him that one time, to send the photo. She was proud of me, and wanted him to know that I existed. She wanted to give him another chance to watch me grow up. But he never responded, and so she never sent him anything else. She refused to even tell me his name until just a few years ago."

"What changed?"

Stacey looked down at the floor, taking a deep breath at the same time.

"She got cancer," she said, her voice trembling. "When she realized she didn't have a lot of time left, she told me. Said I deserved to know and could do whatever I wanted with the information. She warned me, though, that he might not want anything to do with me. That he sometimes wasn't the nicest guy."

"I'm so sorry," I said.

A tear slipped down Stacey's cheek.

"It's okay," she said. "Mom was ready to go by then, you know? And I didn't do anything right away. I waited. But I did research. I found out how involved Bryan was with training and with the club. I wanted a dog my whole life, but we never had the time, or the money. So I thought maybe that would be a good way to introduce myself. As someone who needed some advice for a first dog."

"What happened?"

"He was so sweet. I know you never really got to see that side of him, but he was really supportive when I asked for advice. He talked to me about different breeds, and we discussed what I was looking for in a dog. I thought Diesel was really cool, and I liked the idea of a Rottweiler for protection. He put me in contact with Diesel's breeder, who just happened to have a litter. Of course, I didn't tell him who I was. I never meant to. Not right then, anyway."

I sensed a 'but' coming. Stacey paused again, looking out the window as she struggled to compose herself. Rush, sensing her distress, stopped playing and trotted over to her, rearing up and placing his front paws next to her on the tabletop. He rested his head in her lap, his stub tail wagging so fast it was little more than a red blur. Simon, miffed at having been abandoned, leapt up on the grooming table next to me and curled up in a tight ball.

"I'm guessing he found out before you were ready?" I said, after more than a minute of silence.

Stacey nodded.

"I was stupid and said something about my mom. I didn't use her name, but it was enough to make him curious. He did some digging and then called me one night, demanding to know what I wanted of him. I told him that I didn't want anything, that I'd just wanted to get to know him a little. I swore I'd never tell anyone. He kind of calmed down after that, and said I was still welcome at the Club and stuff, but he didn't want to work with me personally. He recommended I check out the IGP club, but I really wasn't into that sort of thing."

"It's not for everyone," I allowed, lightly stroking Simon's ears.

"I didn't talk to him again for a few weeks after that. That's when I went to pick up Bruiser. I went to pay the breeder, and she told me that everything was taken care of. I didn't owe anything. And he was not a cheap dog, you know? To be honest, I really couldn't afford him, but things had been so crappy for so long, I just wanted this one thing."

"I get that," I said. And I did. I was in similar circumstances when Rush came into my life three years earlier. And luckily for me, I had a benefactor, too. "It was very generous of him."

"It was," Stacey said, running a finger over the white blaze on Rush's forehead. "I was so grateful. But when I tried to thank him, he just brushed me off and said he didn't want to discuss it. So I didn't. I think he kind of avoided me after that."

Rush poked his nose into Stacey's free hand, and in response she stroked both sides of his head simultaneously. He nuzzled closer, his entire rear end wiggling.

"Have you done any therapy work with him?" Stacey asked. "I bet he'd love it."

"I don't know that he's suited for that kind of work," I said. "People might be a little put off by the full-on dental display he uses as a greeting."

Stacey chuckled.

"Yeah, you have a point there. He really did scare me last night."

We were getting off track.

"You said Bryan avoided you after you brought Bruiser home," I said. "And then what?"

Stacey puffed out her cheeks and exhaled.

"And then I found out I was pregnant," she said. "It was a huge shock for Jeff and me. We hadn't planned on kids for years yet, not until I had a better job, and he was more established in his. He wasn't sure we should keep it. I wasn't either, but I knew I wanted him or her. I thought, maybe Bryan would be willing to help out a little. We weren't asking for much, and even though Bryan didn't really want a relationship with me, I hoped that he might feel differently about a grandchild."

"I'm guessing he didn't."

"No," Stacey said. "Jeff kept pressuring me to keep after Bryan, to not leave him alone until he agreed to help us out. I think he was under the impression that Bryan was rich or something."

"Dog training isn't the most lucrative field," I said.

"I tried to tell that to Jeff, but he wouldn't listen. When we got the ultrasound picture two weeks ago, he said we should show it to him. He was expecting it to soften Bryan's heart a little. I didn't think it would work. Mom tried the same thing with me as a baby, after all. But that wasn't what Jeff intended. The day after your first class, we were alone in the training building. He showed the photo to Bryan and said we were going to get a DNA test done, proving that he was the grandfather. Jeff said we'd go public unless he gave us the money we'd asked for."

My mouth dropped open. I couldn't help it. But holy shih tzus, that was bold.

"I gather Bryan didn't take that well."

"He got so angry. He — he scared me. He said that I was just like my mother, and he was going to say the same thing to me that he said to her, which was that this was my mess and my responsibility."

Stacey swiped at her eyes. I looked around the room for some tissues or paper towels, but there was nothing.

"I'd never seen Jeff like that before. He took a swing at Bryan, and Bryan hit him back and then —" Stacey broke off, sobbing.

I hopped off the table and grabbed one of the folded towels in a nearby laundry basket. After shaking off the dust and dog hair, I brought it over to Stacey.

"Thanks," she said, burying her face in the fabric.

"What happened next?" I asked, slipping my hand into the pocket of my sweatshirt and curling my fingers around my phone.

Stacey shook her head.

"Nothing," she said. "Bryan kind of gave Jeff a shove and

said he wasn't worth his time. And then he told us to get out of his office. So, we did."

"Wh — really?" I blurted. "Are you sure?"

Stacey wiped her nose with the towel.

"Sure of what?"

"Bryan was alive when you left," I said, both for my benefit and Dan's.

"Yes," Stacey said. "I swear he was."

"And you didn't see anyone else in the building."

"I don't think so. But I was so upset by what he said, and I was crying so hard that I couldn't even see where I was going when we left. Jeff had to steer me outside. I didn't even realize we left the photo there until after Bryan died."

Stacey dissolved into tears once more. I circled an arm around her back, comforting her as best I could.

"I just wanted to see my baby again," she sobbed. "Jeff kept trying to find it, and every time someone would see us. People thought he was sneaking around, but he was just trying to get our picture back. It was the only copy I had, and I'd look at it every night and imagine ..." she trailed off and buried her face in the towel.

"But how — who?" I stammered.

"Stacey," a voice said from across the room. Simon leapt to his feet and gave a warning bark. "Is she bothering you?"

I whirled around. Kyle was standing in the center of the room, blocking the exit. In his hand he held the shiny, silvery pair of Japanese shears.

Chapter 37

"Kyle," I said, trying to keep my voice low and calm, as though I were dealing with an agitated dog, "What are you doing with those shears?"

Kyle's hand clenched around the handles.

"I won't let anyone hurt Stacey," he said. "I won't let anyone make her cry."

"I'm not making Stacey cry," I said, still calm. "I'm trying to help her."

"Liar!" Kyle shouted, loud enough that all four of us jumped. "I heard you! You made her cry, just like Bryan did."

Simon leapt off the grooming table and sat next to me, ears back and eyes wide.

"And you protected Stacey from Bryan," I said. I could feel Stacey's leg trembling next to me, and I laid a hand on her knee to still it. I didn't want Kyle to think she was afraid of him.

"I tried to talk to him," Kyle said, lowering the shears slightly. "I tried. But he wouldn't listen. He just kept saying bad things about Stacey. Calling her names. I couldn't let him do that."

"Of course you couldn't," I murmured, trying to calculate the distance to the door. Hopefully Dan had already called the police. Help was on the way. It had to be.

"It was hard," Kyle said, lowering the shears a little more. "Bryan was the first friend I made at this club. He helped me out with Remi so much. And Katherine was always asking if I had enough to eat. She'd invite me for dinner all the time, and would send me home with enough leftovers for a week."

"And you tried to tell her you were sorry, didn't you?"

Kyle gave a slight nod, though his eyes remained fixed on mine.

"I sent her flowers. And a card. I wanted her to know that I didn't mean for it to happen. I didn't want her to be mad at me."

Good greyhounds, he sounded like a little kid there for a second. He wasn't one, though. He likely killed two people. And was threatening two more. I considered making a dash for the doorway. The dogs would make it, easy, I was sure. I wasn't so confident about my own abilities. And Stacey, seated as she was on the table, would have the hardest time.

"I'm sure she understands," I said, motioning for the dogs to stand along the wall so that they weren't underfoot. "Did you leave a note for me, too, Kyle?"

"I was so mad at you after you made Stacey run away crying last night," he said. "Just like Bryan. And Jeff."

"Did you ... protect ... Stacey from Jeff, too?"

"I had to. He made her cry. He hit her. I saw it when they were in the training building yesterday. There was a red mark on her face, and she was crying."

I gave Stacey's sleeve a tug, hoping she'd understand that I wanted her to slide off the table. She did, landing quietly at my side. I steered her behind me, and took a sideways step toward the door, my back to the wall. Kyle didn't seem to notice.

"I didn't want to hurt anyone else," he repeated. "But you

kept on snooping. And talking to the police. I thought if you were scared enough, you'd stop. So I followed you a little. Messed with your van."

"And my dogs," I said, more forcefully than I intended. Kyle suddenly lifted the shears. My inching closer to the door came to an abrupt halt.

"I thought they'd stay close," he said. "Remi would have."

And they very well might have done, if someone hadn't been chasing them.

"None of that worked, though. So I played around with your brake line a little."

"And dropped your keychain in the process," I said, taking another small step. Stacey and the dogs moved with me.

"I figured you'd find it, so I stole Adrienne's, just in case. She never seemed to like hers anyway. She didn't even notice. No one ever notices me. I know all the places to hide, so I can see everything. And I saw you last night. That's why I put the book in your car. I thought maybe that would scare you, and you'd stop. But that wasn't enough. You came here again and made Stacey cry."

His weight shifted to the balls of his feet, and his gaze locked onto mine. I'd worked with enough aggressive dogs to know the signs that preceded an attack. We were running out of time. I took one more step, this time in Kyle's direction, angling my body so that there was a clearer path to the door.

"Run," I muttered to Stacey, out of the corner of my mouth.

She only managed a step before Kyle raised the shears high over his head and lunged forward, the blades glinting in the sunlight streaming through the windows. I couldn't block him. I had nowhere else to go.

And then, suddenly, I was being shoved to the side. I crashed into one of the grooming tables, gripping the metal lined edge to keep from tumbling to the ground.

Dan gave a sharp cry of pain, his phone clattering to the floor, a red stain blooming over his shirtsleeve as he fell. I steadied myself, knowing that my only hope was to try to disarm Kyle while he was distracted.

Kyle staggered back from Dan's crumpled form, spinning in my direction, raising the shears once again. A growl sounded from my right, and out of the corner of my eye I saw Rush, my sweet, happy-go-lucky, love-everyone-he-meets guy. He flew through the air, teeth bared. He wasn't smiling this time.

Rush connected with Kyle in a full body tackle. Kyle lost his grip on the shears, and they fell to the floor with a metallic clank. I flung myself forward, kicking the shears even farther away.

"Lie down!" I commanded, and Rush hit the floor.

I threw myself on top of Kyle, using all of my strength and weight to try and pin him down. Never before had I been grateful for that pesky twenty pounds I'd never been able to lose. Kyle squirmed beneath me, and extra twenty pounds or no, I knew he was stronger than I was.

"The leashes!" I yelled.

Stacey darted forward to where I draped Rush and Simon's leashes over the arm of the table I was sitting on. I jammed a knee into Kyle's lower back, and as he let out a gasp of surprise and pain, I wrenched his arms behind him. Stacey tied his wrists and ankles, and we cautiously stepped back. Stacey's hands shook, and I was ready to pounce should the knots not hold.

They held. Kyle squirmed and tried to kick, but try as he might, he wasn't able to free himself. Stacey wasn't fooling around. I called Rush over to me so that I could check for any wounds. His shining white and red coat was as pristine as ever. He pressed himself against me as soon as I'd finished, whining softly. I hugged him tight, telling him he was brilliant. A low groan sounded behind me. Police sirens wailed faintly in the distance.

"Watch him," I said to Stacey waving a hand toward Kyle, and dropped to my knees next to Dan.

He struggled to sit up, clutching his injured shoulder.

"Let me see," I said, peeling back the tatters of his shirt-sleeve. The wound was deep, but nothing was spurting. If anything, the bleeding seemed to be slowing down.

"I think you'll live," I said, helping Dan prop himself against a kennel. He craned his neck to check out his arm, and paled.

"Whoa," I said, hurriedly covering the wound with a towel Stacey handed me. "Take it easy."

Dan closed his eyes and turned away.

"I've never been great with blood," he said.

"You check your blood sugar like, ten times a day."

"Six times. Usually. And there's a big difference between one drop of blood and an entire sleeve."

"Well, stop looking at it, then."

"Your bedside manner is," Dan made a circle with the thumb and forefinger of his good hand, "A-plus."

The approaching sirens grew louder.

"I'll let them know where we are," Stacey said, ducking out of the room.

Kyle's eyes tracked Stacey until she was out of sight, and then he let out a deep sigh, sagging against his bonds. He seemed to give up.

"You were right about her," Dan said, he eyes still tightly closed.

I blew out a breath.

"Yeah, I guess. But I had no idea about ..." I trailed off, gesturing in Kyle's direction.

Even though his eyes were still closed Dan seemed to get the idea.

"I don't think anyone did," he said.

He was probably right. But I still couldn't help thinking of the danger I'd put Stacey, not to mention Rush and Simon, in.

"Thank you," I said to Dan, blinking back the tears that had suddenly filled my eyes. "For coming in when you did."

Dan sat up a little straighter, cautiously opening his eyes, fixing his gaze on me and avoiding his injured arm.

"Does this mean you forgive me?"

Chapter 38

I looked out over white peaks of the Cascades against the clear, blue sky. In just a week, the weather had gone from wavering between winter and spring to going all in for spring. I turned my face toward the sun, glorying in the feel of the warmth on my skin.

"Nell!" Clarice called, from several long picnic tables away. "Did you by chance see if there were any more napkins inside? People are going wild over this barbeque."

"As well they should be!" Adrienne responded, from where she was manning (womaning?) the grills. "It's a secret family recipe!"

Remi, Brent's little black lab mix, was tethered at her side. Brent's one phone call after his arrest was to Adrienne, begging her to care for Remi. She'd agreed and had then promptly arranged a lawyer for him.

Brent most certainly needed to pay for what he'd done; but it was also apparent that he was very disturbed and needed help. Adrienne was intent on making sure he received the help he needed while serving his sentence. Meanwhile, Remi was adjusting to life with a wild pack of huskies. Adrienne was already talking about which position Remi would take on the mushing crew. After all, Remi's DNA test had come back as thirteen percent husky.

I watched as Adrienne expertly flipped two pieces of chicken at once. She seemed to be well over the flu she was fighting those first weeks after Bryan's death. I was glad she never found out that I suspected her of being pregnant with Bryan's baby. That would have been all kind of awkward.

"Nell?" Clarice called again.

"Right!" I said, "I'm on it!"

Rush and Simon, ever ready for action, leapt up as I scooted off the bench I was sharing with Julianne. Rush seemed none the worse for wear after his stint as hero of the day. He accepted the resultant praise and fawning as his due and went right back to loving every creature he came across. Usually with overwhelming enthusiasm. And smiles. Always smiles.

The three of us moved as a unit, jogging across the paths, and passing the *Come Celebrate Spring with the Cascade Canine Club!* banner that hung from the main training building. I knew exactly where the extra napkins were, since I was the one who set up the table earlier in the day. I made a beeline in that direction without turning any lights on.

Calvin and Jared jumped apart, sheepish looks on their faces as I rounded the corner.

"Get a room, you two," I said, rolling my eyes as I grabbed the napkins.

"We thought we had one," Calvin said.

"The lights were supposed to be our alarm system," Jared added. "Would have worked perfectly if some creeper hadn't been sneaking around in the dark."

"The supply room? Really? Could you be more cliché?"

Jared made a shooing motion with one hand. I saluted him with my stack of napkins and left them to it.

Pausing outside the door, I surveyed the growing crowd. Even though we overestimated the number of supplies we'd need for the open house, it was going to be close. I wasn't going to kid myself by denying that a large portion of the crowd showed up out of sheer curiosity about the murders. I probably would have been nosey myself if I wasn't so close to this particular case.

Detective Rodriguez, still in his suit jacket, his tie knotted tightly under his chin despite the heat, appeared at our table while I'd been on my mission. I watched as Julianne offered him my empty seat. He sat down, looking from Liam to Julianne as they both started talking to him at once. Trying not to stare, or cause Detective Rodriguez to feel as though he had to give up his place, I took a roundabout way back to Clarice to deliver the napkins.

"Hey, Nell!" a voice called out as I filled the napkin holder. I turned to see Katherine and Stacey approaching, each carrying a full plate of food.

"Have a seat," I said, indicating an empty table next to the one with supplies. "Wait 'till you try that chicken. Adrienne is a genius."

"Oh, we've already tried it," Katherine assured me. "This is round two."

Stacey flushed slightly and looked away.

"The baby is hungry today," she said.

I introduced the two of them on a whim, a few days after the events in the grooming building. Katherine and Stacey bonded instantly. Katherine offered Stacey a place to stay while she got back on her feet. It was plain to see that they were filling a void for each other and were growing quite close.

"Don't feel bad," I said. "My nephew, Liam, has already been to the buffet table three times. It's a party. Enjoy yourself!"

I left them alone and nearly ran headlong into Felicia.

"Oh, Nell!" she exclaimed, narrowly preventing her cob of corn from rolling off her plate. "I was looking for you. Do you have a minute?"

"Sure," I said, following her a few yards away from the crowd. "What's up?"

"I just wanted to let you know that I won't be asking you to help with any more agility classes."

"Okay," I said slowly. My class schedule was picking up, so I wasn't entirely certain that I had time for it anyway, but I hadn't discussed anything with Felicia.

"A client came to me and said she'd pull out of all of her classes and go elsewhere if you were at another class," Felica said glumly.

I could only stare at her in shock.

"No one thinks you did anything wrong," she went on quickly. "But this person takes a lot of classes with both me and Deanna, and since we'd never finalized anything about you helping out, we figured it would be easy enough to avoid."

"Is it Heather Shultz?" I asked.

Felicia gave a barely perceptible nod.

"We've had some difficulties before," she said. "She generally will throw a tantrum like this and then calm down and forget about it. Otherwise, she is a good member and a big donor."

There it was.

"She contributes a lot, from helping with the trials we hold here on the grounds to helping Linh with the rescue side of things. And you know what rescue is like. There's never enough to go around."

"I know it," I acknowledged.

"So, you're okay with this?"

"Okay is a strong word," I said. "But I get it."

"Between you and me, I think this is insane," Felicia said. "We're hoping it will all blow over. She mentioned you leaving during class again, and also that you ridiculed her breed choice."

"I would never!" I protested. "I was complimenting her dog!"

"I know, I know. I talked to Jared, and he's very firmly on your side. We've just got to ride this out. I'm sure it will blow over soon."

"If you say so," I said.

We chatted a while longer, before Felica wandered off in search of more hot sauce. Still thoroughly disgruntled, I decided to give myself a minute to cool off before returning to the party. I leaned against the trunk of a juniper tree, wondering how in the world I'd unintentionally managed to offend a client so deeply.

A familiar white Subaru entered from the driveway, pulling into a parking spot next to the newly repaired Green Machine. I pushed away from the tree and headed in that direction as Dan stepped out of the car. He held his left arm gingerly, guarding against excessive movement. In his right hand, he held a folded newspaper.

Rush immediately began whining at my side, and gave a single screech of joy as I gave him permission to run ahead. Simon followed. Rush greeted Dan as though they were long-lost brothers. Even Simon gravely submitted to a pat on the head. Just one. But still. It was more acknowledgement that he gave to most people.

"How's the shoulder?" I asked.

"Coming along," Dan said, giving it a shrug. "This looks like quite the party."

"It is," I said. "You'd better grab some food before it's gone."

"In a second," he said. "I wanted to show you something, first. My retraction. Hot off the press."

He unfolded the newspaper and showed me the front page.

There was a color photo of me with Simon and Rush, looking over the vastness of the canyon we hiked with Calvin. I wasn't even aware he included me in the picture he took. That wasn't what caught my attention, though. It was the headline that demanded all of my focus.

Hero Dog Trainer Solves Double Murder.

"Well?" Dan asked.

"It's a little dramatic for a retraction, don't you think?"

Dan shook his head, rolling up the paper.

"Everyone's a critic."

"Oh, you poor, abused reporter," I said. "Come on. Let's go get some food. And you can show that to the rest of the guests and get some unbiased opinions."

He placed the hand holding the newspaper on my shoulder, stopping me from moving forward.

"What if I only came here for one opinion?" he asked, his dark brown eyes searching my face, trying to gauge my response.

I gently extricated myself from his grip.

"Well?"

I was saved from answering when woman in her mid-twenties, her dark hair gathered in a high ponytail that just brushed her shoulders, jogged up to us.

"Nell McLinton?" she asked.

"That's me," I said.

"Hey," she said, skidding to a stop at my side. "I'm Faiza Patel. I work at the vet clinic just down the road."

"Sagebrush Veterinary Hospital," I said, familiar with the name after driving past it for the past few weeks. The vet clinic and the Club were the only two businesses along the private road.

"That's right," she said. "Do you have a minute?"

"I'll go grab some food," Dan said, tucking the newspaper under his good arm and setting off in the direction of the grills. Rush whined softly as he walked away, then turned his attention hopefully in Faiza's direction.

"Can he say hi?" she asked.

I sent him over with a wave of one hand. Simon remained at my side.

"I'm one of the veterinary technicians at Sagebrush," Faiza said, her voice slightly muffled as she and Rush embraced on a patch of grass. "I'm scheduled to take a trip to Ecuador with World Vets for a two-week clinic and spay and neuter trip."

"Cool!" I said. "I did that once, about five years ago. It was amazing."

"This will be my third time," Faiza said. "It's such great experience."

"It is," I agreed.

Faiza stood up, still scratching beneath Rush's chin with one hand as she continued speaking.

"The reason I'm telling you all of this is because the person who was going to cover for me is no longer able. It's hard to find someone for two weeks of relief on such short notice. I asked Clarice if there was anyone in the Club with experience, and she told me to find you."

"I've done plenty of work in vet clinics," I said. "Day practices and ER."

"Great! What's your availability starting next week?"

I thought for a moment. It had been a while since I'd worked at a veterinary clinic, and I missed it. And my next round of classes was mostly nights and weekends, so technically my weekdays would be free. It wouldn't leave much time for anything else, though, and I knew things were starting to heat up with Maeve's custody battle. Still, it was only for two weeks. The extra money would come in handy.

"I could probably work something out," I said.

"Great!" Faiza smiled broadly. "Come down to the clinic on Monday, and you can meet everyone and see if it would be a good fit. I think you already know one of the people you'll be working with."

"Oh, really? Who?" I asked, trying hard to remember if any of the Club members I met over the past few weeks mentioned working at a veterinary clinic. It would be nice to see a familiar face during my shifts.

Faiza pointed to a group of people gathered near the agility building. My heart sank a little at the realization that the only person I recognized in that group was Heather Shultz.

Seeming to sense my gaze, Heather looked up. I gave a small smile and waved in her direction. She turned away.

Shih tzus.

If you enjoyed *The Rottweiler Howls at Midnight* and are interested in learning exactly why Heather has it in for Nell, pre-order Book 2 of the Cascade Canine Club Mystery series: *Murder in a Pug's Eye*.

For a free bonus interview with the author by *The Central Oregon Chronicle's* own intrepid reporter, Dan Friedman, as well as current news, bonus content, and a chance to win a cameo for your dog in a future Cascade Canine Club Mystery!

Visit the author's website: www.rachelleorcelletto.com